The Captive Flesh

The Captive Flesh
Cleo Cordell

This book is a work of fiction.
In real life, make sure you practise safe, sane and consensual sex.

First Published by Black Lace 1993

2 4 6 8 10 9 7 5 3 1

This edition first published in Great Britain in 2009 by
Black Lace
Virgin Books
Random House, 20 Vauxhall Bridge Road,
London SW1V 2SA

www.blacklace.co.uk
www.virginbooks.com
www.rbooks.co.uk

Addresses for companies within The Random House Group Limited can be found at: www.randomhouse.co.uk/offices.htm

The Random House Group Limited Reg. No. 954009

A CIP catalogue record for this book is available from the British Library

ISBN 9780352345295

The Random House Group Limited supports The Forest Stewardship Council [FSC], the leading international forest certification organisation. All our titles that are printed on Greenpeace-approved FSC-certified paper carry the FSC logo. Our paper procurement policy can be found at www.rbooks.co.uk/environment

Printed and bound in Great Britain by CPI Bookmarque Ltd, Croydon CR0 4TD

Introduction

When I wrote *The Captive Flesh* back in 1993 you would have been hard pressed to find any erotic fiction written by women. Apart from a couple of literary luminaries such as Anais Nin, the overwhelming majority of erotica available was produced – and published – by men, albeit with female pen names. Black Lace books changed all that. These were books written by people who knew what female sexuality was all about – women themselves. Women who knew what they wanted and what turned them on. Women have always known that good sex can be down and dirty, risky and exciting, satisfying and loving – and a lot more besides.

The Captive Flesh was one of the first books published under the Black Lace imprint. It was an exciting time to be writing erotica, and I had a strong sense of being a pioneer in the genre. The language of women's erotica was newborn and this book was a journey for me as well as my characters. I chose the harem setting for the story because I wanted a place of opulence and pleasure, where my characters could explore their sensual sides to the full. Here, there would be no distractions. The commonplace and the everyday would not intrude. I wanted to explore the many shades and levels of sexual experience and interaction between the sexes. As the characters came alive for me I found the tension between master and slave to be complex and exciting, and about far more than dominance and submission.

The Captive Flesh is a novel fuelled by sexual fantasies – those of my own and of the many women I spoke to while writing it. It is sumptuous, highly charged and yet tender. My intention was, and is, for the readers to lose themselves in the imaginary sheltered world, where Marietta and Claudine discover unparalleled pleasures.

I hope you enjoy it.

Cleo Cordell, January 2002

1

Marietta clung to Claudine in the darkness. The deck of the Spanish trading ship, their rescuer, pitched under their feet, slippery and treacherous.

Exhausted and half frozen, Marietta watched sadly as the little ship which had been speeding her homewards from Nantes, sank without trace under the heaving waters of the Bay of Biscay. The storm raged still. The rescue ship seemed small and fragile, surrounded as it was by the roiling waves. She was shivering so much that she could barely stand.

'Where is Sister Anna?' Claudine said. 'I cannot see her with the others.'

Marietta shuddered, remembering how she had seen the nun swept overboard. 'She is gone. Drowned I fear, poor thing. We are alone now. Come, we must go below. Find shelter.'

Together they fought their way forwards. The sailors paid them no attention, intent on helping the other passengers. Marietta felt a strong hand take hold of her arm. Above the crashing of wind and waves, came a deep voice close to her ear.

'Come with me. You may have the use of my cabin. The hold will be crammed to bursting with people and baggage. Young ladies of breeding have need of their privacy.'

She stammered her heartfelt thanks. Claudine was beyond speech. Her face was white, her lips blue with cold. Marietta leaned on the stranger's arm as he half-carried, half-dragged them both below deck and along a narrow corridor.

'Best to strip those wet clothes off before you take a chill,' he said, throwing Marietta two large towels. 'There are dry clothes in that trunk. I'll leave you to change. My help is needed on deck. Make yourself comfortable. Use whatever you wish.'

'Thank you. You are very kind. May I ask your name—' Marietta began.

But he had gone. The door slammed shut behind him.

Gratefully she stripped off her sodden dress, bustle and petticoats, then rubbed her limbs until they glowed. Claudine wrapped herself in a towel and did the same. They sat side by side on the narrow bunk. Both were subdued by the loss of their chaperone. Marietta spoke a silent prayer for the soul of Sister Anna but she could not help feeling a sense of relief.

'I'm glad she's gone. The cold fish!' Claudine said suddenly.

Marietta looked at her friend in shocked amazement. Then suddenly they both began to laugh. Sister Anna had been a stern and humourless woman with repressed sexual hungers. Marietta remembered all the times the nun had ill-treated her. Even now the thought of what she'd made her do brought a blush to her cheeks. She had told no one of these encounters. Not even Claudine.

Claudine apparently, hated Sister Anna for her own private reasons.

'Is there ... any brandy?' Claudine said now, her teeth chattering. She was sitting swathed in the towel, her long red hair hung in tangles over her creamy bare shoulders.

Marietta looked around for any alcohol. The cabin

was large and luxurious and a charcoal brazier gave out warmth. An oil lamp, swinging violently from the ceiling, cast a reddish glow and lent the wood panelling a polished depth. There was no brandy, but she found a pot of water and coffee.

'Our rescuer is no drinker,' she said, 'but he must be a cultured man. Rich too.' She spooned ground coffee beans into a long-handled pot, added water, and set it over the brazier. 'There is fresh fruit on the table and that bowl is gold. And look at these embroidered silk bed hangings.'

Claudine sank to her knees and opened a trunk. 'He was well spoken, with a charming accent. Is he a merchant do you think? Perhaps he is the owner of this vessel. As to his wealth, I think you are right. Look.'

She delved into the chest and scooped up armful after armful of rich and exotic clothes. There were pastel-coloured silks, velvets, gauze veils, figured brocades. She smiled, cheered as she always was by the sight of beauty or luxury. Marietta recalled that there had been precious little of either for the two of them in the past six years.

Marietta grinned. 'What clothes are these? Theatre costumes surely.'

'Does it matter? He said we could make use of anything we found in the trunk. And we need dry clothes.'

Claudine pulled out a silken tunic of pale yellow, a deeper yellow skirt, and an embroidered and jewelled sash. She pulled the tunic over her head, then wriggled out from the towel, keeping her bare back turned to the cabin wall. While she dressed she kept her eyelids lowered.

Marietta was surprised by her modesty. Claudine had no need to be ashamed of her lovely body. They had been friends since childhood and had seen each other naked many times. They were alone now, but Marietta supposed that convent habits died hard.

Claudine dug back into the chest. 'Let me choose for you. Ah, yes. Plum-coloured velvet, a wide-necked silk tunic and loose full trousers, gathered in at the ankle. How daring! Wear these, do. The colour contrasts so well with your pale colouring and light hair. There is jewellery here too.'

Her enthusiasm was infectious. Marietta laughed at Claudine's childlike delight and pulled on the outfit, feeling strange without her usual layers of petticoats and the bustle pad on her hips. The silk felt cool and exciting against her bare breasts. There was a looking-glass in the cabin and the two young women admired their reflections, revelling in the lovely fabrics and the way their limbs gleamed through the thin silk. They giggled, twirling so that the fine silk billowed out like fairy wings, thinking how shocked the sisters at the convent would have been if they could have seen them.

Soon the smell of coffee filled the cabin. They had hardly finished dressing and were sipping coffee from shallow dishes when their rescuer returned. There had not been time for Marietta to study him earlier. Now she saw that he was tall and dark, with pale skin and a strong-featured, angular, face.

He smiled. 'You are recovered, I see. Good. And you have made coffee. I shall join you if I may; I am in need of the warmth.'

'Please do, Mr . . .?' Marietta said.

'You may call me Kasim. And you are . . .?'

'Marietta de Nerval, and this is my dearest friend and companion, Claudine Dupont.'

'Ah, you are French,' he said knowingly.

'Creole to be exact,' she said, smiling. 'We are indebted to you, Mr ... Kasim. This cabin is very comfortable. I hope you do not mind, but we borrowed these clothes from your trunk.'

He waved a hand. 'I meant you to. I wish you to keep them. They were bought as gifts for ... for my family. But the colours might have been chosen for you. You both have such unusual colouring. Claudine with her golden skin and red-gold hair. And yourself, so pale, with silver-blonde hair and blue eyes. What a feast for any painter, indeed for any connoisseur of the arts.' He spread his hands and smiled disarmingly. 'Now, I insist that you keep these things. How could anyone else do such justice to them?'

'Thank you, *monsieur*. Most of our clothes were lost in the storm. You are most kind.' Claudine smiled fetchingly, showing her dimples.

Kasim sipped his coffee. 'I am always kind to beautiful women. Especially young ladies in distress. Oh, dear. There I go again. I'm sure you must think me very bold.'

His well-shaped mouth curved in a smile, but his dark eyes on Marietta were intense. She felt a delicious little shiver snake up her back; he really was most attractive.

'Perhaps not bold but a little ... too honest?' she countered.

He laughed. 'Yes, I am that. Truthful to a fault, always.'

There was something languid, though not soft, in his refined features. The light of a keen intelligence was written clearly on his pale, broad brow. Marietta knew instinctively that this was a man who could be dangerous. She found the fact at once disquieting and compelling.

'We are not exactly in distress now, *monsieur*,' Claudine said with spirit, breaking into her thoughts.

'No? But is it not true that you lost your companion in the storm and are unaccompanied?'

'Yes—'

Then I insist that you allow me to oversee your welfare. I have a large house in Algiers close to the port where we are bound. It will give me great pleasure if you would consent to be my guests until passage home can be organised for you. I can arrange for a message to be dispatched to any relatives who may be worrying about you.'

Marietta looked at Claudine. Her friend had her hand to her mouth. Her lovely light-brown eyes were as round as saucers. She gave a slight nod. Marietta responded eagerly. It was wrong, she knew. They should not accept the invitation. But who was to know? Sister Anna was no more and where else would they stay while they awaited the arrival of a suitable ship to carry them home? Far better to stay with Kasim than to have to comb the unknown town for a suitable boarding house.

'Thank you, *monsieur*,' Marietta said, speaking for them both. 'We shall be delighted to accept your kind invitation.'

Kasim finished his coffee and lifted one dark eyebrow. 'So, you are travelling to Martinique, you say? You have families there?'

Marietta nodded, thinking of the large white house at Pointe Royale. 'My father has sugar plantations there. Claudine lives with my family. We are travelling back from the convent at Nantes, where we have been completing our education.'

'Ah, I have heard of this place,' Kasim said. 'A finishing school for young ladies, is it not? And of a some-what severe regime?'

Marietta blushed. He could not know how severe, surely. Could he?

'After the spartan surroundings and simple food you must be ready for a little luxury. You must allow me to spoil you. Rest assured that your every need will be catered for at my house.'

Claudine dimpled. 'It sounds wonderful. I am heart-ily sick of serviceable blue serge gowns, plain food, and bare chambers with stone walls. The mere mention of luxury makes my mouth water!'

Kasim laughed. 'Soon we shall reach Algiers. I will show you around the souk with its spice, perfume, and jewellery stalls. At my house you shall drink fruit sherbet while fountains play and the scent of jasmine and rose surrounds you. Ah, my dear young ladies, there is so much I am eager to show you.'

There was such promise in his deep velvety voice that Marietta felt another delicious little shiver creep down her back. Claudine slanted her a scandalised glance and laughed throatily. Both of them were eager to reach Algiers, sensing somehow that their lives were about to change forever.

Kasim stood up, tossing back the heavy cowl of his cloak, and crossed the cabin to the door. 'Forgive my thoughtlessness. You must both be exhausted by your ordeal. I shall leave you to sleep.'

Marietta did not feel tired. On the contrary, she felt exhilarated. She had never met anyone with such charm, such presence, and felt Kasim was something special. He seemed to radiate a magnetic energy. She was disappointed that their conversation must end, even for a short while. Kasim was so visually attractive. His thick dark hair fell in waves onto his shoulders.

The voluminous dark clothes he wore concealed his form but, from the way he moved, it was evident that his body, though lean, was heavily muscled.

She felt a stirring in her blood. During the years at the convent her eyes had been starved for the sight of a man. Now fate or destiny had sent Kasim to her. And such a man. Claudine was watching him, the front of her silk tunic rising and falling over the motion of her full bosom.

'I will give orders that you are not to be disturbed,' Kasim said. 'I wish you good night. In the morning, if you will permit it, we shall breakfast together. Nothing would give me greater pleasure.'

His face was open now, friendly. Marietta was seered by his charm, but she did not entirely trust him. She wished she knew more about men. Kasim was subtle and sophisticated; dangerous, too, and effortlessly attractive. Too complex a creature for a convent girl to fathom. But Claudine seemed to be won over totally.

'But ... but where will you sleep?' Marietta asked him.

He flashed her a grin over his shoulder. 'Do not concern yourself on my part, *mademoiselle* Marietta. I shall share my servant's cabin next door. But it is kind of you to think of my welfare. I thank you for your concern.'

Marietta felt an odd little flutter between her thighs as his dark eyes looked deeply into hers for an instant. There was something unreadable in their depths.

Then Kasim turned, and was gone.

Claudine talked of nothing else but Kasim.

'He is so striking, so cultured. I have never met anyone like him. And his manners are perfect. Such a gentleman. What is his nationality, do you think? Spanish? No. His name – Kasim – it sounds Arabic. Turkish perhaps. Do you think he liked me? He said I had pretty colouring. Many men do not care for red-blonde hair and freckles. He liked you too, more than me I think, but then you have always had admirers ...'

And on and on it went, while Marietta nodded and commented as Claudine paused for breath. She smiled inwardly. Her friend had not been so animated in months. And if she was honest, she too was flattered by Kasim's obvious regard. Flattered and intrigued.

Claudine yawned. 'The bunk is fairly wide. I think there will be room for us both.'

'It will be more comfortable than the narrow beds in the dormitory,' Marietta said. 'I hated the nights there most. That cold cheerless room. The thin scratchy blankets. And I hated having to lie rigidly on my back, my arms outside the sheets, even in the coldest weather.'

'Just in case we were tempted to explore our own sinful bodies!' Claudine snorted. 'What disgusting hypocrisy.'

Marietta paused, a suspicion flaring in her mind. 'What do you mean?'

'Oh, come now. Now that we are going home there is no need to keep up the pretence. We all know what Sister Anna was.'

Marietta's cheeks flamed. She could not reply.

'Did you think it was a secret? That you were the only one she liked to torment? Do not look so dismayed. It is nothing to be ashamed of. She did those things to all the prettiest young women. After a time I ... I grew to like the things she did to me.'

Marietta's head snapped up. 'Claudine!'

Then her eyes widened as Claudine dropped the single garment she wore and turned around, giving

9

Marietta a view of her naked back. She saw now what Claudine had been hiding earlier. There were vivid red stripes across her shapely round buttocks. The weals were raised and, she realised with a shock, beautiful against the pale golden skin of Claudine's lush flesh.

She gasped. 'You too? But when? Those marks look fresh.'

'Two days ago. When you thought I was walking on deck Sister Anna summoned me to her cabin. She said I needed to be reminded that chastisement purifies the soul. She said that I was a wanton creature, but she'd beat the sin out of me, as she'd done many times at the convent. I was afraid of her. She was so stern, so rigidly controlled. She made me lie across her lap and bury my face in the musty folds of her robe, so that my groans were muffled. Every stroke burned the tender skin of my bottom, so that I squirmed and cried out. But then ... before each new stroke my skin began to itch and throb. It was as if I waited for each new smart of the switch. As if I welcomed the pain.'

Claudine paused. Her cheeks flushed a deep pink. 'I think Sister Anna knew how I felt because she didn't just beat me. After she finished and I was sobbing with the pain of it, she ... she rubbed the handle of the dog whip between my thighs. And then she thrust her hard cold fingers into my body. I couldn't help myself. As she moved her fingers in and out, I writhed against her hand, my cheeks flaming, while my buttocks burned and throbbed still. She called me disgusting, in that soft harsh voice of hers. She said I felt soft and juicy like a rotten fruit and that I smelt like a whore. But I seemed to revel in her insults. The more she reviled me, the more I enjoyed it. My breath came fast. I felt such an explosion of pleasure that I almost fainted. When I'd finished, she made me suck her fingers clean.

Then she pushed me off her lap without a word and went out, leaving me lying sobbing on the floor. Oh, Marietta. And now she is dead. I ... I don't know what I feel ...'

Tears glistened in Claudine's light-brown eyes. Despite her earlier bravado her full lips trembled. Marietta took her in her arms and stroked her soft hair. A single tear rolled down Claudine's cheek.

'Hush now. You have nothing to reproach yourself for. I wish we had spoken of this sooner. How many of the others did she mistreat? I thought it was only me. I dared not speak out, lest she find some new way to torment me.'

'Did she beat you?'

'No. She chose other ways to humiliate me. Come, you must be cold without your clothes. Let's get into bed. I'll tell you about it when we're tucked up warm.'

Claudine climbed into the bunk while Marietta threw off the last of her clothes and crept in beside her. They lay with their arms entwined. Claudine's full breasts were warm and soft against Marietta's own and she was shorter than her friend. The top of her head fitted comfortably under Marietta's chin. Marietta breathed in Claudine's sweet odour of clean hair and skin.

'This is nice,' Claudine said, making a little sound of contentment and snuggling into her friend's neck. 'It reminds me of when we were children and I would creep into your bed when I had a bad dream.'

Marietta smiled, feeling safe and secure also. Claudine's young firm flesh against her own was pleasant – more than pleasant, if she was honest. She tried not to dwell on the feel of it, but it served to emphasise her own memories of Sister Anna's thin spare body; her long humourless face; the faint dusty lavender smell of her skin and the rasping sound of her cold chapped hands as she rubbed them together.

'What did she do to you?' Claudine whispered, as if she'd read her mind. 'Tell me. Let us exorcise all the bad memories, then the old harridan will have no more power over us.'

Marietta's mouth was dry. The shame rose hot within her. Surely she could not ... But perhaps it was time to lay old ghosts to rest. She forced herself to speak.

'It began soon after we arrived at the convent. I thought she didn't like me. She would find fault with everything I did. Always criticising, picking at me. She would wait until we were alone, then she would insist on asking me intimate questions. Like, had I washed all over that day? She would make me open my mouth so that she could see if my teeth were clean, and look in my ears, tugging at the lobes. Sometimes she would make me raise my skirts so that she could inspect my chemise for stains. Once she made me unbraid my hair, then she replaited it, pinning it so tightly to my head that my head ached. Gradually I realised that she was jealous of my youth.'

'Of your beauty, you mean. How could she not be jealous? She was so plain. Surely no one ever looked at her with desire. No need to be modest, Marietta. The poor repressed bitch must have wanted to eat you up!'

Marietta blushed hotly. 'That's ... almost what she did. I had been given the task of cleaning her room. I used to dread it but I dared not complain. What reason could I give for refusing? She made me scrub and dust every inch of it. The worst thing was cleaning the floor. I had to scrub the stone whilst on my knees. Sister Anna would watch. She ... she made me pin up my dress and chemise. Pin them up high above my waist and secure them out of the way, so that my naked buttocks were exposed. She said this was to protect my clothes from the wet floor. I had to move backwards and forwards, scrubbing vigorously, knowing that her eyes were on my swaying buttocks and that she could see the dark valley between them. I would almost weep with mortification.'

'But she never used the lash on you? I am surprised. What a delectable sight you must have been! I almost wish I could have seen you! Is that all she did?'

'At first. It seemed enough for her to humiliate me. Then one day she was in an odd mood. Her eyes seemed to burn into mine. There was a sort of leashed tension in her thin harsh body. I sensed that something was about to happen. I scrubbed the floor in the usual way, then I stood up to go. My face was red with shame. I longed to pull down my skirts and cover myself, but Sister Anna did not dismiss me. She kept looking at the triangle between my thighs, her eyes roving restlessly over my exposed hips and belly so that I became uneasy and longed to cover myself with my hands. But I dared not move. She told me to leave my dress and chemise pinned up. Then she called me over to where she sat on a wooden bench. She told me to sit astride it, facing her. I was acutely conscious of my half-naked state and I hesitated. She grew angry and said that if I did not obey her implicitly she would punish me severely. Then she said that I looked untidy and asked again if I had been neglecting to wash myself thoroughly. I insisted that I had not. Indeed, I had bathed just an hour or so before I began my tasks. She did not believe me. She said my hair was a mess and made me unbraid it. She brushed it out and spread it around my shoulders.'

Marietta stopped and took a breath. Then went on:

'All the time that she was brushing and teasing strands of my hair through her fingers, I was aware of the hardness of the bench under my parted thighs. I longed to close them together, to hide the triangle of hair and my intimate parts that were revealed by my position. My thighs trembled, but if I made the slightest move to adjust my position she slapped my legs, hard. After a while she ordered me to lie on the wooden bench and said that she intended to examine me. Oh, Claudine . . . I can hardly go on.'

Claudine's gentle fingers caressed Marietta's back. Her firm thighs opened. She drew one of Marietta's legs into her embrace and closed her legs around it, squeezing gently. Marietta felt the soft fleece of Claudine's sex against her upper thigh. She felt heat too and a slight dampness.

Her friend's voice, when it came, was light and a little breathless. 'Please go on, Marietta. Tell me everything.'

'I laid on the narrow bench. My shirts still looped up past my waist. My thighs were together, knees pressed so tightly against each other that my muscles ached. Sister Anna examined my bare feet. She pushed her fingers between my toes, separating each one roughly, stroking and pulling at them. Then her hands slid up my ankles and stroked my calves. They felt horribly rough and dry on my skin. Her fingers were always cold. She felt behind my knees, examining the creases, all the time commenting on the texture of my skin. She lingered on my upper legs, parting my thighs a little, stroking and pinching the surfaces – hard. The pain brought tears to my eyes. I made a sound of protest and shrank away, clamping my legs together with even more force. She slapped my face. "Lie still," she hissed, sternly, pulling at my thighs so that I loosened them again. I was frightened. She had the strangest look on her face. There was a faint colour in her thin pale cheeks. I lay still, not daring to move, while her cold hard eyes fastened on the place between my thighs. "Spread your legs, rest them one either side of the bench," she ordered. "Do not resist me, lest you wish to feel the lash. I want to see if you have washed that disgraceful fount of temptation."'

Claudine's breath came faster. Marietta felt the heat of her sex against her thigh increase as Claudine began to move, rubbing herself on the firm flesh. Claudine placed her lips on Marietta's cheek, covering it with tiny butterfly-light kisses.

'I cannot help myself,' she whispered. 'It is the thought of your lovely body, lying there so open and exposed. And you are so fresh and beautiful. It arouses me madly. Go on, I beg you. Continue. This is a gift to wash me clean from the memories. Do you mind, my darling, if I use you just a little? My pleasure will not be long in coming to its zenith.'

Marietta did not mind. Indeed she too was aroused by Claudine's sinuous movements. The hard little peaks of the erect nipples pressed against her own as Claudine moved her breasts back and forth. The liquid warmth of the heavy breasts lashed her own nipples into a state of matching rigidity. She tried to concentrate, to finish her account of Sister Anna's mistreatment.

'You can imagine my shame as I did as she asked. The room was cold. I felt cool air on my most tender flesh as I parted my legs and draped one either side of the narrow bench. My buttocks were flattened against the hard wood and my sex was pushed forward and slightly upturned. No one had ever seen me in such an intimate position. I thought the heat of my face would erupt through the skin. Surely this was enough. She could see that I was clean. Now she would let me up. I felt a sensation like relief; this would be over soon. But she was not satisfied yet. I closed my eyes as Sister Anna bent close. I could not bear to see her eyes, hot now, glistening with what was surely enjoyment. She put her palms on the inner surfaces of my outspread thighs and pressed, spreading my legs wider apart.

'Then I felt her fingers take hold of the lips of my sex. She held them open, parting them and pressing, so that the inner surface stood proud. Tears gathered behind my closed eyelids. I hated what she was doing, but I could not deny that a warm sensation was spreading out from my lower belly.

'"Ah, yes, it needs washing," Sister Anna rapped, in a voice I hardly recognised. "I will attend to it."

'Then I almost recoiled as I felt the most exquisite sensation. I dared not open my eyes but something warm and wet was worming its way inside my body's opening! It was a moment before I realised that it was Sister Anna's tongue. At that my eyes flew open, but she was beyond taking me to task. Her head moved back and forth as she "cleaned" me in long leisurely licks. She tongued the rolled-back surfaces of the lips she held open, then turned her attention to the soft inner flesh. Soon it was swollen and aching. I could not help myself. I moaned and raised my hips, rubbing against her thin dry mouth. She laughed and called me wanton, but she did not seem displeased. I felt a gathering, a pooling of sensation, as she continued to lick and suck my sex. Now and then she bit me, but not enough to really hurt; it only added to my pleasure. Then, as she plunged her tongue deep inside me again, I felt her fingers between my buttocks, searching for that other, tighter orifice.

'She thrust two dry bony fingers into me, hurting me. I spasmed on the instant, my legs raising up, falling back against my chest, my back arching, my belly thrusting against her mouth. Sister Anna was breathing fast. She rested her hands on my thighs for a moment longer. They were trembling violently. She stood up.

'"There. You are clean now," she said, dismissively. "Pull your skirts down and get out."

'I went as fast as my shaking legs would carry me. I was so ashamed that I enjoyed the feeling of her mouth on my flesh. But the next time I was – dare I admit it – eager for her attentions. That . . . was the first of many similar incidents.'

'Oh, Marietta,' Claudine moaned, grasping her around the waist and clenching her buttocks. She rubbed her hot little sex harder and harder against Marietta's thigh. 'I am almost there. Kiss me. Kiss me on the mouth, I beg you.'

Marietta pressed her mouth to Claudine's in a long and melting kiss. Their tongues met for the first time, tentatively. The sensation was wonderful. Subtle. Delicate. Marietta's blood caught fire as Claudine bucked and spasmed. Her friend's moan of ultimate pleasure vibrated down her throat.

Gradually Claudine quieted. Her fingers fluttered on Marietta's back as she subsided against her body. Marietta cradled her close. She felt exhausted, spent. All the fear and loathing, and the other confusing mixed emotions she felt for Sister Anna, seemed to have left her. She was glad that Claudine had found pleasure in the recounting of her secret.

Claudine's fresh young beauty, the straightforward way she took pleasure in her sexuality, seemed to have washed her clean. Marietta felt renewed. Now she would sleep.

And tomorrow ... there was Kasim.

In the night Marietta woke.

Though she tried to dismiss it, the image of Kasim haunted her dreams. It seemed that she had always known him, or someone very like him. He could easily have been the darkly handsome man she had conjured often in her imagination; the one who had rescued her from the boredom and repression, the long nights in the chilly dormitory.

She imagined him leaning over her in the darkness, his angular face vivid and intense in the moonlight. Shadows hollowed his cheekbones and eye sockets. Though bleached of colour his lips looked swollen, as if bruised by kisses. One pale hand reached out to pull the covers from her. The silk sheets slid down, exposing her shoulders, the tops of her breasts. His fingers were cool against her bare skin ...

She drew back from the image, lest she draw him to her by the power of her thoughts. It was easy to imagine that there was a silver thread joining their two minds, reaching through the salt impregnated wood of the cabins. Was he as aware of her, as she was of him? Surely not. He seemed far too controlled to give way to such emotion. But she could not help it: he was like a lamp in her thoughts.

She was afraid, but it was an enticing kind of fear. A fear that drew her on so that she felt breathless with longing. Her body, aroused by Claudine's actions, simmered and pulsed. Beside her, Claudine's breathing was deep and even. She looked at her friend's face, so smooth and peaceful, and her panic receded.

She must calm herself. Was she not born of a good

French family? She had breeding, poise, even if she was a little wilful; a little spoilt. She had always prided herself on her composure. Even the spectre of Sister Anna had not haunted her nights at the convent. The dread – the shameful anticipation – of the nun's actions was confined to the day time. Why should this man have such an effect on her that he disturbed her sleep?

She put her arms around Claudine and fitted herself against her warm curved back. Claudine's firm peachy buttocks rested against her bent thighs. Gradually she relaxed.

Her reaction to Kasim – to his aura of deep sensuality – made her realise how innocent of men she actually was. It made her realise also that she was ready to lose that innocence.

With that disquieting thought, she slipped at last into a deep and dreamless sleep.

Throughout the rest of the journey Kasim allowed the two young women the use of his cabin and all its facilities. They took many of their meals with him and spent long hours in conversation together.

He was charming and attentive, interested in all they had to say, yet they learned almost nothing about him. Whenever the conversation turned to himself, he steered it away again with such consummate skill that, at first, Marietta did not notice. Then she began to watch for the many small evasions: the sardonic little smile that accompanied his silences and the shuttered look to his face that told her he was lying by omission. He had told her that he was honest to a fault, had seemed proud of the fact. Was this how he safeguarded his privacy, by avoiding questions he could not answer honestly?

But even this she found attractive. The secrecy about

his background made him even more intriguing. All she learned of him was that he travelled widely, was wealthy, and that he had a large house in Algiers.

Kasim's servants cooked, cleaned and waited on them all. One man, handsome and dark-skinned, named Mehmet, seemed to be Kasim's confidant. They were often together. Marietta supposed that they were discussing business or Kasim's instructions to the other servants.

One morning, Marietta was alone in the cabin while Claudine was walking on deck. Marietta was attempting to dress her hair in a way that was the height of fashion in Paris. She puffed it out into a froth of curls and began to arrange it in a full halo around her shoulders.

Kasim entered the cabin silently but she saw the movement in the looking-glass and gave a start.

He laughed softly. 'Forgive me. I did not mean to startle you. I thought my cabin was empty. But I am glad you are alone, beautiful one.'

Before she could speak, he reached out and meshed his fingers in her hair. He admired the fluffy confection of it, then penetrated through the thick mass of curls to her scalp. For an instant she felt his long fingers stroking her skull, cupping the back of it where the roundness descended to the slender column of her neck. Then he drew away a little and lifted a few curls onto his spread fingers.

'Your hair is so pale, like strands of spun sugar,' he said, tangling a curl around one long white finger. 'Never have I seen hair like it.'

She held her breath while he trailed his other hand slowly up her pleated dress sleeve and across the stiffly-boned bodice. He brought his fingertips to rest lightly at the neckline, then moved aside the printed cambric scarf that draped her bosom. His fingers met the flesh on the exposed part of her rounded breast showing above the low neckline, and outlined a tiny circle on the outswell of flesh.

'Such skin. Like thick cream, with the slightest touch of honey.'

His touch was no more than a whisper, but Marietta could not suppress a violent shudder. His fingertips were warm and they sent an immediate thrill scudding through her veins. Kasim laughed again, throatily – a sound that held much promise. Their eyes met in the mirror. Marietta's dropped first. Her cheeks were flushed a deep pink; her lips trembled.

'You are a flower in bud, Marietta. Do you know how enticing you are? An innocent. What a challenge you present to a man! Ah, how difficult it is to hold back. I want to show you what an instrument of pleasure the body can be. But ... I shall wait. You shall tell me when the time is right.'

She stared at him, caught in the blackness of his gaze. In the looking-glass her eyes were wide blue pools. She did not know how to reply – or if she were able to. Her throat had closed with alarm. His words were shocking. She ought to be crying out for help, berating him for his forwardness, but she could only bite her lip. Her fingers clutched at the folds of her dress, burying into the creases, twisting and snagging the grey-violet sprigged cotton.

Kasim smiled long and lazily, his glance sweeping over her face, measuring her reactions, then he touched her curls to his lips, moved away and leant against the wall panelling.

Marietta felt relieved, but also, perversely, disappointed. For a moment she could not move. Her skin felt hot then cold and she tried to control her rapid breathing, wishing that she had not laced her gown so tightly.

There was a brief silence while Marietta regained her composure. She took up the brush and began to repair the damage to her coiffure, but her hand shook so much that Kasim must surely notice. She put down the brush and began pinning silk flowers and ribbons amongst the pale curls.

In a thoughtful, dreamy tone Kasim said, 'You look charming in your own clothes. Mehmet has made them as good as new. Yet I prefer you in the silks and gauzes from the trunk. Such beauty should be decorated with jewels: pearls, emeralds, sapphires and gold chains. Ah, yes, lots of delicate gold chains. You are most decorative, Mademoiselle de Nerval. What a delight to my eyes you will be while you are my guest.'

The predatory sensuality had quite disappeared. She could almost believe she had dreamt his earlier words. Almost . . .

'Th . . . thank you,' she stammered, not sure how else to reply to the effusive compliments. She was confused by his quicksilver change of mood.

He seemed about to say more, but just then a cry went up.

'Land! We have sighted land!'

Kasim threw her a final glance before hurrying up the ladder to the deck. 'Come, Marietta, I want to share this moment with you. You shall have your first glance of the Barbary coast, my homeland.'

She grabbed for her bonnet then, tying the wide ribbons under her chin, followed Kasim up on deck. Her knees felt weak. She could feel the spot where his fingertips had touched her breasts and she closed her hands into fists. A strange sensation spread through her stomach, warm and pulsing. Anticipation? Yes. But whether it was for the sight of the gleaming coastline, or for whatever she would find at Kasim's house, she could not tell.

Claudine was leaning over the rail already. In the near distance there was a hillside piled with the dazzling white cubes of buildings. Cypress trees were everywhere, looking like dark-green candle-flames. There were spires and towers of pink stone and the sun on the waves that broke on the shore turned them to sparkling turquoise.

'It is so beautiful,' Marietta whispered.

'Wait until you see my house,' Kasim said, standing at her elbow. 'It is far more lovely. But you and Claudine will outshine all of my treasures. You will love it there. Both of you.'

Claudine threw Marietta a look of excitement There was no time for words; the other passengers were crowding the deck, collecting together relatives and possessions. Kasim turned suddenly and stood with his back to the sea. Something passed over his face; it looked like hunger – then was quickly gone.

'Will you and Claudine indulge me? Algiers can be a dangerous place for unveiled women. Only whores display their naked faces, indeed, any part of their bodies. Though you will be safe enough with me and my retinue, you will attract an undesirable amount of attention dressed as you are. Will you consent to wear the traditional garments of concealment?'

Claudine laughed merrily. 'Really, *monsieur*, is that necessary? Ah, you seek to flatter us by telling us how special we are, no? Perhaps you wish to cage us and keep us for your pleasure alone. Oh La! We are free young women, not birds of paradise!'

They all laughed.

'Claudine's sense of humour is preposterous at

times,' said Marietta, indulgently. 'But I think we should agree. I do not relish being the centre of so much attention. Claudine?'

'Of course, I agree also. I spoke only in jest. Where are these garments we should wear?' Claudine smiled at Kasim.

Kasim smiled back, but his eyes glittered with some contained emotion. Marietta did not think that he was amused. He seemed edgy, impatient for them to leave the ship.

She felt again that small dart of fear. Their conversation, below decks a few minutes before seemed unreal. This man was sophisticated, wealthy, used to getting what he wanted. Should they go with him? It was not too late to refuse. It might be possible to seek the protection of one of the other passengers.

For Kasim could be ruthless – even cruel – she sensed it with utter certainty.

Then he smiled and the warmth suffused his angular features, turning him from being merely striking to being completely breathtaking. Ah, he was so beguiling. His presence was a forbidden fruit – the temptation of Eve.

It was impossible to refuse his invitation.

Marietta's stomach turned over.

One could forgive such a man anything.

2

Kasim stood in the shadows, listening, as Marietta and Claudine packed their few belongings and prepared to leave the ship.

Folded across his arms were a pile of black garments – two capes, veils and long black gloves. In a moment he would go into the cabin and give the robes to the young women to wear. But first he waited.

He wanted to savour the moment. It seemed impossible that in a short time he would step off the ship and be on his way to his house with such charming guests. His head seemed full of all the wonderful possibilities. Such things they would do together.

Claudine now – she would not be difficult. It would be easy to win her. She was a creature who responded to pleasure. Delightful in her way, and lovely; undeniably so. Who could not want to feel the tickle of that sleek red-gold hair on his bare skin? Or to lay hands on the luscious rounded curves of her body. To part the globes of her fine whip-marked buttocks and explore the scented, shadowed valley therein.

He recalled the sight of her, naked, as she showed the whip marks to Marietta the night before. Through the hole in the cabin wall he had seen everything. He had seen Marietta's nakedness also, all too briefly. But it was enough to inflame him.

Ah, how fine she was. Sleeker, less opulently curved than her friend, and with that hesitancy, that self-fear that he found utterly compelling. He heard the recounting of Sister Anna's ministrations; the hesitancy and the shame as both young women confided in each other. How delightful it had been.

And how convenient that the bedclothes had slipped aside, so that he glimpsed the curve of Claudine's thigh, flexing and releasing as she rubbed herself to a climax against Marietta's body. He had seen the swell of her heavy breasts as she crushed them against Marietta. The nipples were quite small. Pale, a colour like coffee mixed with peach. They looked new, tender.

His erect penis jumped at the thought of them. There was a pleasing pressure in his scrotum. Since he first laid eyes on the two of them he had been in a permanent state of arousal. It made him feel vital, truly alive. He savoured the heaviness, the engorgement at his groin. The pleasure-ache of it. Prolonging that sensation was what pleased him most; the final release could be delayed indefinitely. It was just a matter of being strong enough to keep the level of arousal restrained.

Restrained. He liked the word. It described him admirably. He was controlled, self-disciplined to a fault. Not many people ever guessed at the torrent of passion he kept leashed. The quick release, the dissipation of pleasure into brief uncontrolled ejaculations, random miltings, were not for him.

He had long ago discovered a world of refinement. A world where the level of pleasure was fed by surroundings of the utmost sensual luxury – where pleasure and pain could mix, if one so desired, and be transformed into ecstasy.

And Marietta, Claudine too, might be invited to share that world.

He thought of how Marietta had looked when he walked into the cabin just before land was sighted. She looked charming in the ridiculous western clothes. The pale grey-violet gown suited her perfectly. Her slim throat rose from the gauzy white scarf which was criss-crossed over the low-cut bodice and tied at the small of her back. She had her arms raised to dress her hair. The tight sleeves, flaring out from the elbow, had fallen back to cover her upper arms and expose her slender forearms and wrists.

He found the sight of the constricting bodice and flaring skirt captivating. The thought of all that cool satin-smooth flesh, restricted by the boned bodice and tight sleeves, and the many layers of stiffened skirts, made him feel hot.

His cock stirred, the swollen end pulsing, nudging at the heavy belt he wore at his waist. There was a tightness in his stomach and he was more aware of the skin between his thighs.

He had not meant to touch her, but could not resist. Her skull felt so delicate as he cupped it in his palm. The cloud of her hair surrounding his hand had been warm, feather-light, hay-scented and slightly sticky with salt. He could not wait for it to be washed in soft soap and perfumed with sandalwood. Then he would gather its pale mass in his two hands and bury his head in the softness.

Her hair had stirred him to take greater liberties. There was the tiny circle he traced on her breast. Ah, how enticingly they swelled from the constriction of the bodice. The skin was smooth, milky. He could hardly contain himself. He had been tempted to dip into the bodice, hook his fingers under one breast and draw out the nipple. He imagined it jutting over the bodice offered to him like a ripe fruit – by the fabric pushing up hard against the underswell. His lips itched to taste the nipple. He longed to gaze at its unique colour, polish it with his tongue, until it glistened; to suck the smooth silky tip until it grew turgid. A peak to tease with teeth and tongue.

It had taken a supreme effort to refrain from touching her; to simply walk across the room. Marietta's eyes in the looking-glass had been beguiling beyond measure. So wide and blue, innocent but pleading. Her fresh pink lips had trembled, fearful and bereft. Did she know that she was ready to be opened? He thought she fought that knowledge.

All the better.

The moment, when it came, would be worth the wait. For both of them. And the moment *would* come, he was certain of it.

He took a step forward and advanced on the open doorway of the cabin. 'Here are the robes of concealment,' he said, his voice perfectly calm and level. 'Are you both ready to leave?'

Marietta looked around in amazement. Algiers was a place of vivid contrasts and the heat was suffocating. Smells of dust and jasmine mingled with the savoury smells of roast meat and spiced pastries. Kasim's entourage made its way through the cobbled streets, passing the stalls of street vendors. Many of them called out, holding up strings of glass beads and lengths of brightly coloured fabrics.

Doorways, dark and mysterious, peppered the crooked stone walls that lined the narrow streets. In some places blue-tiled courtyards could be glimpsed, nestling behind archways hung with embroidered calico curtains. There, too, flowering shrubs stood in pots and fig trees clustered around stone fountains.

Elsewhere they passed dark stinking alleyways, the entrances slimy with filth. Rats scurried over piles of rotting food. Next to butchers' stalls grimy barefoot children played with tangles of still-bleeding entrails, while nearby a group of old men sat drinking and fanning a charcoal brazier.

Marietta devoured the many sights from behind the black gauze veil that swathed her head and face. A shapeless black cape covered her body and long black gloves ensured that every part of her was hidden from public view. Claudine walked some way ahead, partly obscured from view by the bulky figure of Mehmet. Marietta could just see the top of Claudine's swathed form. Like herself she was a cipher, featureless in this vibrant, dangerous place. Kasim was at the head of the retinue, two slaves walking at either side. One held a parasol above his head, the other wielded a huge fan made of peacock feathers.

Marietta could not help noticing how a way cleared for them as if by magic. People stopped what they were doing to let them pass. Some bowed their heads, or touched hands to foreheads and lips in a form of greeting. Many curious looks came their way. Some hostile ones, too, mainly from groups of painted slatternly women.

She was glad of the anonymity of the costume, though the dark cloth drew the heat and brought beads of perspiration out all over her body. She had insisted that she wear her own clothes under the cloak, but now she wished she had listened to Kasim. The loose flowing garments from the chest would have been more comfortable than her cotton gown, laced tightly over stays and the bustle pad at her hips.

As they approached what seemed to be a market, a roar of noise greeted them. A crowd had gathered to watch some spectacle. The slaves on either side of Marietta nudged each other and grinned, pointing towards a raised wooden platform. The crowd cleared a space for the entourage. Kasim gave the order to halt. The slaves gathered around the two women, shielding their backs but allowing them a clear view of the platform.

Four men ascended the steps, dragging a fifth between them. It took the strength of all four to hold the struggling man, though his hands were bound behind his back. Marietta suppressed a gasp; the captive was strikingly handsome, and he was naked. He was also tall and strongly built and every inch of his well-made body was covered in hard muscle. The air rang with his curses as he struggled with his captors but, despite his best efforts, he was soon secured to two stout wooden posts. The prisoner glared defiance at the crowd, twisting and straining against the shackles which secured his wrists.

Marietta supposed that the man must be a criminal. He had a wild rakish look about him. He was so close that she could see his clear grey eyes, narrow with contempt. Whatever his crime, he was not contrite. He held up his chin and threw his chest out proudly. She admired the sheer animal force of him. He was like a lion; beautiful and dangerous.

Her eyes lingered on his body; on the straight muscular limbs, the flat stomach, slim hips; and especially on the thick phallus and sac at his groin. The skin on the cock-stem was darker than on his body. She was fascinated, never having seen a man naked before. The prisoner's private parts were surrounded by a dark blond thatch. The curls had been brushed out into a crisp halo and shone as if they had been oiled. A thick mane of light yellow hair tumbled unbound over his powerful shoulders. Over the whole of his body the skin had a light sheen as if it had been polished.

Someone had taken pains to see that the prisoner's body was groomed to perfection for the public spectacle of his punishment. A fact that seemed odd to Marietta.

'Magnificent, isn't he?' Kasim whispered, close to Marietta's ear.

'Yes, he is,' she breathed, unthinkingly. Then she caught the brief flare of interest on Kasim's lean face. Was he jealous? How ridiculous. She almost laughed, but something stopped her. Kasim was not a man to be laughed at.

'What ... what is the man's crime? Do you know?' she asked.

Kasim laughed, 'Certainly I know. He is a runaway slave. His name is Gabriel. He belongs to a merchant friend of mine.'

On Martinique her father had kept slaves, but no one had ever run away. It was the most serious crime, next to murder. She feared for Gabriel. So aptly named, for he was as beautiful as an angel. Slavery must be a hard yoke for one such as he. For an instant Gabriel's restless grey eyes lingered on her. She felt the sudden urge to pull aside the veil, to look him full in the face and let him see her distaste for this public spectacle.

As if he sensed her thoughts Kasim laid his hand on her arm. Marietta turned towards him and saw that his face looked slightly flushed. The tip of his tongue snaked out to moisten his mouth.

'Have you ever witnessed a beating?' said Kasim.

'No. Father never beat our slaves,' replied Marietta.

'Indeed? How strange. Then you missed a rare treat.'

She looked at him with horror, thinking she had misunderstod. 'You enjoy watching such a thing?'

He chuckled. 'But of course. A measure of pain is a potent spice to stir the senses. And not only to those who witness the act. Do not look too concerned; he will not be badly hurt. That is not the intention. Watch Gabriel closely. You will see what I mean.'

Marietta trembled. Half of her was revolted by Kasim's words, but a larger part of her being was morbidly fascinated.

A thickset man, holding a lash, ascended the steps. He took up his position behind Gabriel. He put down the lash on the boards, then grasped the thick flaxen hair and pulled Gabriel's head back. The prisoner's chest was forced outwards, his back curved like a bow, while his neat buttocks were thrust into prominence. Laughing, the thickset man ran a meaty hand over Gabriel's chest, massaging his muscles, pinching his nipples until they stood up. He flicked them in turn, between finger and thumb. Soon they glowed a deep red-brown.

Marietta thought how awful, how humiliating it must be to be pawed openly in this way.

The coarse, thick-fingered hand moved down over the prisoner's flat belly and circled the navel. Travelling to the groin the fingers began tugging at the pubic curls. Gabriel had closed his eyes, but Marietta knew that he could not help hearing the roars of appreciation from the crowd. The roars redoubled when the thick hand closed around the penis, jerking it crudely upright and beginning to pump it with firm strokes.

As it stiffened and stood proud, the crowd went wild. Gabriel's hair was released, his head grasped and his neck bent forward so that he could watch while the thickset man worked the glowing member up and down.

How does he stand it? Marietta thought, appalled. But, like the crowd, she could not take her eyes from the rigid stem crowned by the tight swollen bulb.

After a while the man picked up the whip. He stood

to one side of Gabriel, grinning and running his tongue around his thick fleshy lips. Gabriel mouthed an obscenity and the man laughed. Grasping the erect stem and scrotum in one hand, the man wrapped the lash tightly around the root, under the sac. The organs were now painfully exposed. Gabriel's shame was tangible. For a time the man tormented him further, tapping the head of the cock with the end of the whip, beating it lightly down its length.

The crowd jeered and cheered. Judging the mood of the audience, and picking his moment, the man released Gabriel's organs. Then he trailed the whip over his shoulders and walked around Gabriel to stand behind him.

'You want more?' he shouted, suddenly, grabbing Gabriel's buttocks in both hands and dragging them apart. The phallus stirred, jerking. It was dark red, suffused with blood.

Gabriel winced as the thick fingers pulled at him, exposing the tight puckered anus, surrounded by damp blonde curls. The crowd were delighted.

'Lash him! Lash him now!' Someone began. Others took up the cry.

The thickset man grinned. 'Oh, you've had enough of just looking. Right then,' he said.

Marietta could not tear her eyes away from Gabriel's beautiful face. His jutting cheekbones were set, flushed darkly with shame, and ready now for the first biting sting of the lash. His mouth – full and tender – was still curled with disdain.

Her thoughts rioted within her. Suddenly she wanted to see his expression change; to see him slimed with sweat, his beauty broken as he sobbed with pain. Ah, then she would love to cradle his proud head in her arms. Kiss his bruised mouth . . .

She was alarmed by the darkness inside her. Where had such thoughts come from? Did she know instinctively what Kasim spoke of?

Yes. All at once, she knew. Sister Anna had awoken hungers – not planted them. Her senses had been slumbering only. What a startling discovery. She needed space to think, to encompass this new revelation. But she had no time to wonder at herself.

The beating began.

The sound of the lash hitting flesh broke the air. It was a soft sound; there was not too much force behind the blow. A sigh went up from the crowd. Marietta saw Gabriel's head jerk back, but his expression did not change. Another blow. The lash tip curled around his waist. She saw the slight weal it left, pink against the white flesh. Beads of sweat broke out on Gabriel's forehead.

She wondered at his tension. The blows could not be very painful. A third blow. Then another. The people standing behind the prisoner must have seen how the marks coloured his white skin. Pink and white. Such symmetry. She would have liked to see that too. But she had his face. That was even better.

Now the cords stood out in Gabriel's neck. The blows came often and he strained against his bonds. Marietta saw how the shackles cut into his wrists. His hands were curled into fists, the fingers pale and bloodless. His chest swelled. The copper-brown nipples were stiffly erect, small and tight. At the next blow he drew in a great breath. His ribcage gaped and his belly grew concave. Tremors ran down his thighs. A sheen of sweat pearled his limbs, running down his legs like rain down glass.

She was intent on his face, watching as it slackened. He could not hold back his reaction. Oh, Gabriel, you are even more beautiful in your distress. She was almost moved to tears, longing to kiss his hot face, to smooth the hair back from his cheek where a damp yellow strand was plastered to his cheekbone.

Gabriel's lips trembled. His bravado crumbled, inevitably. He twisted his head round to rest on one shoulder and buried his face in his outstretched arm. As he began to groan Marietta felt heat gather between her thighs.

'The phallus,' Kasim whispered.

She watched as Gabriel's member grew even more rigidly erect. His sac contracted, becoming two firm stones. Surely every woman who watched wanted him. People began shouting obscenities. She wanted them to stop. Such a sight should be enjoyed in reverent silence. Her legs felt weak. Each of Gabriel's groans went like a dart straight to her stomach and an insistent pulsing began in her lower belly. Under her bodice her breasts swelled until they ached. She felt a sound gathering in her throat and caged it behind her teeth.

Kasim laughed softly, knowingly, one hand snaking around her waist as he drew her against him. He took her weight on his arm, whispering:

'I knew I would not regret bringing you to my house. Feast your eyes, Marietta. Let your passions rise. Look into Gabriel's face. Is he not a marvellous animal? Watch him lose all control. He cannot help it. Though he tries to withhold himself to punish the crowd, he cannot – and they know it. That is why they jeer. That is the spectacle they come to see. They love him for his frailty. Look at them. You can see it on their faces.'

It was true. Every face was avid. While they berated the bound man and enjoyed his suffering, they admired him. Some probably envied him. Many of the men had shining eyes, slack mouths. A woman with dyed red hair and a painted mouth pulled down her tunic, exposing ripe breasts with large brown nipples. She lifted them as if offering them to Gabriel. Flinging back her head she laughed, showing strong white teeth. Then she turned to a man wearing a butcher's apron. He grasped her around the waist, suckling at her breasts eagerly to the great delight of the crowd.

From the corner of her eye Marietta saw a man lift a whore's skirts and slide into her from the rear. Even while the whore protested, demanding payment, he thrust at her. His groans of pleasure were muffled against the bunched-up material around her shoulders. The many coarse gestures, the open sexuality of the crowd, inflamed Marietta's passions further.

Gabriel, rapt in his battle with his own responses, tossed his head from side to side. His long hair was wet, soaked with sweat. Droplets flew out, sparkling in the sunlight. Marietta felt the hot drops land on her face, tasted the salt of his sweat on her lips, and realised that Kasim had pulled the veil down, exposing her eyes, nose and mouth. His fingers were a vice around her arm. She felt his other hand caress her neck and move upwards to cup her chin.

Then the tips of his fingers found her mouth. She parted her lips eagerly and he thrust his thumb between her teeth, rubbing the fleshy pad over her tongue. She tasted salt on his skin.

Kasim's breath came in a harsh shallow rhythm. As Marietta sucked on his thumb she felt his sexual excitement mounting. His eyes were fastened on the spectacle before them. The rigid tension was evident in every line of his body and his narrow angular face looked as if carved from marble.

Marietta's tension matched his. She had never felt so aroused. A shameless hunger rose in her. She envied the whore. Her womb throbbed, sending signals of readiness to her moist slit. She wanted to be filled, impaled, torn into. Kasim's thumb moved, probing the soft flesh inside her mouth. She drew it deeply into her throat, circling it with her ravenous tongue.

She could not look away from the platform. Gabriel's hips thrust forward each time the lash stroked his back. His distended member beat against his stomach. The exposed glans was shiny, moist and purplish, collared by the ruched cock-skin. A single clear drop, like a tear, trembled on the tip. The skin on his organ looked stretched it was so engorged. Surely he could not contain himself much longer.

The tip of the lash snaked around Gabriel's inner thigh, marking him lightly from thigh to groin. He bucked and jerked his wrists against his bonds, then the lash curled around his pubic hair, licking his balls. And again. A harsh groan escaped him. His breath was ragged now, his teeth bared in a rictus of shame and pleasure. The crowd groaned in unison.

'He breaks. Now!' Kasim hissed in Marietta's ear, drawing out his thumb and rubbing the damp tip of it across her parted lips.

She felt a gathering of excitement. Her heart beat fast. Yes. Oh, Yes.

Gabriel threw back his head and roared. Every muscle in his body was strained to breaking point. The swollen veins were visible under his golden skin. His phallus jumped, his balls tightened, and a great jet of seed spurted across the platform, followed by another, and another.

'Oh, God,' Marietta whispered against the back of Kasim's hand, as, at that precise moment, she locked eyes with Gabriel.

The troubled grey eyes fastened on her face, became

focused, and remained. She looked deep into him, projecting her admiration, her arousal, her soul towards him. The barest flicker of acknowledgement passed over his face. His mouth trembled, pulling away at the corners. And she knew that he was on the brink of tears.

She felt her body respond with the force of a furnace.

She loved his self-hatred, his shame, the way he sagged in defeat. Only the shackles at his wrists supported him. Without them, he would have fallen in the dust. She could see how he longed desperately to hide; how he hated the eyes watching his every move. A silent darkened room must have seemed like paradise to him at that moment. Oh, he was achingly beautiful in his sweat and pain.

She held his eyes by the force of her will as she leaned against the wooden edge of the platform. Kasim was silent, locked in private appreciation of Gabriel. She meshed her black-gloved fingers, gripping them tight, pressing them into the hollow between her thighs. Suddenly her climax wracked her, washing over her in great wrenching spasms, leaving her weak and spent.

Kasim's hard body supported her still. He was fully aware of what had happened. He said something under his breath and the hand that rested on her waist trembled. He too desired Gabriel, she could feel it. The thought excited her beyond measure. Could men be lovers? What things would they do together?

Kasim and Gabriel. The darkest night and the sun. She imagined their bodies locked in a fierce embrace, and glimpsed a world of jewelled delights, hitherto unknown to her.

She felt quite faint. Though her body was sated for the moment, she was confused by all she had experienced. The tight lacing of her gown restricted her movements and she could hardly draw breath for the tightness of her throat. Her responses alarmed her. Suddenly the crowd seemed to lose its fascination. She wanted to get away from the crush of people.

But poor Gabriel remained a prisoner.

For a moment longer she looked at him. A thin trickle of semen ran down one thigh. Even as she watched, a last pearly droplet fell from the tip of his cock. Tremors jerked across his chest. He was sweating so much he looked oiled.

The man with the lash drew away, grinning. The spectacle was over. She realised, belatedly, that the whipping had been incidental. There was no blood and the marks, though pink, were not raised, and plainly not too painful.

Humiliation had been Gabriel's punishment – not the lash.

His master must have known him well to have chosen such a refined chastisement. As well, it seemed, as Kasim was beginning to know her.

'Come, Marietta. It is hot and dusty. There is nothing here for us now,' Kasim said shortly, drawing her away.

Marietta looked over her shoulder at Gabriel, who was still watching her. She mouthed 'Thank you' to him.

Surprise, then the ghost of a smile passed over his remarkable face before his head sagged forward a last time and dropped onto his chest.

Gabriel lifted his head and stared after the figure of the woman who had watched him.

He felt grateful to her. Her presence in the crowd had dissipated some of his agony of mind. It had seemed, at the last moment before the explosion of pleasure came, that he was on show just for her – and it had not been so very bad. He had pretended they were alone, and the reflection of himself – which he had seen in her shining face – had made him proud to be beautiful. Proud that, though he could not hold on, and the crowd would have their satisfaction at his expense, he could give himself to her.

The crowd did not matter. Only *she* mattered.

And she had understood that, accepting what he gave her. She had even thanked him, shaping her lovely mouth around the silent word. Even through the haze of exhaustion and the shame which still burned in every line of his abused body, he held onto her image. While they untied him and led him away, he thought only of her.

That perfect oval face, framed all in black, and the big blue eyes. Blue as the summer sky. Blue as flax flowers. Who was she? He had not heard of a blue-eyed slave. Such a one would be noticed. She had been with Kasim Dey, and Kasim was a friend of his master, Selim the jewel merchant.

The merchant went often to Kasim's house to do business. Gabriel might be taken, too, if he took pains to engineer events. He smiled, the strong well-shaped mouth curving richly. He knew what he must do to influence his master. Tonight he would beg to be allowed to pleasure Selim, protesting his contrition after the public punishment.

Selim could resist him nothing when he had his buttocks pressed to Gabriel's groin and Gabriel's hand working up and down his hungry shaft.

Ah, it was more than possible that he would meet the woman. He hoped fervently that it would be soon.

3

The crowd began dispersing rapidly.

The ranks of slaves closed around Marietta and Claudine. Safely hemmed in by strong black bodies they moved on. There was no time for Marietta to see what happened to Gabriel. The market and platform of punishment were soon far behind them.

Kasim walked by her side, supporting her elbow in one strong slender hand, a gesture that to outward appearances looked innocent enough, but she felt the tightly leashed power in his fingers. His profile was stern, the set of the strong mouth severe. Those refined nostrils were white-tipped, flaring just a fraction, the only hint of his contained inner turmoil.

He was still aroused by the sight they had witnessed, she was certain of it and the thought excited her.

She had the feeling that he would like to tear the clothes from her body. Even to punish her a little for her shameless enjoyment, for the way the wicked pleasure had rolled over her without the need for anyone's touch. She would have liked that, welcomed it even, though she feared the strength of Kasim's reactions.

She was a little afraid of herself too; the docile convent girl was fast undergoing a transformation. It was a heady sensation, this self-discovery. She longed to talk to Claudine, to confide in her.

For some time they walked in silence and Gabriel's face invaded Marietta's thoughts. She knew that she would not forget him but Kasim's insistent presence surrounded her. Even the memory of the beautiful prisoner took second place to her charming companion.

The fans and parasols waved over her head and she smelt salt on the warm breeze that blew in from the sea. The streets were wider here, the cobbles clean. They passed the walls of great houses; sheer and white, reaching up high overhead. Balconies, boxed in by ornate screens, jutted out over the street. Soon they came to a stone gate; it was huge and ornately carved. Two burly soldiers stood on guard. Mehmet knocked on the gate with his staff; it opened and they entered into a cool shady courtyard. More guards were apparent; they saluted Kasim.

'Welcome to my home,' Kasim said bowing to his guests. 'All that I have is yours.'

'Thank you. You are most kind,' Claudine replied at Marietta's side.

Servants came out to welcome their master home. Marietta was aware of many eyes studying them from windows that looked out on to the courtyard. Shadowy veiled shapes peered through the carved screens. A woman's hand protruded from a small arch. The hand was long and slender and covered in some sort of painted design. Gold bracelets were clustered on her wrist and on her middle finger she wore an enormous emerald ring.

Kasim looked up toward the owner of the hand. He smiled briefly, made a subtle gesture of greeting, then turned his attention back to Marietta and Claudine.

'Take my guests to the women's quarter,' he ordered a slave. 'Leyla is to be given charge of them.'

Taking hold of Marietta's gloved hand he carried it to his lips, then did the same to Claudine.

'I have business to see to for the moment. Leyla will

see to it that you are bathed and made comfortable. In the cool of the evening I shall join you in the garden.'

'I shall look forward to it,' Marietta said.

Kasim bowed, then walked towards a stone tower with Mehmet. The rest of the entourage followed him.

'Please to come this way,' the slave said, leading them both towards a side entrance.

There were guards patrolling the forecourt and yet more guards stood to either side of the small brass-bound door.

'What riches Kasim must have to need so many men to guard him,' Claudine said.

Marietta had been thinking the same thing. As they passed through the brass-bound door, the guards stood aside. Neither of them glanced at the two women. The door was pulled to and slammed shut behind them. Marietta whirled, suddenly feeling panicky; there was such an air of finality about the dull clang.

The slave waited patiently, silently, until she collected herself and walked forward.

'What is it?' Claudine said.

'I ... I don't know. But this is not what I expected. It's almost as if we are locked in. It seems a strange way to treat one's guests.'

Claudine smiled. 'I expect it is the custom here. I find it all fascinating. I'm sure that Kasim is just being protective. Now stop worrying. I must confess that the thought of a bath and a place to rest has quite pushed all other worries out of my mind.'

Marietta shrugged. Perhaps her friend was right. She too welcomed the thought of bathing. She realised how tired she felt. Her nerves seemed a little ragged, and no wonder after the spectacle and her response at the marketplace. They were led down corridors and passageways. Slaves hurried to and fro on various errands.

There were many of them, of various races, and all women or girls. They hardly glanced at Marietta and Claudine.

Marietta could not explain why, but she still felt uneasy. Though the surroundings were luxurious in the extreme, there was a cloistered feel about the place. Somehow it reminded her of the convent. The air smelt of sweet spices, perfume, and aromatic smoke. Once, as they crossed an inner courtyard, she glimpsed the town, framed in an open archway. It seemed very far away.

They followed the silent slave across endless tiled floors and stone paving. It seemed a long time before they stopped at the entrance to a chamber. The slave bowed and gestured that they might go in.

Marietta parted the beaded curtain that draped the archway. She and Claudine stepped into the most beautiful room they had ever seen. Embroidered silks framed the low divans, where a number of women reclined. Some were talking, others played board games or nibbled sweetmeats. Slaves served the women with dishes of food and drink.

They were welcomed and drawn into the room. All activity stopped as everyone crowded around. Marietta smiled nervously, speaking words of greeting. Someone held out their arms for the concealing outer clothes. She and Claudine disrobed and a silence fell when the lovely pale faces were revealed. Then a great noise broke out as everyone began speaking at once.

There was much giggling over the French clothes and hairstyles. Marietta stood uncomfortably while the women ran their hands over her hair, plucking at the spray of silk flowers and ribbons, drawing her pale curls through their thin brown fingers. But it was her clear-blue eyes that drew the most admiring glances.

She smiled hesitantly, looking round with lowered eyelids, a becoming pink flush staining her cheeks.

Marietta noticed one woman in particular, studying her with avid interest. But this woman did not smile with delight; instead her eyes were wide and appreciative. She was exotically beautiful. Her face, a perfect oval, was dominated by long almond eyes so dark they seemed to be black. A crown of night-black plaits was wrapped around her head and rubies glinted amidst the heavy coils of hair. Her painted red lips stood out against her astonishing white skin.

After a few moments, the dark woman stood up and clapped her hands for silence. The noise subsided and the women drew away a little.

'I am Leyla,' the dark woman said. 'Kasim Dey asks that I take care of you until you become accustomed to our ways. May we know your names?'

They introduced themselves. Claudine commented on how thoughtful it was of Kasim to think of their welfare.

'We shall not be staying very long,' she added. 'Just until our passage is arranged to Martinique.'

Some of the women exchanged glances. Leyla looked warningly at them. She smiled. 'Of course. But for now you are our guests. It is an honour to welcome you. First you must eat and take your ease. After, I will show you where you may sleep. Then you may wish to bathe.'

She clapped her hands. Marietta and Claudine were led to a divan and made comfortable amongst embroidered silk cushions. Food soon arrived, served in dishes on low tables of carved and gilded wood. There was no cutlery and Marietta hesitated to eat with her fingers. Leyla saw her embarrassment and, dipping her fingers into a bowl, showed them both how it was done.

Marietta was famished and ate everything put in front of her. The food was delicious: aubergines stuffed with peppers and onions; fish in a delicately spiced sauce; fluffy rice; and sherbets, cool fruit drinks. After eating they washed their hands in bowls of rose-scented water. Across the room a woman began playing a musical instrument. Another sang.

Claudine relaxed against the cushions. A tray of sugared nuts was placed beside her and something that looked like a brass lamp, entwined by a snake. Leyla explained that it was a *nargileh*, a water pipe. Marietta was fascinated to see that the women smoked it with relish. They offered it to Claudine. Giggling she tried it and, finding it to her taste, began to smoke with enthusiasm.

'Do try it, Marietta. It is quite delightful. The tobacco is perfumed and very cool.'

Marietta declined to smoke.

'Would you like to bathe then?' Leyla said. 'Your friend is comfortable here. Let us leave her to entertain the women. We do not have many visitors. Any diversion is welcome.'

Claudine waved the pipe tube, looking completely at ease. 'You go, Marietta,' she said, 'I'll join you later.'

She was plainly flattered by all the attention. A group of women had gathered around her, admiring her pale skin, stroking her red-gold hair. The golden freckles on the skin above her neckline caused many comments. One of the women unwound a sparkling blue sash from her waist and held it up against Claudine's skin.

'Women of your fair colouring are a rarity in these regions,' Leyla said to Marietta. 'You will be made much of here. But others will be jealous. Stay close to me. I will protect you.'

Protect her from what? Marietta wondered, and was about to ask, but Leyla was leading the way across the room, her slim sandalled feet making no sound on the thick colourful rugs. Claudine's infectious bell-like laugh rang out. It seemed that this place, with its luxury and promise of sensual delights, was already working its spell on her friend.

'Come, Marietta,' Leyla said, in her soft husky voice. 'I will take you to the hammam where all worries and fears are put aside for a time, and there is only the enjoyment of the perfumed water. If you are tired, you will be invigorated. If you are tense, you will become relaxed.'

It was just what Marietta needed to hear. She went with Leyla, gladly.

'This is the hammam – the baths,' Leyla explained. 'It is more than a place of cleansing. Here we meet to relax and exchange gossip. Only women are allowed. The men have separate baths in different parts of the house.'

The ballroom at Marietta's house in Martinique was not as fine. Here, tall narrow columns soared up to a coloured skylight and the walls and floors were inlaid with tiles. A dense perfumed vapour hung over the room and a plunge pool occupied the centre of it. The surface of the water was level with the floor.

A number of women, naked or partially clothed, were being attended by slaves holding dishes of sweet-meats. Some of them swam in the pool, others sat on the sides drying their hair with fluffy towels. More of them sat around talking or reclining on cushioned platforms.

They were all beautiful.

A woman walked up to Leyla wearing only a pair of

bath shoes and a loose gauze robe. A jewelled sash was tied loosely on her hips. She had a large-framed voluptuous body, all of it clearly visible through the thin gauze. Propping one hand on her hip, she exchanged a few friendly words with Leyla. When she laughed her breasts jiggled.

Marietta averted her eyes, trying not to stare. She had never seen so many naked women. When bathing, at the convent, she had been made to wear a voluminous calico robe. All bodily contact between the young women was frowned upon, so she was doubly shocked when the woman gave Leyla a lingering kiss on the mouth before tottering away on her stilted shoes.

Leyla smiled. 'I have kept you waiting. Forgive me. Come then, we must disrobe. First we wash and make our bodies beautiful. Then after, we can talk and drink sherbet.'

Two female slaves stood ready to wait on them. They were both young and comely, and naked except for their jewellery. Chains and strings of metal discs adorned the slaves' necks and chests. And peeking, through all this finery, were their upright young breasts, each gilded nipple jutting out provocatively. Despite Marietta's censorious thoughts, she found all the nakedness arousing.

The slaves disrobed Leyla. Her perfect body drew Marietta's eyes, as earlier Gabriel's had done. Leyla's limbs were long and rounded – the skin pale, glowing softly like a pearl. She had large breasts, full and slightly up-tilted, with prominent wine-red nipples. Her waist was narrow, tapering to lushly flaring hips. The smooth indentation that swooped down to her groin, on either side of her flat belly, was particularly lovely. Marietta swept her eyes over Leyla's body in appreciation, realising that, to her utter amazement, there was no body hair.

She found herself staring openly at the smoothly naked mound, where the slit of Leyla's sex was plainly visible. It looked strange to her. The little pouting mound was somehow childlike, yet distinctly womanly at the same time. The pink inner lips showed slightly through the closed flesh-lips and, as Leyla moved, Marietta saw the tip of what looked like a darker pink bud protruding. It was most enticing.

Leyla caught her looking. She did not seem to mind. Turning around in a circle, she said, without a trace of modesty, 'I am beautiful, yes? You like me, Marietta? That is good. For I find you beautiful too. We shall find pleasure in each other.'

Her words were strange. They promised something unknown; Marietta felt excited and fearful in equal measure.

Leyla watched closely as Marietta was undressed. Marietta squirmed under the directness of those long black eyes, but she did not protest. It seemed foolish to protest when everyone else was naked, or partly so, but as the final garments were taken from her, she could not help hunching over a little and holding her cupped hands over the lightly shadowed mound at the joining of her thighs.

Leyla laughed huskily. 'But no,' she said. 'Do not hide yourself. Let me look.'

She took hold of Marietta's wrists and gently but firmly pulled her arms out to the sides and held them there. Marietta's cheeks felt hot and she longed to cover herself. The two slave girls watched, smiling slightly. Her embarrassment mounted as Leyla studied her intently.

'Ah. You have no need of the magic of cosmetics. Your body is beautiful. Such pretty breasts, so high and round, and the nipples, pink and tender, waiting for the touch of hands or mouth. Your waist is small, very small. That device of bones and laces you wear is to make a small waist, yes? Your hips are shapely; they flare out beautifully.'

She exerted pressure on Marietta's arm so that she made a half-turn. 'Your bottom is high and round too; nicely plump. And your thighs are long and firm. Why are you ashamed to be naked? You have a body which must give you much pleasure when you touch it and bring yourself to a melting peak.'

Marietta's cheeks burned. She knew that her whole face was red. Never had anyone spoken to her in such a direct way. And she had never touched herself in the way Leyla described. It had never occurred to her to do so. But she knew what pleasure Leyla spoke of. Sister Anna had first shown her.

She had to admit she was pleased, flattered, that Leyla thought she was comely. Leyla was very beautiful herself. A far cry from the stern humourless nun who had used Marietta's body for her own twisted pleasure. She felt a stirring within her as Leyla's sultry eyes lingered on her naked flesh, as if she was unwilling to look away.

When Leyla let go of her arms she left them as they were, letting Leyla continue her examination at her leisure. She was more intrigued with each passing moment by the fact that Leyla found her desirable. It was not something that she had given thought to in the convent. Now she felt a new pride beginning. The obvious interest and admiration shown by the slave girls added to her feeling of being special.

'The soft fleece on your sex is so pretty,' Leyla said.

'So unusual. Pale, like spun gold. It is a pity that it must be removed. Here it is considered to be a sin to have hair on one's female parts but I like the mystery it gives. Your sex is concealed from the casual gaze and must be discovered by close inspection – perhaps only by touch. How a lover must long to spread you and feast on your secret flesh. Charming. So charming.'

She touched Marietta's mound with gentle hands, pulling at the fine silky hair which covered it, letting the curls kiss her fingers. Then she slid one finger down the slit of the sex and dipped inside the lips momentarily before removing her hand. Marietta was speechless with shock at the casual intimacy of Leyla's gesture, but too surprised to brush her away.

Leyla withdrew her hand. She laughed. 'I forget myself. We are here to bathe. After ... we shall see. Come.'

Leyla began to pull on a pair of stilted bath shoes. Only when Marietta sat down and did the same did she absorb the other woman's words. Was she too expected to submit to the process of being denuded of all body hair – as it seemed was the custom here? She decided right away that she would refuse to submit to such an indignity. Surely guests were not expected to be bound by such customs?

Leyla and Marietta entered a side room of the bath house. The slaves came after them, carrying soft towels, perfumes and oils. There were no tubs of hot water as Marietta expected but deep basins lined the stone walls. Heated water flowed directly into the basins from brass taps set above them. The square-shaped plunge pool in the larger room was visible through a line of pillared archways.

Leyla and Marietta sat on stools, which resembled wicker cages.

'I will attend you,' Leyla said in her lovely husky voice, picking up a silver bowl and using it to pour perfumed water over Marietta's shoulders. 'Let me introduce you to the potent pleasures of the bath, beautiful Marietta.'

The water was very hot, but Marietta soon grew used to it. More disturbing was the feel of Leyla's soft hands on her skin. Sitting behind Marietta, her parted knees brushing the sides of her hips, Leyla rubbed a creamy perfumed concoction into Marietta's arms, then gradually worked her way down Marietta's body. Leyla's hands made small circles up and down her back. She encircled Marietta's waist, using a rotating motion of her fingers and thumbs to massage the skin, then she cupped Marietta's buttocks, one in each hand, and began kneading them.

As Leyla pulled at the globes of flesh, Marietta felt an indirect pressure on her sex. Her buttocks opened and closed, parting the flesh-lips slightly. At each movement that drew back her buttocks the flesh-lips were drawn a little way towards Leyla's hand. The warm steamy air of the baths penetrated the deep valley between Marietta's buttocks, playing over the damp skin and the tight little nether mouth. The seat of the stool was cool and firm and it provided a pleasant friction on the whole of Marietta's secret sensitive area. It was most disquieting. She drew away from Leyla's fingers a little.

'What is it? You do not like?'

'Yes ... I like. But ...'

Leyla laughed. 'Ah, you wish to offer me the same services, is that not it? Perhaps you think I am offended because I serve you like a slave? But I like to do this ... Wait. I know what we shall do.'

She stood up and adjusted the position of her stool.

Then she sat down facing Marietta. 'There. Now we can attend each other.'

Leyla turned her attention to the front of Marietta's body, describing creamy circles around her throat and jaw, then progressing down to her shoulders and chest. In another moment Leyla would close her hands over Marietta's breasts. Marietta felt a moment's panic and, in confusion, dipped her hand into the bowl of scented cream and began to apply it to Leyla's arms, neck and shoulders. But rather than calming her, the feel of Leyla's petal-soft skin only confused her further. Marietta concentrated on lathering Leyla's body, staring blankly into space over her shoulder, trying not to dwell on the feel of Leyla's hands on her skin. Nor would she look directly at the signs of pleasure on Leyla's lovely face, but she could not help seeing the loosely parted lips, the slight flush on the pale cheeks, the soft gleam in the sultry dark eyes.

The languid stroking went on. Marietta copied Leyla's movements, mirroring the pace and pressure of the other woman's hands. The movements were hypnotic. It was like a slow dance. Through the thick steam she caught brief glimpses of other bathers engaged in similar activities. Pairs of women were pouring water over each other. Some were washing each other's hair. Others were lying together on low platforms. She heard sighs and gasps near at hand. The sound of skin moving on skin. Little breathless moans. Subtle erotic sounds.

Marietta dared not look at the women who made these noises, yet she wanted to, badly. The air seemed scented with the musk of so many female bodies. She felt it surround her, as if sinking into her pores.

'You have a gentle touch, Marietta,' Leyla said on a sigh.

Marietta could not reply. Her mouth was dry. However much she concentrated on what she was doing, she could not ignore the feel of Leyla's touch or her own body's reaction to Leyla's close proximity. Her breasts were swollen, and the nipples had gathered into hard, aching peaks. The thick steam swirled around the two of them, screening them in a small private world.

Droplets had gathered on Leyla's black hair and the thick ebony ropes seemed to have a silver sheen. More droplets trembled on her sooty lashes. Her face was turned to the side, so that the straight, slightly-long nose was shown in profile. The delicate nostrils quivered. The dark shapely mouth, with its full, slightly puckered lips, looked shiny, moist and inviting. There was a darker brownish-red line running around the edge of Leyla's rouged mouth, delineating the edge of her lips, making its shape all the more startling against her white skin. Leyla opened her mouth, and nipped the corner of her bottom lip between her teeth; the small teeth gleamed like pearls.

Marieta shivered. She had never thought to find a woman so utterly desirable, or to find such pleasure in a woman's touch.

She was unable to stop herself, though she knew that she should. Under her palms Leyla's nipples hardened. Crested by the creamy suds, they looked like cherries in milk. Marietta itched to taste them, to draw the little round nubs into her mouth and collar them with the rolled curve of her tongue. Leyla's lovely mouth looked ripe for kisses and the liquid weight of her firm breasts filled Marietta's hands.

With a soft sigh, Leyla leaned forward into Marietta's grasp, throwing back her head in shameless enjoyment. The long sweet curve of her throat was revealed; a tiny pool of moisture had settled in the hollow of her neck.

Marietta felt the urge to bend forward, to lap at that little salty pool with her tongue. Drops of scented steam silvered Leyla's face, wetting her curved black brows, meshing on the fine down that grew above her full top lip. Tiny curls of springy black hair stuck to her damp forehead.

We should stop this, Marietta thought again. But it felt wonderful; Leyla was more than willing, and who was to see? Her body seemed to have come alive and the whole of her skin felt acutely sensitive. A pulse ticked between her legs.

Leyla lifted her head and smiled sweetly. Her hands slid over the swell of Marietta's stomach, massaged the slight pout of it for a time, then dipped between her parted thighs.

Marietta trembled violently as the creamy fingers threaded through the hair on her mound. They rubbed and teased, drawing out strands of moistened pale hair, playing lightly up and down the outside edges of the fleecy lips where they joined the creases of her groin. Then the fingers moved in to the centre. Gently Leyla parted the lips of Marietta's sex and began to caress the secret flesh with an expert touch. Her parted fingers rubbed either side of Marietta's hidden bud.

Marietta locked eyes with Leyla. A moan of pleasure was rising in her throat.

'No ... Please,' she whispered, but her back arched and her thighs opened more widely. She could not help pushing towards Leyla's hand.

Leyla smiled into her eyes. 'No? Lovely Marietta,' she said, tugging very gently on the little hood of flesh that covered the bud. 'Your mind says no, but your body wishes it. Let it have its way. Give yourself up to pleasure. Learn to take that pleasure wherever you can, as I have done. The hours here can seem so long.

Boredom is the enemy of the women in the harem. Why not take what is free and enjoyable?'

Marietta let out the groan she had been trying to hold in. She smiled. Where was the harm? She felt suddenly wicked, lascivious, and greatly daring.

'You mean, like this?' Marietta said, teasingly.

Leyla gave a hoarse little gasp as Marietta attempted a more intimate caress; a sound that acted like a goad to her own rising passion.

'Oh, so divinely enjoyable,' Leyla purred. 'Do you like it when I stroke you thus and when I insert my finger here?'

She slid one finger in and out of Marietta's body, assessing her wetness and readiness. Then she slipped another into her, exclaiming at the silky tightness. Marietta could not concentrate on what Leyla was saying. She knew only that the tone of her voice, husky and melodious, was like silk against her skin. Her flesh sucked at Leyla's fingers, unwilling to relinquish them even for an instant, though she must, for each new inward thrust. Her hips began to move, the buttocks flexing as she pushed forward, sheathing herself on Leyla's slippery fingers. Leyla's knuckles pressed the liquidly soft inner lips as she curved her fingers inwards, drawing Marietta's sex up towards her.

Ah, what a practised seductress she is, Marietta thought on a wave of sensation. The fingers circled her, moving round the silky inner walls, drawing out her feminine moisture.

'Do it to me too, beautiful one,' Leyla whispered. 'Can you feel how ready I am? Under your touch I am like a ripe fig. A split fruit ready to be suckled, so that the juice runs down the fleshy cleft. Yes. That's it. Spread my sex open. Rub me there. Oh, yes. Like that. Gently. Yes, on the flesh-covered bud. Just there. Feel how hard the little kernel has become, how it juts out? The fruit ripens for you, fair one. How it swells. What delight Kasim will have in you.'

'Kasim?' Marietta said dreamily, thinking only of the way Leyla's fingers worked away inside her.

At the same time Leyla had pressed the pad of her thumb to the stiffly swollen bud inside Marietta's flesh-lips, rotating it delightfully. Her passionate words were almost poetic, spreading magic through Marietta's mind as her fingers cast a spell over her body.

Marietta loved the feel of Leyla's naked sex against her hand. The swollen flesh-lips, so smooth without any hair covering, were thickly engorged, slippery. She pinched them gently, squeezing them together, feeling the hard pulsing little bud inside them. Leyla was very wet. Her hot juices felt like melted butter. Her smell of jasmine, salt, and musk made Marietta feel light-headed.

Leyla laughed throatily with abandoned delight. 'You are wonderful, fair one. Your body is a jewel. Perhaps Kasim can be persuaded to enjoy us together. Would that please you?'

Gradually Marietta became aware of what Leyla was saying. Then a word she had mentioned earlier in an unguarded moment rang in her head, discordant, like a cracked bell. Harem? That was it.

Harem! Here was the reason why she had felt so ill at ease. Realisation rushed upon her. She felt cold. Her passion died at once.

She pulled her fingers roughly out of Leyla, who gasped and moaned with disappointment. Marietta drew away, and dashed Leyla's hand away from her. Then she stood up and jerked her stool away.

'Take your hands off me!' she said icily. 'I will bathe myself. And I tell you again, Claudine and I are guests here, not residents. We shall be leaving soon. We are not harem inmates. I expect Kasim asked you to pleasure me, did he? No doubt hoping that I would be won over by the sensuality and riches all around me. He wants me to stay here. Is that it? So that he can use me for his pleasure like a whore!'

She stopped, her blue eyes blazing into Leyla. Leyla's lips trembled.

'It is true that you are beautiful enough to seduce an angel, Leyla. and I will not lie, I do desire you. But I warn you, I am not a pawn to be dallied with at will. Yours or Kasim's! Do not try your wiles on me again!'

In the instant before Marietta grabbed for a towel and swung away she saw the hurt and confusion on Leyla's face. Perhaps she was wrong about her. She hoped she was. She liked Leyla. More than liked. A great deal more, to be truthful. But she was too shaken and disturbed to think clearly.

Leyla called after her. Her voice sounded rough, as if she was suppressing some strong emotion.

'You have entered the harem of Kasim Dey – administrator of the pashalic of Algeria. He is a rich and powerful man. You cannot say him nay. No one escapes from here. It is useless to struggle. Best that you accept your fate, as I have. Only the most beautiful women reside here. You are honoured that Kasim chose you. Bow to kismet, Marietta – as we all must do.'

Marietta was speechless, unable to encompass this information. She saw now what an innocent fool she had been. Claudine and she were not Kasim's honoured guests at all. It all became clear to her. Kasim was a lover of beautiful things, a patron of the arts, and a collector. He had told her so himself, but she had not understood.

She did now.

Claudine and herself were Kasim's latest acquisitions.

4

In the garden, lamps glowed softly.

Lemon trees cast nets of shadows over pots of roses and lilies. Peacocks strutted around the fountains, pecking at seed which the women scattered for them. Marietta closed her eyes, listening to the sound of harp music floating out from an open window somewhere above. Nightingales in gilded cages gave out their sweet songs.

It was so peaceful, so lovely, but she could think of nothing but Kasim and the way he had duped Claudine and herself. She sat tensely on a pile of cushions. Waiting.

There was a sense of contained excitement all around her. The word had passed around that Kasim would be visiting the harem that evening. He had apparently not been too keen to do so of late.

'It is the presence of you and Claudine that draws him here. He is like a moth to your flame,' said Leyla. 'The other women are glad you are here, though you may become rivals. They think that if Kasim visits, he might notice one of them and bestow his favours on her.'

Marietta did not reply, only nodding her head a little stiffly, then felt churlish when Leyla smiled hesitantly. It was not Leyla she was angry with. It was Kasim, and herself. Leyla looked beautiful in dark-green velvet. A lighter green veil covered her long black hair, which hung loosely in thick shining waves to her hips. Her black eyes sought Marietta's face often, their expression pleading for forgiveness. Marietta avoided Leyla's gaze. Though gradually she felt herself soften, she kept her chin up, her head erect, and gave no sign that she intended to speak to Leyla ever again.

Leyla pressed her hands together in her lap.

Her lovely face was anguished. Now and then she glanced across the room at Marietta, who was sitting so stiffly upright, a look of fury on her face. The scorn in the wide blue eyes hurt her. It saddened Leyla that Marietta thought her guilty of manipulating her. True, she knew that Kasim had lured the young women to the harem. No one but a slave, purchased from a trader, came willingly to a life of confinement – and even some slaves were not willing. She shuddered remembering . . .

One day she would tell Marietta her story, if Marietta ever forgave her.

She had been drawn to Marietta for her own reasons. At first she had felt pity for the lovely young woman. She knew that it would be a shock when she discovered that she would never leave this place. The other woman, Claudine, would not find it so difficult. But Marietta would find the path to obedience long and painful.

Leyla saw an echo of a younger, more innocent, self in Marietta. That was why she thought to befriend her, show her how things were done, ease the way forward for her. So that she would accept her new life with the least amount of mental anguish. That was all she *meant* to do.

But when Marietta disrobed, Leyla had been torn by a raging desire to explore her flawless body, so unique with its pale colouring. She wanted to arouse the passions in that cool smooth flesh. But it had all gone wrong. Marietta thought she was Kasim's creature – and in a way it was true – but that was not why she had pleasured Marietta.

The truth was that she was already half in love with the French woman.

Leyla clenched her fingers and pressed her lips together, watching Marietta from the tail of her eye. Unable to stop looking at her – so breathtaking even in the ugly and constricting French gown that she still insisted on wearing.

Claudine rested on a pile of cushions, nibbling sweet-meats. She sucked her sticky fingers, paying great attention to cleaning them one by one.

Marietta felt mildly exasperated. She had expected her friend to be furious with Kasim, to be waiting to challenge him, as she was. But Claudine looked composed and relaxed, perfectly at ease.

It was late when Kasim arrived. Many of the women had grown bored. They were slumped in untidy postures, their clothes crumpled and disarrayed. At Kasim's appearance there was a flurry of activity.

He strode across the tiled courtyard, looking magnificent in robes of mulberry velvet. In one hand he held a fine gold chain and in the other a pliable leather switch. In his wake, attached to the chain by a neck ring, trotted a naked woman. Her face was flushed and tear-streaked. Lash marks were visible on the skin of her belly and thighs.

The harem women ran to meet Kasim, fluttering their hands and smiling, falling over each other to speak words of welcome. They ignored the chained woman who, coming to a halt, stood with her head bowed.

Marietta hid her shock and remained seated, waiting as Kasim walked through the crush of women and approached the cushioned dais. He smiled broadly at her as he seated himself.

'Sit,' he ordered the captive woman, jerking the chain so that she lowered herself to the floor. 'Not like that. As you have been taught. Legs apart. Must I punish you further?'

She lowered her eyes and did as he told her. Marietta watched in astonishment as she squatted on her haunches, her knees wide apart, facing her and Kasim. Though she kept her chin lowered, her back was straight and her breasts thrust forward. Her flat belly sloped down to muscular thighs, and between them was her plump mound and parted sex, hairless as Leyla's had been. The lips were shockingly red and exposed. There were lash marks between her thighs also.

As Marietta looked at the tender rosy skin, She felt a little shock of excitement.

Kasim eyed the kneeling woman, toying with the chain he still held. 'Better,' he said, softly. 'Keep those legs spread. You will not burn the food on the morrow.'

He turned his head and addressed Marietta in a normal conversational tone. 'You have been made comfortable, I see. Good. And by your angry expression I think you have realised where you are and that you will not be allowed to leave. Did Leyla tell you this?'

The kneeling woman and what her presence signified confused Marietta so that she was slow to reply. Before she could answer, Leyla spoke.

'Forgive me. My tongue was careless. It . . . it was at the hammam. I did not mean to . . . I was distracted by the new lady's beauty.'

Kasim laughed thinly. 'Understandable. But that is no excuse. You know what to do.'

Leyla bowed her head. Her lovely pale cheeks were flushed. 'Please, I beg you. Not now. Not in front of—'

Kasim's eyes blazed. 'You dare to question! That remark will earn you a more severe punishment.'

Leyla bit her lip. She stood up slowly, slanting Marietta a look of pointed distress from under her lashes.

'Kasim,' Marietta said, finding her tongue. 'She did nothing wrong. She only told the truth. Was not yours the greater crime? You have made captives of Claudine and myself. We were brought here with lies and empty promises.' As she spoke her temper rose. She rushed on unthinkingly. 'It is you who are at fault. How do you dare punish Leyla!'

There were gasps from the gathered women. They threw Marietta horrified looks, whispering behind their hands. Kasim's lips tightened. Then he grinned.

'Lies and empty promises, you say? Hmmm.' He seemed vastly amused. 'Oh, no. Not empty, my dear Marietta. Never that. All I promised shall come to pass. But what a hypocrite you are. I saw the hunger in your eyes, the knowledge that I found you attractive. Can you say honestly that you expected to be just – a guest?'

She could not meet his eyes. His words were too close to the truth. At that moment she hated him. She could taste the bitterness of it on her tongue. Yet she was still perversely aware of how much she desired him. She determined that she would hold that desire in check. He would never know how much she burned for him. An ember that lust might be, but she would never allow it to become a flame. She lifted her head and found the courage to stare him down.

Kasim looked away first, but the victory was hollow almost nothing. He had let her win. This time.

A muscle twitched in his cheek. There was an implacable set to his mouth. She saw that there was nothing to be gained by angering him; neither would he be moved by any appeal to his better nature. He would not let Claudine and herself go. She felt stunned. Impotent. There must be something she could do? She clenched her hands together to stop them trembling. The shock settled in her stomach like a spiked ball.

The naked woman at Kasim's feet shifted her weight. He tugged at the chain, his lean face dark with displeasure. She threw herself forward and kissed the hem of his robe, raising her naked buttocks in the air. He pushed her away with the toe of his boot. The movement jolted Marietta back to the present.

What would he do to Leyla?

'Will you not forgive Leyla?' she said after a moment, trying to make her voice sound calm and reasonable.

Kasim laughed delightedly, 'How refreshing you are. So wilful. Different indeed to most of these women who were bred to harem life. You are angry with me, very angry, though you hide it well. Yet you seek to protect Leyla.' He laughed again, huskily. 'She will not thank you for that. Though this, and much else, you shall learn. But learn this one thing at once, it will serve you well to heed it: there is never any way to avoid my will.'

Though he smiled, his eyes were hard as jet. She sensed again, as she had on board ship, that he was completely ruthless. The shadow inside her responded to that knowledge. Kasim was a dark jewel and she knew that if she were to look into a single facet of his personality, she would see part of herself reflected there. The flash of insight blinded her. She felt as if she was standing outside herself, watching everything from a new and more acute perspective.

Kasim turned his attention back to Leyla, who had been disrobing as they spoke. Her head was bent, but the deep flush of shame was evident on her slim neck. The green velvet lay in a heap on the floor. Now she wore only thin silk trousers and a transparent shirt reaching to her knees. The dark-red nipples made little peaks in the thin fabric.

'All of it,' Kasim said pleasantly.

No one spoke. Everyone watched Leyla. Soon she stood naked, covered only by her hair.

'Come close,' Kasim said gently.

Trembling she approached him and threw herself at his feet. She clasped the toe of his boot and pressed kisses to it. Almost lazily he wrapped his hand in her long hair, twisting the night-black waves into a rope, pulling her up into a kneeling position. Without being asked to, she spread her knees wide and arched her back. Her buttocks flared from her narrow waist, form ing a perfect heart shape.

She made a sound, partway between a murmur of entreaty and a groan.

Kasim grinned, his eyes looked soft, moist. 'Good, Leyla. You assume the position of willing submission. But it will not save you. Ask me,' he whispered.

Leyla swallowed. Her throat was taut, stretched by Kasim's grip on her hair. Her voice was muffled, husky.

'Please. Not that. Oh, please,' she said.

Kasim raised the switch and ran the tip of it across her breast, toying with each nipple in turn. Leyla twitched like a skittish mare. He ran the notched tip down over her belly and gave a playful tap on each of her thighs.

'Where shall I begin? Tell me,' he said, bending close to Leyla and kissing the tip of her straight nose.

She did not answer. He laughed again.

'Then I shall decide.' He loosed her hair. 'Make the bow.'

Leyla flashed an agonised glance around, but plainly she dared not refuse. Her dark eyes were clouded by shame. The women watching leaned close as Leyla lay flat on the floor. They seemed to know what was about to happen. Marietta realised that this was not an unusual event. The thought caused her heart to quicken. She was bound by fascination, too filled with conflicting emotions to look away. But she could not suppress a little cry when she saw the position Leyla assumed. Her hands were one to either side of her head, palms flat on the floor. Her arms stretched taut to take her weight. Her feet were planted apart and her body was bent over at her backbone so that she presented herself belly up. Her long dark hair plumed out behind her, sweeping across the tiled floor. The bow, indeed.

Marietta was horrified. In that position Leyla's sex was thrust uppermost, looking exposed and vulnerable. The naked pubic lips were slightly parted, pouting and enticing. Marietta recalled the feel of those flesh-lips when they had been thickened by desire and slick with pleasure juice.

Kasim drew in his breath. He walked slowly over to Leyla, slapping the switch against his high leather boots. He stood between her parted knees, looking down on her lovely body, the fine skin stretched tautly over the toned flesh and muscle.

'Beautiful you are, my Leyla,' he crooned. 'Your supple dancer's body shall soon feel the caress of my lash. Do you crave the heat, the smart of it?'

He laid one hand lightly on her stomach, then moved up to pinch a rosy nipple. He laid two fingers in the flattened indentation of her throat, where a pulse was beating rapidly.

'This is obedience,' he said to Marietta over his

shoulder. 'Wherever they are, whoever is present, it is what I require from every one of these women. They yearn to serve me, Marietta. Yes, I see your doubt. This is abhorrent to you, this – servitude. But it is true that they desire it. Soon. Soon, you too will feel that need. For I see myself in you.'

She had no answer. He saw too much. Far too much.

With a movement of his hand he dismissed the other women. They ran from the room uttering cries of disappointment but obviously not daring to stay.

'You too.' He gestured to the chained woman he had led into the garden, now sitting forgotten, her head still bowed in submission. 'Marietta and Claudine only will stay. I wish them to attend me.'

Marietta stood up abruptly, intending to follow the other women from the garden. 'You are insufferable!' she said. 'You may order your harem women about but you will not order me. I am a free French woman. Mistress of myself. I will not stay to witness this act. Claudine, are you coming?'

Claudine hesitated. She looked at Kasim and then at Marietta. Clearly she was excited by the turn of events. Before she could move Kasim spoke.

'Stop!' he said imperiously. 'Leyla will suffer more if you do not stay.'

Marietta turned around. Beaten. He had found the one thing that would influence her. Oh, he was clever. As clever as the devil.

'What must I do?' she said softly, admitting defeat.

Claudine's eyes were bright, her cheeks flushed. When Kasim ordered it, she went to stand next to one of Leyla's bent knees. He gestured to Marietta. Slowly she approached the other knee.

Kasim raised the switch and began laying light strokes across Leyla's taut stomach. She made no sound.

Red lines appeared on her white skin. The switch made a faint whistling noise as it cleaved the air.

Soon Kasim gave his attention to Leyla's thighs, laying the marks neatly across their tops. Leyla's hips squirmed. Her legs shook. The slightly parted lips of her sex were moist. As she thrust her hips back and forth as Kasim beat her, Marietta caught the scent of her sex. It was perfumed with something sweet and flowery, and underlying the perfume was her own heady musk.

'And now . . .' Kasim said, his voice shaky, no longer teasing.

He began stroking the plump little sex with the notched tip of the switch. Not too hard, but hard enough for Leyla to begin to moan. It was the first sound she had made. Marietta could tell how she tried to hold back, but could not. Her moans were of pain and pleasure mixed. The sweat broke out on Marietta's body.

Reaching out, Kasim spread Leyla's naked pubic lips with his fingers. He circled the damp bud, which was thrust from its hood of flesh by the pressure he exerted. The tip of the switch teased the pink inner lips, flicking lightly across the quivering bud. Leyla's opening pulsed as if it hungered for the thrust of his fingers.

Kasim bent swiftly and placed his mouth on her sex. His lips worked as he tasted her and Leyla moaned at the unexpected tenderness of his touch. But before she could draw pleasure from the contact, he drew away and began to place light strokes of the whip on the pouting sex. Again he spread the flesh-lips and now the switch went to work on the tender exposed flesh.

Marietta wanted to cry out for him to stop, but equally she wanted him to continue. She did not want to be here. She wanted to be Leyla. There ... she had admitted it. The shaming heat flooded her cheeks, as her sex swelled and grew damp.

'Ah,' Kasim breathed, absorbed in the sensuality of the punishment. 'See how the pink flesh glistens. How swollen it is. How strongly erect the little kernel of delight is. It is well developed in you, is it not, my Leyla? What a hungry little bud it is, thrusting out for the caress of fingers and tongue. It is like a tiny cock, a salted nipple. And always thirsty for its punishment. How it throbs and stings when I beat it thus. And thus. Does it burn, Leyla? Does it throb? Do you long to be beaten harder?'

For a while longer he gave his attention to caressing the parted sex with firm strokes of the switch. Leyla writhed under his ministrations but her moans were muffled by the long hair stranding across her face. In a swift movement Kasim turned the switch, handle uppermost. It was thick, ridged with leather bands. He delved into Leyla, working the handle in and out of her entrance until it was shiny with her juices. Leyla's legs trembled so much that they seemed on the verge of collapse.

'Hold her. Support her under her hips,' Kasim ordered, his breath coming fast.

Marietta and Claudine reached out and did as he asked. Leyla's buttocks were hot against Marietta's shaking fingers, and the luscious flesh trembled. Kasim withdrew the handle and began lashing the parted sex again, increasing the strength of the strokes with careful control, until the tender flesh was red and swollen and throbbing almost visibly. Leyla writhed, whimpering and sobbing, cringing back from the seeking tongue of the lash tip. Her hair lashed the tiles as she twisted her head from side to side.

'Enough,' Kasim said. His face was flushed, his lips parted. 'Now, Leyla, I shall solace you.'

He turned to Marietta. 'See what a benevolent master I am? Only my favourites are treated thus. Is this not the most sublime punishment? The others vie for such attentions, but seldom are they rewarded. A lifetime of living in the harem has turned many of the women into sheep. They do not know how to be disobedient. Leyla here is different. She was purchased in the slave market. I trained her myself, and I shall train you too. That is why you are so special. Why I wanted you the moment I saw you, soaked and shivering on the deck of the ship. Those who have been free, need the firmest, most exquisite chastisement and discipline. Claudine will bend to the yoke before long I suspect. But you, Marietta ... Ah, you shall be a triumph. And at the end you will be willing.'

His words filled her with utter dread but she had hardly time to ponder on them.

Kasim had been unfastening his belt as he spoke. He reached down and freed his penis. He held it for a moment, stroking it. Waiting. As if he wanted to savour the moment. When he loosed it Marietta saw that it was engorged, stiffly erect. Dark red, as if it too had been beaten. The stem was thick and ridged with prominent veins. It looked strong, vital. The moist swollen head of it was free from any covering of skin, unlike Gabriel's. The scrotum was dark and firm, like a plum.

The sight of Kasim's erect state stirred Marietta strongly. The stem and testicles were surrounded by thick black curls. Evidently the prohibition against pubic hair did not apply to him. She was glad; the hair made his genitals look more exciting, even a little dangerous.

Marietta envied Leyla. Her hungry swollen nether mouth, tortured as it was, was about to be given comfort.

As if Leyla knew what was going to happen, she whispered to Kasim, entreating him to have mercy. But the lovely husky tones of her voice made the words sound like a plea for more.

'Kasim, please. I cannot stand it.'

He gave a throaty laugh and bent his knees. The strong thigh muscles flexed as he thrust his buttocks towards her sex. The cock jutted forward and up.

'You must,' he said sternly. 'Keep those arms straight. Forget your aching muscles. Bear my weight. It is your final ordeal.'

Even now he was not going to let her up. Her chastisement must go on. Her body, bent into that obscene bow, must now receive her master's phallus. Marietta shivered as Kasim thrust forward, nosing the tip of his cock into the pouting, half-opened little slit. The naked pubic lips opened around him as he thrust at the entrance, seeming to suck him in greedily.

Leyla's lack of pubic hair made her look all the more naked. Marietta could not fail to see every movement of her sex. The little kernel of delight, such a deep purplish-red, so strongly erect that indeed it was like a tiny cock, rubbed shamelessly against Kasim as he worked in and out.

Now he leaned into her and thrust deeply. Leyla's juices bathed his stem and glistened on the dark thatch of his pubic hair. He moved slowly in and out, his eyes hooded, his mouth stretched around his teeth.

Leyla moaned loudly. Marietta felt the muscles of her buttocks moving against her own hand as Leyla pushed forward to meet Kasim's thrusts. Her face burned with mortification. She was outraged that he had forced Claudine and herself to witness this – act of debasement. She wanted to run from the room, to blot out the sight of Leyla's painfully exposed sex. To pretend that she was not maddeningly aroused by the sight of Kasim plunging into Leyla's willing flesh.

He had warned Marietta that he would punish her in the same way, bend her to his will. But was it truly punishment when one desired a thing, as Leyla plainly did? Marietta too desired it so intensely that she felt her own pleasure mounting unbearably. But never would she admit the fact to anyone else.

The cadence of Leyla's cries changed. Soft wet sounds came from the two joined bodies.

'Soon, my Leyla, soon,' Kasim said hoarsely.

He placed his hands around Leyla's narrow waist, holding on to her as she thrashed against him now, pubis to pubis. Marietta's arms ached from supporting them, but she dared not let go. Claudine's lovely face wore an avid expression. She bit her lips, not troubling to hide her enjoyment.

Suddenly, Leyla groaned. Her buttocks tensed, and her belly jumped. Kasim stopped dead still. Sweat poured down his face as Leyla bucked against him, sucking her pleasure from the stem buried deeply inside her. He looked wracked by some inner torment and his face wore an expression of exquisite agony. Ah, how much like a bruised angel he looked. Leyla groaned loudly as her spasms faded.

In a moment Kasim withdrew but his cock was hard still and it glistened with Leyla's juice. Marietta realised that he had not spilled his seed. Somehow, with incredible restraint, he had managed to stop at the precise moment of his own release.

Kasim slumped forward, bending over the bow of Leyla's body in a gesture that possessed a singular grace. His cheek lay against her belly, which was soft and relaxed now. A moment later, he sank back onto his haunches.

'You may let her go,' he said shortly, as he adjusted his clothing.

Claudine and Marietta let Leyla down gently. Without their support she would have crashed to the floor. She lay on her back for a moment, taking deep shuddering breaths. Then, ignoring the two women, she scrambled up and walked across to Kasim who had seated himself on a divan.

Grasping the toe of his boot she covered it with kisses, murmuring, adoringly, 'Thank you, my lord. My life. Oh, thank you.'

Still naked, the tears streaking her cheeks, she poured Kasim a glass of sherbet and, on her knees, handed it to him. She assumed the same position of submission Marietta had witnessed earlier – back straight, knees apart and head down. Her black hair flowed in deep waves over her breasts and pooled in her lap, masking the pouting belly with its lash marks and the tender abused sex.

Kasim smiled and cupped her chin, lifting her face to his gaze. With his thumb he wiped away the tears that streaked her scarlet face and tugged playfully at her underlip.

'And now, my Leyla, I shall give you a task to perform. You are to take Marietta and Claudine and train them. I want them to be perfect in all the arts of entertainment and pleasure. I am planning a banquet for my friends in a few weeks' time. These two will perform for me then. If they fail to please me, either of them, you will be chastised. Mark me well. What you have suffered up until now, is nothing beside what I shall do to you then.'

Leyla gave a delicious little shudder. 'All shall be done as you wish it.'

Claudine watched in open admiration. When Kasim smiled at her and beckoned her over, she walked meekly to him and sat at his feet.

Marietta could stand it no more. Her womb burned, crying out for the release that she craved but which she denied wanting. Kasim looked up and pinned her with his long black eyes.

'The first thing Leyla shall do is choose you some beautiful clothes. I do not ever want to see that dress again.'

With those words he had made a gesture of finality. Marietta felt frightened at the thought of being without her stays and boned bodices. It was if by forcing her body to be unconstricted, he would force her mind to follow.

She felt that he saw inside her, knew what was in her very soul. But he would never reach that inner sanctity. She would fight him all the way.

She told herself that with a certainty she did not feel.

Kasim's full mouth stretched in a grin. She saw triumph there, and complete self-assurance. There was nothing she could do.

She whirled around and ran from the garden.

5

The harem was dark, lit only by one flickering oil lamp. Moonlight streamed through the carved window screens, making lacy shadows that loomed across the tiled floor. Soft snores filled the room. Now and then a string of small brass bells, hanging in a draught, gave out a musical tinkling.

In her sleep Marietta tossed and turned, disturbed by coloured images that invaded her mind. Her eyelids fluttered as her brows drew together in a frown. Her lips parted on a single word.

'Kasim.'

Her dreams were full of the scene in the garden. She again saw Kasim standing over Leyla as she bent for him into the obscene bow shape. He was looking down on her pale, sweat-slicked body. Marietta stood at Leyla's side, feeling that mixture of intense shame and excitement as she witnessed the other woman's chastisement.

Then the dream changed. Leyla disappeared. Kasim and Marietta were alone. She was naked, and it was her that Kasim was tormenting.

'Abase yourself,' he ordered. His lean angular features were composed into a frown. 'On your knees.'

And her dream self knelt meekly before him.

The softly scented air played across her skin. Keeping her head bowed, she dipped down gracefully. Straightening her back, she thrust her breasts forward.

Without being asked to, she spread her knees wide

and felt the lips of her sex part as it was presented to his gaze. Though she was acutely self-conscious she gloried in the act of submission. Her mouth trembled as his dark eyes swept over her body, appraising the curves and contours.

'Good. Good little slave,' Kasim said. His face softened, though his dark eyes glistened with cruelty.

He reached out and pinched her nipples. Hard. She winced, but did not look up. The tender peaks gathered under his fingertips as he rolled and tugged at them. They became round like berries, seeming to flame into life, throbbing and burning under his touch.

Then he slapped her breasts lightly, delighting in the way the flesh shook from side to side. He cupped the underswell, lifting each breast as if weighing the flesh, then holding them in his palms, drawing them upwards so firmly that the flesh seemed engorged. The rosy nipples thrust out pertly, shiny with the inner pressure.

'Bend your head, Marietta. Suckle at your breasts. I want to see your mouth working.'

Marietta's dream self hesitated. She could not do it. It was unthinkable. Kasim waited for her to comply. The pressure in her breasts was disconcerting but not frightening. Kasim's grasp, though hard, was not cruel. Her nipples looked bigger than usual, as if swollen to twice their normal size. They were glowing darkly and tingling; two shameless cones, begging to be soothed by a soft mouth.

'Surely you do not refuse?' Kasim said softly. He pulled her breasts a fraction higher.

She gave a gasp of pain and bent her neck, turning her head slightly to one side to reach a nipple. She opened her lips over the swollen peak and began mouthing it.

'Good. Suck gently. Is that not good? Now lick each one. I want to see your tongue.'

She did as he asked, forcing herself to the act, glad that her face was averted. The aching pressure in her breasts became centred on her nipples. Though she hated to be watched, she found pleasure in the act. Her nipples were hot and delicious, tingling in her mouth. The skin was so taut over the hard little pips that it was like licking warm marble. Her tongue circled each one until they were shiny, polished with her saliva. The joint sensations of her tongue on her own nipple-flesh and the hard little nubs questing against the roof of her mouth were unique and tantalising. Her breath quickened.

'Enough,' Kasim said, letting her breasts drop abruptly.

She almost cried out as her pleasure was interrupted. The nipples were jerked from her mouth. Then she gasped at the bruised and heavy weight of her breasts as they settled back high up against her ribcage. She was painfully aware of them, though he no longer touched them. They seemed swollen still, jutting forward pertly. The soft night air teased her wet nipples.

She tensed, not knowing what to expect next, and kept her chin down, closing her eyes, not daring to look as Kasim trailed his fingers down to her belly. He paused and took the softly rounded flesh in one hand. Squeezing and kneading her belly gently, he teased her navel with his thumb, stroking it with the lightest touch of his nail.

'What a delightful little flesh-cup this is,' he crooned, softly. His voice was husky with desire. 'Shall I trickle honey onto your belly and let it pool here in this hollow? Then shall I allow the flow to run down over your plump little mound? How the stickiness of it would cleave to the lips of your sex. It would anoint the flesh-hood and glaze your kernel of delight. I could bid Leyla suck the honey from you. How I would enjoy watching. Would you like that, Marietta? Would you?'

She dared not answer. Her mouth was dry with fear and anticipation. Surely he would not do as he said. She imagined herself spread out, thighs wide apart, while Leyla knelt between them, and Kasim watching with that hard expression on his face, one finger stroking his full mouth while he gave Leyla instructions. She would die with the shame of it.

But the thought of Leyla, holding open the lips of her sex, of her hot tongue, lapping at the honeyed flesh, made her bear down. Her womb contracted and her insides pulsed. The pink inner lips of her sex convulsed. She hoped Kasim did not notice.

Kasim was silent, intent on stroking her. Her navel seemed to have become a new and unexpected pleasure centre. Her belly trembled as he stroked the firm, soft skin. It was an effort not to draw her muscles in, away from his knowing fingers. Poking a finger into the shallow indentation Kasim gripped the rim of the tiny flesh-cup between finger and thumb and tugged on it, rolling it gently, squeezing it together into a tiny tight slit.

Marietta's dream self felt an answering pull deep in her belly. She was aware of her whole body. It seemed that she was in a state of spreading heat. Her nipples were erect, throbbing from the firm pinching. Her breasts were hot and flushed from the slaps and the squeezing of Kasim's strong fingers. They felt heavy and ripe. The insistent, subtle tugging on her navel sent little shocks of pleasure down to her exposed sex. She lifted her head a little, looking away from the hand that rested on her belly, trying to bring order to her emotions and to distance herself from his disturbing touch.

The dream shifted.

From the corner of her eye Marietta caught a movement. A man was standing in the shadow of a fig tree. Watching. He was tall, powerfully built, familiar. Her stomach jigged.

Gabriel.

Gabriel, the beautiful slave she had seen chastised in the marketplace; he who had prompted such devastating emotions in her. How long had he been standing there? The sexual tension was evident in every line of his body. His eyes were intent on her face, as if he understood her inner struggle. The breeze blew his long flaxen hair across his face, masking for a moment the grey eyes which had narrowed and were glistening with desire.

Marietta was at first appalled that her shame was being witnessed by another man. Then she perceived a kind of justice in it. Had she not watched Gabriel's humiliation?

A new and heightened awareness swept over her. The thought of Gabriel's eyes roving over her secret flesh, his perfect body a slave to his desire, added an extra dimension to her torment.

She felt the swelling of her sex-lips and knew that she was growing damp. Kasim would see. They would both see. The pink inner-flesh would grow ever more slick and the clitoris would become erect and thrust against its tiny hood. Even now it had begun to throb strongly, stirring into life, eager to be rubbed and stroked. She remembered how Gabriel had looked while he was being lashed; the intensity of the pleasure-pain on his face as he spilled his seed before the crowd.

Kasim's proximity and Gabriel's presence seemed to

merge in her vision. She felt surrounded by the heat of their sexual energy. Yet in an odd way she felt in control of them. These two strong and enigmatic men desired her strongly.

She was at the centre of this tableaux. It was her responses which prompted their joint fascination. Her naked body, her moistly parted sex, which held them in thrall.

The knowledge stirred within her, powerfully erotic. In the midst of debasement then, there could be strength. Marietta felt a primaeval flutter deep inside her womb. She found herself growing increasingly excited, and could no longer control the tremors in her thighs. Still, she longed to hide the evidence of her arousal. She was too exposed, too open in the most intimate way. It frightened her. If only she could move her hips a little, clench her buttocks, so that her parted flesh-lips could close together. She felt the moisture gathering. But she dared not move. It would be a sign of disobedience and would prompt Kasim to carry out ever more refined humilations. If Kasim beat her in front of Gabriel she could not endure it. Just the very thought of it sent tingles of anguish down her spine.

Her cheeks grew hot with shame as she grew wetter. She felt desperate to close her thighs, to draw back from Kasim's relentless touch and his dark probing eyes. But she stayed as she was, her body open and submissive to him. Her mind was in an agony of torment and helpless arousal.

Kasim lifted her chin and stared directly into her eyes. 'I know that you struggle, lovely one. I am well pleased that you obey me. I knew that you would. It was only a matter of time. And now – I shall reward you.'

He gave her navel a final little tug, then his long

cool fingers moved downwards to stroke her inner thighs. He pinched her gently, then more firmly, so that her eyes watered. From his belt he took a fine leather strap, very long and pliable. He trailed the end of the strap across her parted thighs, then lifted the tip so that it hung between her open sex-lips.

He gave a sound of satisfaction as he stared between her legs. Marietta could not suppress a cry as the dangling strap brushed against her erect bud. Kasim moved the strap so that it played up and down her moist inner petals. She made a tiny movement of her hips, pushing towards the strap's caress. Kasim laughed, low and throatily.

'Did I tell you to move? Such disobedience! I am going to beat you with this strap until you beg me to stop. Is that not a wonderful reward for that lush body which has betrayed you? I know how hungry that little sex of yours is. How wanton. I can smell the musky heat rising from you, see how swollen your pearl of delight is. Your sex is uncontrolled. It must be tamed. As you have been.'

Marietta's breath rose in her throat on a sob. Not that. Oh, no. She couldn't stand it. She knew that she would disgrace herself and reach her peak of pleasure after the first few strokes. Kasim would see her writhing out of control. His hard mouth would curve with satisfaction. Gabriel too would witness her surrender. Oh, no . . . Please, she entreated silently.

She threw an agonised glance towards Gabriel. He was leaning against the tree. He smiled, his full mouth tender. Slowly he moved aside his cloak. Marietta saw that he was naked underneath it. He was strongly erect. The cock stood up from its nest of dark-blond curls. Gabriel curled his hand around the thick stem. As he began working it up and down, moving the heavy balls, he blew her a silent kiss. At the sight of the erect cock, the shiny glans sliding free of the foreskin, the pleasure cramped in Marietta's belly.

Kasim glanced towards Gabriel for the first time. He smiled, a long and sensual smile.

'And now, Marietta, for my delight, and his too, you shall squirm and moan. That thirsty little sex of yours looks ready for the strap.'

His lips thinned. He raised the strap . . .

No! Please. Stop! Marietta jerked awake abruptly.

Early morning sunlight streamed into the room through the stained-glass skylight. For a moment she did not know where she was. Then she remembered. She ran trembling fingers over her face. Her cheeks were damp and flushed.

She did not at first register that she was lying on her back with her knees drawn up and her thighs parted wantonly. With a little cry she turned on her side and pressed her thighs together. She wrapped her arms around herself and drew the pillow close for comfort. The dream had been so vivid and she realised that she had been strongly aroused by it. The place between her legs was very wet.

Her whole body felt warm and languid. The cambric chemise she had slept in was twisted into a tight rope and was pushed up beneath her breasts. The low neckline had slipped off one shoulder. The thin silk bedcover had fallen back leaving her exposed from the waist to the knee. She reddened, pulling down the crumpled garment to cover her hips and thighs. What a sight she must have been, lying there flushed and half-naked, her thighs parted exposing her secret flesh. And what a good thing she had pulled her bed curtains closed.

She raised herself on one elbow and pushed her hair

back from her face. The ribbon and silk flowers had come loose and her hair was all meshed into a tangle of pale curls, as if she had been tossing restlessly on the pillows.

It had been only a dream, after all. Nothing to get upset about. But it was the remembered pleasure that chafed at her. Those things that had been done to her dream self – they were so shameful, so exquisitely lewd. But she had felt a kind of freedom in giving up her will to Kasim, knowing that Gabriel watched and understood. Her dream experience seemed to have prompted her to an inner, unwanted honesty. It was a disquieting discovery. She knew that if she stopped resisting Kasim, she would be lost. She did not want that.

The embroidered bed curtains trembled slightly in the breeze from an open window. She could hear the sounds of the other women rising. There were whispered greetings. Female laughter. Then, the sound of steps drawing close.

Claudine pulled the bed curtains aside. 'Come on, sleepy-head,' she said cheerily. 'Aren't you hungry? There's food set out ready in the next room. Cheese and preserves and olives, and Russian tea to drink. Just fancy! How very civilised everything is here.'

Claudine looked lovely and exotic. She wore a loose robe of figured black silk over voluminous green trousers. Marietta looked at her animated face. She hadn't the heart to tell her friend that she had no appetite, that she did not care how civilised it all seemed, it was still just a fancy prison. She turned over on to her stomach and buried her face in the pillow.

'I'm still tired. I'll join you later,' she said.

Claudine made a sound of assent, a musical little noise in her throat. 'As you wish. Why are you still wearing that old cambric chemise? Did you not find the silk robe which was left for you? It is so pretty. So much more suitable in this heat. That chemise must be hot and uncomfortable. I think you are being perverse, Marietta. I really do.'

Marietta grunted, feigning sleep. To answer would only involve another pointless discussion. She did not feel ready for that. The dream had disturbed her greatly. She wanted time to let it fade, to compose herself before she faced whatever the day held.

Claudine let the curtain drop back into place. Marietta could imagine her friend's eloquent little shrug, her easy dismissal of her peculiar behaviour. She hugged the pillow to her cheek, trying to empty her mind, while her skin remained in a state of heightened sensitivity. She felt every movement of the cambric chemise as she breathed in and out. The lace at the neckline was scratchy, tickling the swell of her half-uncovered breasts. The movement of the silk bedcover was smooth and cool against her calves and bare feet.

It was no good. She could not get the dream and Kasim out of her mind. In disgust she drew herself upright and began to dress.

'Your training starts this day,' Leyla explained as she nibbled a piece of feta cheese. 'But it need not be looked upon as a trial. The first rule is that you are made to feel special. You are ordered to be cosseted. A woman who is aware that her body is lovely to look on becomes a sensuous creature. Her womanly nature blooms. She is a pleasure to herself as well as to others. Quite irresistible in fact. Kasim wishes this for you both. That is not too hard. He is kind, no? And he is very rich. You may ask for anything: a favourite food, jewellery, cosmetics—'

'Freedom?' Marietta cut in, sipping at a glass of Russian tea.

'Ah, no,' Leyla said with a tiny smile. 'You can never leave. But he wants you to be happy. You are to indulge yourselves completely.'

Claudine giggled. 'That won't be too difficult.'

Marietta flashed her friend an angry look. Claudine's lovely mouth was curved with eagerness as she awaited each discovery about her new life.

Marietta's own feelings of impotence and anger had fostered a deep depression. She had been furious to find that her French gown and stays had disappeared. In their place was a comfortable silk robe and wide trousers. With no other choice she had pulled the clothes on over the chemise she had slept in. It felt very odd to be without her stays. Even under the layers of fabric, she felt naked and oddly exposed.

In the room where food was spread, Marietta sat curled into a ball at one end of a divan. The other women were chatting and eating from silver bowls, using the tips of the fingers of their right hands. Marietta did not return their friendly smiles. She surveyed the women with a hostile expression on her face.

The harem women rolled their eyes and grinned at each other, giggling behind their hands, making whispered comments about the bad temper of the newest favourite. Everyone let her be. All except Leyla who tried to coax Marietta to eat or to let someone comb the tangles from her sleep-ruffled hair.

After a time, Leyla too stopped trying to draw Marietta out. Marietta accepted another glass of tea, then sat staring into space. In the midst of all the noise and the bustling women she felt lonely. She had no one to confide in. Claudine and she had shared everything since childhood, but Claudine had become a stranger.

Did Claudine not realise that they were slaves? Perhaps she did not understand that they were to be used in any way that Kasim wished. He desired to wear down their resistance, to erode their free will, to make them serve him as their only master. How degrading that thought was.

And how stimulating...

Across the room, Leyla glanced briefly at the glowering Marietta.

It hurt her to see the French woman's distress. She saw how often Marietta's eyes strayed towards Claudine, but Claudine seemed unaware of it. Claudine was eating a dish of clotted cream with honey, licking her lips like a cat.

Leyla sensed Marietta's loneliness. It was self imposed and could be taken as a sign of haughtiness. But Leyla knew that it was more than that. She understood Marietta's resistance. To Marietta it was a symbol, a way that she could retain her free will. Ah, if only she could be made to understand that the way to find freedom was to lose one's inner-self. Then she would be free to own the secret desires that drove her.

She wanted to take Marietta in her arms and kiss that lovely, sulky mouth. There were violet shadows under the blue eyes and her small nostrils looked slightly pinched. And no wonder. Leyla had heard the sounds from behind Marietta's bed curtains during the night. There were rustlings and soft moans.

At first she had been worried. Was Marietta ill? Intrigued, and a little alarmed, Leyla had crossed the room. Silently she pulled the curtains open a little and looked down at the woman on the bed. Her cheeks grew warm as she remembered how Marietta had looked.

The French woman's face was flushed in sleep, her forehead damp. Her head lay to one side, cushioned on the cloud of her pale hair. The loose neck of her chemise had slipped down, exposing her breasts. The garment was twisted up around her body and lay like a rope around her waist. The silk bedcover was thrown back and lay in a ruched tangle around Marietta's bare legs.

Leyla's fingers tightened on the curtain as she looked at Marietta's body. She lay on her side. Half of her body was in shadow and the bare limbs were pale, silvered by the moonlight. A slight sheen of sweat made them look pearly. Leyla ached to place kisses on that long white neck, to stroke the slim rounded arms.

She knew that she should go back to her own bed. Marietta did not need help. She was not unwell, only dreaming. But Leyla did not leave. She wanted to look at Marietta for a moment longer. The beautiful face was peaceful. The deep eyelids were closed over her intense blue eyes – eyes that held accusation when they were open. Leyla could not bear for Marietta to dislike her. She wanted to be Marietta's friend and confidante, as Claudine was – or had been.

While she slept, Leyla could have the exquisite French woman all to herself. She could imagine that Marietta would wake and be pleased to see her; the sensual little mouth would curve in a smile; the arms reach out to embrace her. Leyla's eyes roved over the high round breasts, the generous curve of hip. How slim were Marietta's ankles and her feet were narrow and well-shaped. Leyla would love to decorate those feet with henna, and slip gold rings on the little pink toes . . .

Marietta had groaned and turned over, facing away from Leyla. She drew her knees up, presenting Leyla with a view of her firm rounded buttocks. Leyla's blood quickened. Between the pale globes she could see the split-plum shape of Marietta's sex. Light golden curls clustered around it.

Hesitantly Leyla reached out with one hand. Dare she touch her? Gently, using just the tips of her fingers, she grazed the lightly furred sex. Her fingers caressed it, rubbing up and down the adorable little slit and disappearing into the crevice between her buttocks, tickling and rifling the blonde curls. She pressed a little more firmly, opening the tight plum and reaching a fingertip inside to the inner moisture.

Leyla's breath grew shallow as she drew her finger up and down the snug little groove. The flesh seemed to suck at her finger. Carefully she ventured deeper and found the rim of Marietta's central opening. She slipped the finger inside just a fraction, feeling the slickness of the flesh-walls. Oh, it was difficult not to do more. She wanted to work on that lovely little tube, to feel the wetness surround her finger. Perhaps slip in one or two more fingers, slip them in deeply and feel the soft flesh-lips bearing down on her knuckles.

She was quite lost in the wonder of her contemplations and the feel of Marietta's inner heat . . .

Suddenly Marietta shuddered and changed position. Her eyelids fluttered. Leyla removed her hand and jumped back. Guilty colour burned in her face. She replaced the curtain and crept back to her own bed. Once there she inhaled the lingering perfume that clung to her fingers. With her other hand she reached down between her thighs and stroked herself, rubbing firmly in a circular motion, bringing herself quickly to a climax.

With a sigh of satisfaction, she snuggled down into the pillows. Before she slept, she made herself a promise: I will win Marietta's love. One day she will come to regard me as the true friend I am. And one day she will welcome me as her lover. For that, she could wait.

Leyla licked the taste of Marietta from her fingers. And with the sweet musky taste of the French woman in her mouth, and those comforting thoughts of the future, she went to sleep.

'We must see to your clothes first, I think. You have finished eating, Marietta? Claudine? Then come with me,' Leyla said, her voice friendly but impersonal.

Claudine followed Leyla eagerly. Marietta sipped the last of her tea and watched as Claudine followed Leyla from the room. She was expected to follow, but she hung back. She wondered what would happen if she refused. Then she knew. It would be Leyla who was punished. She remembered Kasim's threats. Leyla did not deserve to suffer further on her account. Perhaps she would go along with the training for a while.

Besides, if she were truthful, she was rather tired of being sulky. Making a decision, she rose from the divan and followed Leyla and Claudine down a corridor. Soon she entered a large side room where some old women sat sewing lengths of brightly coloured silk.

Leyla flashed Marietta a warm smile, and she returned it briefly.

'You are to choose any fabric you wish,' Leyla said. 'New clothes will be made for you. There is everything here. Silks, velvets, brocades encrusted with gems, gauze veils.'

Claudine cried out with delight and, rushing over to the shelves that lined the walls of the room, began fingering bolts of cloth.

'Oh, Marietta did you ever see such a colour? It is like the sun on water. And this, such a deep green sewn with silver thread.'

Marietta looked at the array of fabric without interest. Claudine's enthusiasm reminded her of when they had plundered the trunk in Kasim's cabin. If only she had realised then what was about to happen. She stood in the arched doorway, watching her friend.

She must be practical. All she possessed, she wore now. She was tempted to be stubborn and insist on remaining dressed as she was. The chemise was the only link left with her old life. But Kasim had expressly ordered her to be dressed in finery for his delight. It was not beyond him to force her to walk around naked if she refused. She approached a shelf reluctantly and pulled out a bolt of garnet-coloured cloth at random.

'This one,' she said tonelessly.

Leyla nodded, encouragingly. 'Choose more. As many colours as you wish.'

'You choose. I care not,' Marietta said.

Leyla looked disappointed, she had obviously hoped that Marietta would be seduced by the array of sumptuous fabrics.

'Come now, Marietta. This is not a punishment,' Claudine laughed.

Marietta shrugged and pointed to three or four other bolts of cloth, then stood placidly while her measurements were taken. Claudine twisted and turned, holding up lengths of fabric and swathing herself in sparkling veils. The old women laughed, nodding to each other and speaking in their own tongue.

'What do they say?' Claudine asked Leyla.

'The say that you were born to the harem,' she smiled. 'Your presence is like the warmth of sunlight after winter chill.'

Claudine dimpled, well pleased. She held a transparent veil up to her face coquettishly, shaking it so that the sparkles danced. Her eyes, the colour of honey, twinkled at the old women. They patted her arm and, taking hold of her hands, kissed the backs of them, chuckling approvingly.

Leyla made a sharp motion with her hand. The old women stopped chattering and began at once to measure and cut cloth. Then Leyla led Marietta and Claudine from the room.

'Later you can choose jewels. While the clothes are made, your bodies will be groomed. Your first dresses will be waiting for you after you return from the hammam,' she said. 'Kasim will want to examine you. He does this with all the new women.'

At the mention of the baths Marietta felt her cheeks grow warm. There were many enticements to her unwilling flesh in that place. She remembered Leyla's gorgeous body; the things they had done together, they had been so sweet ... An image of Leyla's naked body, caressed by runnels of lather, rose in her mind. The singular scent of it came back to her; musky with salt and female arousal, all overlaid with a sweet jasmine fragrance. She was unprepared for the sudden hot pulsing between her thighs.

For a moment, bound by the seductive recollections, Marietta did not absorb all of Leyla's words. Then, realizing what was to happen to her and Claudine, she stiffened.

'Groomed. Examined. And then decked in finery. Does Kasim think we are horses to be added to his stable!'

'It is the custom. And expected,' Leyla said, looking worried. 'Surely you want to wear beautiful clothes and perfumes. What woman does not? And do you not want Kasim to find your body beautiful? Your beauty is a gift from Allah. You must take pride in it. You bestow honour on yourself and Allah when you display your beauty to your master.'

'He is not my master!' Marietta fumed. 'I refuse to be examined. I refuse to behave like ... a ... a meek little lamb!'

'Marietta, please,' Leyla said, in exasperation. 'You distress yourself needlessly. Will you not allow me to show you how good life here can be? I wish you would, for your sake.'

Marietta looked into Leyla's lovely face. Her long dark eyes looked moist and gentle. The full red lips trembled slightly. Her expression was one of genuine concern.

'I will not, I cannot relinquish my freedom,' Marietta said, less stridently. Her voice, less sure, shook just a little.

'But you have no choice,' Leyla said softly. 'Did you not hear Kasim? His word is law. If you do not comply you will be punished. I too, for failing to win you to our ways. And some punishments, lovely one, are much harsher than others.'

Marietta bit her lip. She felt trapped, stifled. The fear rose in her belly, fluttering under her ribs. It was difficult to stay angry. It would be so easy to give in. Leyla was so persuasive. She wished she could trust her.

Leyla took her gently by the arm. 'Come. You shall bathe now, then change into your new clothes. The formalities will not take long. Then perhaps you would like to sleep.'

Marietta's shoulders sagged. Why was she resisting? It was plain that Leyla was trying to be kind. And what was to happen was inevitable. Of course Kasim would want to look at his new slaves. Did not all despots demand complete subjection? All horsemen examine their prize animals?

But, try as she might to destroy the dazzling mental image she carried of Kasim, with these and other unflattering comparisons, she found that she could not do it. He remained stubbornly compelling, invading her dreams, filling her thoughts with his dark angular beauty, his vibrant presence. He was quite simply the most desirable, the most fascinating man she had ever met.

She must continue to resist him, to face what was to come with all the strength and fortitude she could muster. There was no alternative. If only she did not feel so morally fragile. Nothing in her life had prepared her for the potent enticements of Kasim's harem. Kasim was the bigger part of it, but Leyla too drew her strongly. Leyla, so gentle and kind. So compelling, in quite a different way.

She knew that she desired them both. But neither of them would ever own her. And besides the potent pull of physical attraction, there was that other deep dark – and oh so beguiling – threat. The threat of what Kasim would do to her if she angered him. She knew that he would beat and humiliate her. By all that she held holy, she hoped she could resist the delicious pull of such chastisement.

She was weary suddenly of thinking. Enough of introspection. Leyla had said that after the 'grooming' she might rest. She longed to close out everything, for a while at least, in sleep. She prayed that this time she would not dream.

'I'm ready for the curry comb. And you may plait my mane if you wish,' she said icily to Leyla.

At which point Marietta had the satisfaction of seeing sparks of humour and admiration mix in Leyla's bewitching black eyes.

6

In the hammam two slaves scrubbed Marietta's skin with pumice stone and then rubbed her limbs with the same creamy concoction that Leyla had used on her.

Marietta sat on the basketwork stool, surrounded by scented steam. Claudine sat nearby, her eyes closed and her head tilted back as slave women washed her thick mass of red-gold hair, massaging her scalp with a mixture that smelt of cloves. Leyla too was naked. She was also being soaped and rinsed.

The shock of being naked was not so bad as that first time, but Marietta was still strongly affected by the sight of Leyla's and Claudine's unclothed bodies. There was something so erotic about the silky smooth female skin, buffed to rosiness by the pumice. The contours and hollows of both bodies, beautiful in their separate ways, were overflowing with runnels of creamy lather.

The long wet tresses – deepest-black and honey-auburn – streamed down their backs. Marietta found herself looking from one to the other admiringly. Claudine's body was as lush and curvaceous as Leyla's. Leyla was all pale skin, smooth and hairless, the only colour being her large wine-red nipples.

Claudine had a gold tint to her skin, emphasised by the abundant freckles that covered her shoulders and arms. She looked as if she wore gold coins on her skin. Her nipples were light in colour, the pigmented area not clearly defined from the colour of her breast skin.

The cluster of light-brown curls at her armpits and groin was startling next to Leyla's smoothness.

The lash marks on Leyla's belly and thighs were faintly red, but not raised. Leyla ran her hand over them, stroking them with her fingers as she massaged suds into her skin. Her full underlip was pushed out slightly as she contemplated the marks. She seemed proud of them. As if, Marietta thought, she valued them like a sort of trophy.

It was an aspect of Leyla's punishment that Marietta had not considered. She saw that there was a hidden and profound subtlety to Leyla's relationship with Kasim. Something in her responded to that knowledge but she pushed the thought aside. It was too troubling.

Claudine followed Leyla's hand movements as if mesmerised, her eyes opening wider as Leyla parted her thighs and began washing her hairless sex. Marietta looked away, alarmed by the pleasure it gave her just to look at Leyla's body. She could not help being conscious that Leyla too was watching her closely, gauging her reactions.

Claudine commented on the nakedness of Leyla's sex. Her voice was slightly rough, a little breathelss. 'It ... it is strangely compelling. Are all women here without hair at the base of their belly?'

Leyla smiled. 'It is the custom. After the bath you too shall have all your body hair removed.'

Claudine gave a little shiver. 'It makes me feel a little afraid. I shall be so – exposed.'

Marietta did not speak. Claudine sounded quite delighted at the prospect of having her body hair removed. It did not occur to her to question the practice. Well, there would be a few angry faces when it came to her own turn. The slaves spent a long time attending to the three women. The combination of being steamed, scrubbed, and massaged with scented soap left them all quite exhausted. When they were all petal-soft and sweetly fragranced, they were wrapped in large towels and led into a side room.

There were many small tables with trays of food and glasses of sherbet. Carved and decorated screens were placed around the walls. Silk draped divans and tables were arranged for the purpose of massage and beauty treatments. Slaves brought trays of perfumed oil, cosmetics, and paint.

Marietta was asked to lie face down. A slave began to massage her body with perfumed oil. Another blotted her hair and swathed it in a soft cloth. Yet another brought her a glass of pomegranate sherbet. Marietta sipped the brilliant red drink; it was sharp and refreshing and smelt of orange blossom.

Marietta relaxed on the divan, laid her cheek on the backs of her hands and closed her eyes. The slave's strong hands began to work upwards from her feet. Her calves were squeezed gently and the backs of her knees were pinched, ever so lightly. The circular movements, the scent of the oil, the gentle sounds of her companions' breathing acted like balm on Marietta's senses. She gave herself up to the delicious sensation of being massaged.

Now the fingers stroked up the sides of her thighs, describing more small circles on the firm flesh. Marietta sighed with pleasure. Her body had become a leaden weight. There was a brief pause while the slave rested one hand lightly on the underswell of her buttock. She assumed that the slave was reaching for more of the warm oil, then the soothing rhythm was resumed with both hands.

The pressure of the hands was subtly different, firmer but still gentle, knowing. Long strokes progressed up to her waist and then on to her shoulders. Her arms were smoothed with warm oil and stroked and kneaded firmly. Her neck was circled and the slight indentations at the base of her skull were massaged with tiny circling movements. Marietta closed her eyes, feeling as if she could drift off to sleep. The hands now retraced their path, lingering on the flesh of her buttocks.

The firm flesh was kneaded, then lifted gently and rolled. The pressure was increased slightly, the slave's palms pressing outwards. This caused the underswell of her buttocks to be forced gently upwards and her twin globes to be pulled apart. Before she had time to feel dismay, the movement was completed. Her bottom-cheeks were closed and squeezed together.

She felt less drowsy. The warm strong fingers on her buttocks were stimulating. The outward pressing movement began all over again, and though she tensed slightly just before the moment when her shadowed valley was opened to reveal its secrets, she relaxed into the rhythm. It went on and on. It was as if the slave was unwilling to move her hands further upwards. There was the squeezing and the gentle pressure, then the upward pushing and the opening. And the knowledge that the puckered brown rose of her anus was revealed momentarily, before the lush globes were allowed to fall back and close. Her oil-slick inner surfaces rubbed together, creating an exciting friction.

Marietta began to feel aroused. The tight little mouth between her bottom-cheeks grew warm, the crevice grew more soft and damp. Sometimes when the thumbs were exerting their pressure to force the cheeks upwards, she felt the slightest scrape of a nail on her flesh-valley. And once a nail tip trailed across the tight brown rose.

Marietta turned her face into her hands and bit gently on her fingers. She felt ashamed that her sex had begun to swell and the tender bud within her folds was pulsing strongly. Her face was hot. She felt a sort of delighted shame in the pleasure she felt. It was a secret pleasure, known only to her. That fact aroused her strongly.

She found that she was tensing, holding her breath for the moment when her buttocks were splayed apart – more widely it seemed as time went on – and the pressure forced the tight little bottom-mouth to give and gape just a little. Her body's openness fascinated her. She had never dreamt that this orifice could be so wanton. It seemed to be pushing itself out, clamouring for attention. For a while she was lost in contemplation of this new discovery and, while she watched herself with her conscious mind, her body seemed to soften and become languid. It was as if every muscle in her body responded to that slow stroking, squeezing and pulling apart, then rolling together and squeezing again. Moisture gathered between the lips of her sex. Her nipples, which were pressed to the table beneath her, grew hard.

Then she felt a different sensation. More warm oil was applied to her buttocks. Quite a lot of it, so that it ran down into her valley. The earlier sensations were heightened by the slippery feel of her flesh. It took great control not to raise her hips, arch her back, and push back against those strong, expert hands.

The massage went on and Marietta feared that she would moan aloud. She prayed that the slave would travel upwards and begin to work on her waist, saving her from the building sensations of pleasure. Conversely, she wanted the massage to go on. She was having difficulty keeping her breathing even.

Then her buttocks were grasped firmly, and rolled wide apart. She felt the edges of two strong thumbs rubbing either side of her anus. Fingers held her spread while the oily thumbs probed the tight little mouth, slipping around and across it. Marietta's eyes opened wide, as suddenly, both thumbs entered her and began working in and out. The pleasure was tinged with pain as the flesh-ring was stretched and teased. She winced and writhed against the intrusion. Her first instinct was to protest, then leap from the table in shock.

As if the slave had sensed her consternation, Marietta felt another pair of gentle hands on her, holding her down.

'Do not struggle, Marietta,' came Leyla's voice. 'This is part of the grooming. Your body is being assessed to see how much pleasure it will give.'

Fear crawled in Marietta's belly, but it was a hot-tipped exciting kind of emotion. They were testing her and she could not hide her responses. She sensed that someone was standing next to Leyla, beside the slave. Then the slave spoke.

'This one is very tight, my lady. The orifice must be trained, worked in this way often, until it will give pleasure willingly.'

Marietta made a sound, meant to be of protest, but it was more like a groan. Leyla's voice came again, thick and husky.

'It will be done. I will see to it myself. See how she fights her responses? But she cannot win. Her body is too eager for pleasure, her senses too voluptuous. Is she not entrancing to watch? If I was to touch her here . . .'

She slid her hand under Marietta's hips and between the parted legs. 'Ah, yes. As I thought. Her sex is swollen, hungry. It weeps and burns for the touch of a lover. Good. Very Good. We make progress.'

Marietta hid her burning face in her hands. It was as if a shameful secret had been laid bare. Yet they spoke about her with something like awe. Using glowing terms, they discussed her responses; the perfection of her buttocks; the texture of the skin in her secret valley; the colour and tightness of her anus.

It was as if she was some rare morsel. In an odd sort of way she felt honoured by so much attention. The feeling confused her.

She could almost feel the eyes on her bottom, as if their gaze raked her skin. And now the busy thumbs delved more deeply into her body and, aided by the oil, were distending and loosening her tight flesh-ring. The thumbs slid in and out, over and around the opening. More oil was applied, then the unwelcome intrusion continued. She squirmed with humiliation and her buttocks trembled as she tried desperately to clench together against the restraining fingers.

She could not hold back a moan. 'Stop. Please.'

Leyla's cool hand stroked gently, soothingly, down her backbone. 'Hush, lovely one. It will get better for you. I will show you ways to pleasure this little mouth that will give you much delight.'

Marietta could find no answer. She lay pressed to the table, her face hot and red, until the oily thumbs were slowly withdrawn and her buttocks allowed to close. Her ring throbbed and burned between her oiled bottom-cheeks. She let out a sigh of relief, thinking that the examination was finished. Then her heart sank at Leyla's next words.

'Enough. Turn her onto her back.'

Marietta had the impression that one of the slaves left the room, then she saw a swift movement behind one of the carved screens. The slave seemed very tall and dressed in dark robes. A suspicion formed in her mind. Her heart began to beat fast.

Then eager hands turned her over, slipping cushions under her so that she was lying comfortably with her upper body raised and her knees apart.

'Before the examination continues she must be depilated,' Leyla said. 'Bring the paste.'

Marietta brought her knees together, clenching her thighs modestly. A mulish look came over her face. This was too much. Let them bring the paste. They were going to get a surprise.

Claudine, lying face down on a table nearby, hardly noticed what was happening to her friend.

She closed her eyes and let out a long ragged sigh.

Her body felt like it was on fire. She writhed under the ministrations of the slaves. The thumbs had been removed from between her buttocks and a carved ivory phallus had been inserted carefully.

She did not trouble to hide her pleasure. Why should she? Everyone here wanted her to enjoy herself. She arched her back and rocked her hips in time with the thrusts of the oiled object. Ah, this was a wonderful place. Here she could indulge herself in every way possible. She had rather regretted the death of Sister Anna, thinking she had lost the source of a quite delicious ilicit pleasure. Now, here in the harem, was the promise of fleshly delights beyond her wildest dreams. It was almost too much to encompass.

One of the slaves slipped a hand between Claudine's legs and took a firm hold of the wet sex. Holding the flesh-lips closed the slave massaged the firm little plum in a circular motion.

Claudine's breath came fast. The slaves were well

trained in coaxing pleasure from womens' bodies. She loved the fingers that were working on her; they knew exactly what to do. Wonderful sensations radiated from her swollen vulva. The movement of her closed flesh-lips exerted a referred pressure on her swollen clitoris. It flicked from side to side in a subtle and maddening rhythm. The phallus, moving deeply inside her anus, pressed against the place behind her pleasure bud, separated from her cunny by only a thin membrane. Warm drops of oil mixed with her musky juices and ran down her thighs, pooling on the cloth spread beneath her.

The slave holding the phallus laughed and twisted it gently. She pulled it out almost completely and rimmed the tight little mouth with the round carved head. Delicious shivers spread up Claudine's back. She gasped. The whole of her sex felt pincered by sensation.

The erect pleasure bud strained from its flesh-hood. It pulsed and throbbed, trapped within the pinched together sex-lips, tortured by the firm circular movements of the slave's strong fingers. Two other slaves began to lightly spank her buttocks. The slaps were firm, making a crisp sound as they connected with her flesh. The sound, the pain, the heat of the sore buttocks, poured sensation on top of sensation.

Claudine lost control. She began to moan and clutch the edge of the draped table. She thrust her buttocks high into the air and spread her thighs wide. She did not care that the whole of her open flesh-valley was held clear of the table.

Her sex oozed. The slave's grasp was slick. The movements of her hand against the still-closed flesh-lips had become hot and silken. Claudine felt as if all her nerve ends were on fire. She did not care either, that her buttocks were spread wide; that her distended anus, collared by light brown curls, was pushed out lewdly and moistly for all to see as it sheathed the head of the oiled phallus.

She moaned aloud, loving the sound as it mixed with the sounds of the slaps. Her womb contracted suddenly. Waves of pleasure spread to her belly, the warmth radiating to her buttocks and trembling thighs. The climax was heavy and deep and a sweet ache encompassed the whole area from her belly to her thighs. She collapsed on to the table, her cheek against the rumpled silk. Her body felt boneless.

As her breath began to return to normal, the slaves patted and stroked her, congratulating her on her total abandonment.

'Kasim Dey will be delighted with you,' they whispered, as they took away the phallus, then wiped her with clean towels and sweet oil.

Claudine felt a new pleasure in that knowledge. Kasim promised to lead her to new heights. She looked forward eagerly to the time when he would summon her.

The slaves, still complimenting and flattering her, asked that she turn over. They propped her up with cushions. Claudine became aware, only then, that Marietta was uttering sounds of protest as she was laid on her back. A slave brought a bowl of paste and set it down next to her friend. Then Marietta seemed to lose her head.

'Take that stuff away!' she yelled, kicking out at the slaves, ordering them to let her be. She insisted that she would not be depilated.

Claudine had never seen her friend so angry. Leyla was trying to calm her, looking quite distressed. But Marietta was not to be placated.

Claudine was tempted to intervene. She felt exasperated. What did it matter if they were denuded of their body hair? She thought it would be exciting to be naked there, like a child. She could not wait to see how she would look. She shrugged and sipped at the glass of sherbet she was offered. Marietta would come to her senses in her own time. She knew how stubborn her friend was and it was always better to let her fits of temper run their course.

She was sorry that Marietta brought such distress on herself. She truly wished that her friend would grasp what was offered. For what could be better than the life of pleasure at Kasim's harem? It was free from care, free from worries. All they had to do was to reach into themselves and allow their secret natures to surface. This was something Claudine was more than willing to do.

When the slaves brought the paste to Claudine, she smiled, settling back against the cushions and parting her thighs helpfully. She stretched her arms overhead, so that they might spread the paste onto her armpits, and bit down on the sugared plum that a slave had placed in her mouth.

'Mmm,' she said. 'I'll have another sweetmeat. And may I have a mirror to watch as I am laid bare?'

'Marietta! Stop that noise at once!' Kasim rapped, stepping out from behind a screen.

Marietta pulled the cushions over her body to hide her nakedness in a futile gesture of protection. She looked up at Kasim without surprise, knowing that he had already seen her naked. He had probably watched them all in the hammam. She also knew who it was who had given her the massage.

'So. Now you show yourself,' she said coldly, fighting

to keep her temper. 'Did it please you to violate my body just now? To have me held down while you ... you ...'

'Yes. It did,' he said without inflection. 'It pleased me to plunder those lovely buttocks while you were unaware that I was doing so. And I felt the way your flesh awoke too, despite your efforts to hide the fact. Really. What do you expect, Marietta? An apology. Ah, you still do not see, do you? I do exactly as I please. Always. And now ... I expect my orders to be carried out.'

He drew close to the divan and looked down at her. She wrapped her arms around her knees, drawing them up to her chin, and glared up at him. A tiny smile played at the corner of his mouth.

'So. You will not consent to be depilated? Is that golden fleece of yours so important to you? Then I must look at it more closely.'

He made a movement to the slaves, who hurried to take the flimsy protection of the cushions from Marietta, and to press her back against the divan. She made a sound of protest and resisted them, trying to roll into a ball.

'Do not presume too much on my good nature,' Kasim said harshly. 'Your display just now is enough to earn you a beating with the strap! Now, I wish you to show me that you know the meaning of obedience. Has Leyla not even made a beginning with you? Brace your upper body. Spread your knees and place the soles of your feet together. Do it. Now!'

The mention of Leyla penetrated Marietta's fury. She uncurled her legs slowly and sat as he asked, resting her upper body back against the piled cushions. He watched with cold dark eyes. Her legs trembling, she parted her knees a little.

'Open them wide,' he said.

She flexed her knees and allowed them to fall open. 'Wider!'

She felt the strain at her groin as her knees relaxed to lay flat on the divan. The soles of her feet met. She gave a little shudder and, as if it were possible to shield even part of herself from him, she crossed her arms on her bare breasts and closed her eyes tight.

Kasim gave a low chuckle. 'Such charming modesty.' He moved closer. 'Ah, and here is the centre of your lovely body. I have been watching you in the hammam, feasting my eyes on your beauty, and I have been anticipating the pleasure of doing – this.'

He reached out to tug gently at the light growth of pale blonde curls on her mound. He drew them out with his fingertips, testing the springiness and texture of the hair.

'Lovely,' he breathed. 'Never have I seen a prettier little sex.'

Marietta kept her eyes closed tightly as his fingers brushed lightly across the parted sex-lips. It was her dream of last night, come true. Her body was completely open to his gaze. Half of her recoiled in horror at the knowledge that he could do as he wished with her. The other half melted into a sort of welcome submission.

Kasim bent over and inhaled deeply. 'You have a fine woman's smell. No doubt you taste sweet too. I would sample you. But that can wait for another time. Open your eyes, Marietta. I want you to see the pleasure on my face. And now, I want you to spread those adorable gold-furred lips, with your own fingers, so that I may gaze fully on your most intimate secrets.'

Marietta's eyes flew open in horror. She had thought

there could be nothing worse than being offered up to his gaze like this. But he was going to spare her nothing. He wished her to participate in her own debasement. She saw Leyla watching with a look of sympathy. It gave her the strength to do as Kasim asked.

Her mouth was dry and a pulse beat heavily and insistently deep within her stomach. Slowly she moved her hands downwards then, using two fingers on each hand, she spread her flesh-lips open.

'Wider,' Kasim said. 'And pull upwards slightly. I want to see the little kernel of delight. Ah, yes. There. The tip of it slips from the flesh-hood.'

He reached forward and took hold of the little nub between his finger and thumb. Pinching gently, he worked the hood back and forth. Marietta shuddered. Despite her anger, her feelings of helplessness, she felt her body begin to respond. Kasim kept up the torment until her clitoris was pink and fully erect.

'Excellent,' he said. 'You may remove your fingers. But leave your legs spread.'

Marietta drew a shuddering breath. She had expected far worse. She had tensed ready for the inward plunge of his fingers and was almost disappointed when he drew away. Then she realised her mistake. He had only just started to humiliate her.

Her fear and excitement mounted to a new pitch as Kasim slowly rolled back the loose cuffs of his black tunic.

'You may keep your golden fleece. The novelty of it pleases me,' he said pleasantly. 'I should like for it to be oiled and decorated. And it is to remain prominently on display at all times. Leyla, I wish Marietta to wear clothes that leave bare or enhance this unique treasure of hers.'

'As you wish, my lord,' Leyla said.

'It is settled then. But you are to be chastised none-theless, Marietta. Do you know why?'

Numbly she shook her head. She was close to tears.

'I alone make all decisions concerning your person. You keep your fleece only because I wish it. Understand? But you will still be punished for refusing to be depi-lated. Now. Stay as you are. Accept your punishment.'

Marietta remembered his words to her in the garden, 'There is never any way to avoid my will.'

Now she was to have evidence of that. Using the flat of his hand, Kasim began to slap Marietta on the insides of her thighs. He flicked his hand back and forth, so that the backs and then the fronts of his fingers struck her in turn. He slapped lightly at first, the sound of his hand hitting her flesh clean and crisp. Then he applied the strokes with increasing strength.

The shock of it, more than the pain, stole Marietta's breath. She had never been beaten in her life, and for it to be before an audience was doubly shaming. Leyla, Claudine, and all the slaves were watching. She bowed her head before the disgrace of it.

Let it be over soon. She did not think she could bear it although she realised that it had been inevitable. But at least Leyla had not been punished. She flinched at each stinging double stroke. The pain increased as her skin grew sore, but still he slapped her. Her thighs began to feel warm and the marks of Kasim's fingers were plain on the white skin.

He paused and she thought it was over. Her inner thighs felt hot as a furnace. The soreness was fading already, leaving only a deep flush on her skin. It had not been so bad.

'This time only, your breasts will be spared. Turn onto your belly,' Kasim ordered.

Unable to stop herself giving a sob of dismay, she obeyed. At least she could hide from all those eyes and close her legs. She felt a moment's relief as she stretched out. The skin of her inner thighs stung and tingled but she hardly had time to concentrate on the discomfort, or to catch her breath.

Kasim began to spank her buttocks with loud, deliberate slaps. She gave a sob of renewed distress, squirming under his hand, pressing her belly into the divan. The cool silk caressed her as she bucked and twisted, unable to escape the stinging slaps.

Her bottom grew hot, the skin glowed and smarted, and still he smacked her. Then, unbelievably, through the pain she began to feel a sort of spiked pleasure. When he spread her buttocks and began spanking the inner surfaces of the cheeks she made a convulsive movement. There seemed to be a building of pressure within her. Her erect nub, wakened by Kasim's touch earlier, began pulsing. Kasim smacked the abused bottom-mouth now. Her throat felt raw with holding in her moans. She bit her lips, afraid that any sound, if it escaped, would be a groan of pleasure.

It was the dream all over again. Her flesh was being led unwillingly into further realms of passion. She hated that he knew this, that he somehow perceived how she hungered for the strokes of his hand.

It was punishment indeed to be shown what she was.

She began to sob aloud as he proceeded. He smacked her past soreness, past the time when she could catch her breath between slaps. A riot of warm pain suffused her from the waist down. It seemed to go on and on, until, at last, he was satisfied.

Kasim stopped; he was breathing hard. 'Get up,' he said. Slowly she did so. Her face was tear-streaked and flaming with colour. She looked up at him with brimming eyes and saw with intense satisfaction that his pale face was flushed high along his prominent cheekbones. Her abused buttocks throbbed and burned. She wanted nothing more than to run and hide. Surely now he would allow her to seek the sanctuary of her curtained divan.

But Kasim had still not finished.

'Leyla. Come,' he said.

Marietta's heart sank. Oh, no. Leyla was not to escape. This was her fault. If she had consented to have the hair removed none of this would have happened. She slanted a look at Leyla, who had paled. She wanted to apologise but there was not time.

Leyla smiled shakily back at her. She seemed to know what was required. Without a word, she raised her thin gauze bath robe to waist level and leaned across the nearest empty divan.

Marietta stood upright painfully. The skin of her buttocks felt stiff. Even her sex hurt, but it was a ravenous, hungry sort of feeling. She looked at Leyla's prone figure; at the lovely rounded buttocks, the shapely thighs. Had she looked that enticing?

Then she reeled at Kasim's next words.

'Marietta. Come here. You are to chastise Leyla. I want you to feel the heat of her skin, the trembling, as she cries out under your hand. Then you will truly appreciate the twin pleasures of chastisement. Leyla is ready for you. Begin.'

She took a step back. Something in her withdrew from the idea of laying hands on Leyla. It was too tempting, too close to what she wanted to do. She could not explain. The complexity of her emotions confused her.

'I . . . I cannot. Please, Kasim, I beg you. Do not make me,' Marietta said, the tears running freely down her cheeks.

Kasim's dark brows flew together. 'Such disobedience,' he said through clenched teeth. 'A stronger lesson is needed.'

He reached into his tunic and approached Marietta. She stood trembling as he encircled her neck with a thick leather collar. The collar forced her to hold her chin high. There was a gold ring attached to the front of the collar. Kasim attached a lead to the ring. Jerking on the lead, he forced her to follow him.

'Leyla, you come too. You shall watch and learn. As you seem to have let Marietta do as she likes, you must also be taught a lesson. Marietta's training will take place in my chambers. Under my supervision.'

He strode out of the side room without another word, leaving Marietta to stumble after him. The tiles were cool under her bare feet as she half ran after Kasim, trotting behind him down the corridors that led to his private apartments. She was acutely aware of her bouncing breasts, her abused thighs which burned as they rubbed together, and her buttocks which jiggled as she hurried along. Her damp hair spilled in a tangle of curls over her shoulders and down her bare back, the headcloth having slipped off when Kasim dragged her from the room. Even the touch of the curling strands, brushing against her buttocks, caused her to bite her lips with pain.

Leyla hurried after her and Kasim. Marietta thought how terrible it was that the other woman was to observe her humiliation. Of course, that was Kasim's intention. It seemed that, each time she thought Kasim had done his worst, he was moved to new refinements, new ways to degrade her. Just the thought of Leyla, watching her being half-dragged, naked and sobbing after Kasim, caused her to squirm with humiliation.

Once, Marietta felt the touch of Leyla's cool hand on her boiling buttocks. The touch was gentle, lingering a little too long to be merely comforting. Leyla seemed to be savouring the heat in the sore flesh. Marietta winced. She knew that her bottom-cheeks must be a vibrant red. And that they bounced enticingly with every hurried step.

Marietta was very afraid of what was to come. But Leyla's presence gave her some courage. She knew that, despite her disobedience, which intimated Leyla's failure to teach her humility, Leyla bore her no hatred. She remained her friend. More than a friend.

Leyla's touch also promised to coax a wealth of new sensations from her sore flesh. She trembled inwardly. The journey down the corridor seemed endless and her nakedness and the unyielding leather collar emphasised her helplessness.

Marietta's tears flowed freely. There was no escape, no one to aid her. Leyla would do as Kasim bade her because she must. And because she adored him. Both she and Leyla were at his mercy.

Then, she realised for the first time, she would be at the mercy of her own senses. Kasim would not allow her to hide her pleasure from him. She had learned already that he demanded her complete submission. More than that. He would force her to acknowledge that she enjoyed what he did to her.

That was the greatest fear. The fear of herself. In this place, not only her body had been stripped bare.

7

Kasim strode down the corridor. The soles of his knee-high boots struck the tiles with a hard staccato sound and Marietta's lead was clutched tight in his eager fingers.

He quickened his pace so that she had to hurry to keep up with him. She was breathing fast and making little sobs of distress.

Kasim tugged on the lead. 'Lift your knees and keep that chin up,' he rapped. 'I want those breasts and buttocks to bounce. Don't fall behind or I shall be forced to stop and spank you again! Do you understand?'

'Y . . . yes. Ohh.'

Her answer was muffled by a moan as he jerked the lead again, pulling her head forward so that she lost her step and almost stumbled. Her feet scuffed at the tiles with a sound like a sigh.

How those subtle sounds warmed him. He resisted the temptation to glance behind him. It was difficult. He longed to look at her, to drink in all that troubled beauty, but there would be time enough for that. As much time as he wished, but for now he intended to give her a lesson she would never forget. Soon she would find pleasure in obeying him completely, even find a certain freedom in the act of submission. But not too soon. Marietta must suffer; her character demanded it. And her own release would be hard won.

He relished the taming of her, the drawing out of her hidden responses. Ah, she was even more tempting than Leyla had been. What a treasure. Worthy indeed of his affection.

He almost turned and smiled at her. He felt grateful – almost humbly so – for the spark she had kindled in him. It was so easy to grow bored when you had everything you wanted; when women kissed the ground you walked on. But he would resist the urge to soften towards Marietta. Her fear would heighten her responses, adding a depth to her pleasure that most women could only dream of. Such refinements must be cultivated.

All she saw was a master who punished his slaves. She could not know how much *he* was enslaved by his nature, by his own need to be worshipped, and by the potent drug of inflicting pleasure-pain on those who had discovered the delights of complete submission.

He thought that Marietta must almost hate him, but the knowledge did not distress him; Leyla had once thought that way.

They were almost at his rooms. He slowed a little, savouring the last few moments of the journey. He allowed his mind to wander back a little. Marietta had looked so desirable spread out on the divan for the massage. He had meant only to watch her being pre-pared, but the sight of her lying naked and relaxed had prompted him to lay hands on her. He smiled as he thought of her outrage when she discovered that it had been he who had oiled her body, spread her bottom-cheeks, and plunged his thumbs into her tight little anus.

How she had turned on him when he revealed himself. Her anger was delightful to him. The prospect of chastising her had him hard immediately. And when he slapped those creamy thighs and felt the firm flesh grow hot under his hand, the sweet ache in his cock-stem had seemed almost unbearable. Her little gasps of pain were music to his ears. That lovely face, all anguished and tear-stained, aroused him further.

Ah, how she twisted and writhed, yet her knees had remained far apart, displaying the delicate pink folds surrounded by that fleece – never had he seen such pale pubic hair. Though she longed to, she had not drawn her knees together. That pleased him. She had begun already to learn obedience.

He had felt an almost uncontrollable urge to mouth her pretty sex and then to plunge his cock deep inside her; ride her, until she cried out for mercy. But it was too soon. Penetration – that most intimate contact – would be her final reward – his too. He trembled at the thought of what would come to pass. It was only a matter of time. One day she would be willing to open her body and mind to him, to abase herself completely, then . . .

But for now, such a rebellious slave must be treated harshly. Tenderness must wait. And, though she did not realise it, the waiting would be an equal ordeal for him. He had kept his face impassive in the hammam while his cock-tip had stirred against his belly, weeping salty moisture into the dark hair that grew thickly around it.

He was pleased with himself for thinking to bring her back to his apartments. He had shown admirable restraint up until now. It was time to enjoy himself a little.

Now, leading Marietta behind him, he made his way across a courtyard and entered another corridor. He was erect still, the swollen cock-tip rubbing maddeningly against the thick leather belt at his waist. It was sweet torture to contemplate the many delights to come.

For what could compare to the delight of seeing her flesh awake under his expert touch? How she fought him, even when she knew that there was no hope of escape. He respected her spirit. What a soldier she would have made! And what a prisoner of her own flesh she was.

He had sensed early on that she set restrictions for herself, but this seemed to be a thing she was unaware of. It was as if she was two people. For, certainly, her body knew things that her mind did not. When his thumbs explored between her buttocks – so tight and hot was the tiny hole – he had felt the reluctant pulsing of her flesh, the trembling of those parted cheeks. She had been shamed by her responses, hiding her face in her hands as if she could deny her pleasure, her moans held in by the fingers pressed to her mouth.

How different Marietta was from Claudine. He smiled as he remembered the other French woman rolling and grinding in complete abandon against the slave woman's hands. There was no need to hold back with that one. He would take his pleasure with her soon. There was no need to prepare her further, or to punish her. An opportunity missed, sadly. For Claudine was a creature born for pleasure. He anticipated how it would feel to have her luscious body writhing under him. He felt eager to try her. But somehow he did not burn for her as he did for Marietta.

Ah, they were here. He stopped at the entrance to his apartments. Behind him Marietta came to an abrupt halt. He heard her breathing falter. His cock jerked. Little tremors of sensations ran up his engorged stem and gathered in the swollen tip. With a small smile playing about his hard mouth he stepped into the room.

* * *

Marietta lifted her knees and stepped out smartly across the enormous room. The stiff leather collar kept her chin high and her head pointing forward, so that her vision was filled by Kasim's broad velvet-clad shoulders.

The room smelt of incense and orange blossom. She felt the softness of thick carpets under her feet. As Kasim led her to the far end of the room she glanced to one side and took in details of her surroundings. This was his private place. Though she was afraid, she was intrigued. The walls were panelled with screens of carved painted wood, gilded and set with precious stones. Many candles gave the room a soft glow and deepened the colours of carpets and tiles. It was a beautiful room, but she felt threatened by its cold richness. It seemed to her that it reflected Kasim's personality to perfection.

Kasim led her over to an alcove where marble pillars framed a platform which was draped and covered with cushions. Stained glass spilled patterns of colour on to the rich silks and satins. Kasim stopped. Gripping her shoulders, he positioned her so that she faced the centre of the room. In front of her, a few choice pieces of furniture were arranged around a large carpeted area. They seemed to have been placed so that guests could watch entertainments.

Leyla came to stand beside Marietta. She tried to catch her eye, but Marietta avoided looking at her. She kept her eyes downcast, and was red-faced with humiliation as Kasim secured the lead to one of the slim pillars.

'Lift your arms,' he ordered.

Marietta did so although she fought the urge to struggle. It would only be worse if she angered him further. He secured her wrists to a hook so that she was pressed face-forwards against the pillar. She felt the cold marble against her breasts and belly and leaned against the pillar as if it might offer comfort.

'Leyla, come,' Kasim said.

Marietta pressed her burning face to the marble. She looked around fearfully as Leyla walked across to the platform but Kasim seemed to have forgotten her for the moment. She knew him well enough already to know that her respite would be brief.

Leyla's face was flushed, her full dark lips were slightly parted. She looked eager, excited. She still wore the flimsy bath robe. Her damp hair was wrapped in a gauze cloth although one strand of her night-black hair had come loose. The heavy coil of it hung over one shoulder, reaching down past her waist.

In contrast, Kasim was dressed all in black. His tunic was velvet and the loose trousers, tucked into his boots, were made of softest leather. Kasim drew one long finger around Leyla's jawline, then cupped her chin. He put out his tongue and licked her full underlip. Leyla drew his tongue into her mouth, suckling greedily.

Kasim drew the bath robe from her shoulders and let it fall at her feet. The headcloth slipped off as she let her head fall back. Her hair cascaded down to her hips. She stood facing Kasim, arms at her sides. Waiting. Grasping her heavy breasts, Kasim squeezed them, teasing the rouged nipples until they stood out as hard as small stones.

Leyla gasped as he mouthed her breasts, biting at her nipples, slapping the up-swell gently so that the breasts quivered. For a few moments he toyed with her, licking the deep cleavage, pressing the globes together so that he could suck both nipples at once. Then he pressed down on Leyla's shoulders, so that she sank to her knees.

She dipped her chin and arranged herself into the submissive posture, linking her hands behind her back, straightening her shoulders so that her breasts jutted forward. Then she arched her back, and parted her knees widely, displaying the naked sex-lips and moist inner flesh.

'Are you watching, Marietta?' Kasim said softly. 'I want you to take notice. Whenever I order it, you will assume this posture. Wherever you are, whoever is present. Understand?'

'Yes,' she said hesitantly, thinking how dreadful it was to display oneself in that way.

At a word from Kasim, Leyla began kissing his leather-encased thighs. She rubbed her chin cat-like against his leg. Without changing position, she took the fabric into her mouth, biting into the flesh of his inner thighs. Her tongue drew wet trails across the leather as she licked and sucked at it. Slowly she worked inwards to mouth the bulge at his groin. Keeping her hands clasped behind her back, she leaned forward, working over his tumescence. Up and down, her busy wet mouth moved. Her open lips slid over the hidden cock-stem, unable to surround it but biting gently, teasing the swollen head which was clearly visible through the thin leather.

Then Leyla bent her head to nuzzle Kasim's testicles. She opened her mouth wide, her tongue snaking out to spread heat and spittle around the firmly encased bag. She lifted the balls on the point of her tongue, stroking firmly up the centre division and dipping beneath his thighs to lap at the root. A spasm passed over Kasim's face and he stroked Leyla's loose hair. She began again to slide her lips back and forth over the leather-covered bulge. The cock-tip jerked as Kasim pressed towards her mouth. Leyla nosed at the opening of the loose trousers.

Kasim shuddered and pushed her head away. 'Not yet, my Leyla. Soon,' he said.

He hooked her under her armpits and lifted her, bringing her up his body. She stood on tiptoe as he bent his head and began biting her nipples. She squirmed, thrusting out her backside and clasping his thigh between her legs. He worked his mouth up her neck and placed biting kisses along her jaw. She turned her mouth towards him but he twisted away laughing, and bit her sharply on the earlobe.

Leyla gasped and sagged against him, her head falling back to reveal the long white sweep of her throat. Her hands were still clasped behind her. She did not bring them forward but closed her eyes and leaned into Kasim as he probed between her parted thighs.

'Open wide to me,' he ordered.

Leyla spread her legs, bending her knees slightly to allow him greater access. Kasim plunged his fingers inside her, while she moaned and rubbed her pubis against his knuckles. When her buttocks began to flex and release, he withdrew his fingers.

'Before you reach your peak of pleasure you must earn the right to your release,' he said. 'You know what you must do? You will obey me? Let me hear you say it.'

'I will obey you gladly, my lord. Always,' Leyla breathed.

Putting her from him, Kasim walked over to Marietta. Leyla stood with her chin down, breathing hard, waiting for his command. Kasim leaned close to Marietta. She could smell his breath; it was scented with cinnamon and lemon.

'This wicked slave must be chastised. What shall we do with her?' Kasim's voice took on a harsher note.

Marietta tensed, ready for his touch. The scene she

had just witnessed had affected her strongly. Leyla's lovely body, bent in obeisance, the graceful way she had used her mouth and tongue, could not fail to be arousing. Watching her, Marietta had found her own desire mounting. She also found herself wondering what it would be like to be in Leyla's place.

When Kasim stroked her face she smelt Leyla's musk on his fingers. He rubbed his fingertips over her mouth, smearing the moisture and perfume into her skin. When he took a step back, she waited, her whole body cringing, for the expected slap to her breasts or buttocks.

The touch, when it came, was gentle. Kasim lifted the heavy mass of her hair and laid it to fall over one shoulder. For just an instant, so brief that she thought she imagined it, Marietta felt his lips touch the back of her neck, just under the leather strap. He kissed the prominent nubs of her spine, licking the places where the skin was stretched thinly over bone.

'You refused to chastise Leyla, thinking to save her. But it was of no avail. She accepts her punishment gladly. And know this: she will never show you the same mercy.'

Kasim reached for a thin pliable switch. He ran it down Marietta's backbone and trailed the end of it into the cleft of her buttocks.

'Spread your legs,' he ordered. And when she did so, hesitantly, he probed with the switch, tickling the still-sore flesh of her thighs and teasing the abused little bottom-mouth. She gasped as the pliable end probed between the slightly parted sex-lips, stroking the tender flesh with a delicate touch. Kasim flicked the notched end lightly from side to side, easing the moist lips more open with each stroke and reaching up so that it licked against the flesh-hood.

'Wider. Bend your knees. Embrace the pillar between your thighs.'

Marietta bit her lip. Awkwardly, she bent her knees and spread her legs. The marble was cold, soothing against her glowing thighs. As she pulled downwards, her wrist bonds tightened, exerting pressure on her arms and forcing her underarms into prominent hollows. At the same time her breasts were pulled up tightly, the underswell was lifted and the slim pillar was pressed between her cleavage, so that one breast was forced to either side.

'Part your buttocks and push down so that your flesh-lips open and your bud is laid directly against the pillar,' Kasim said, probing ever more deeply with the switch-tip.

Marietta felt the tip enter her body as she bore down on to it. Her vulva convulsed at the invasion, but she dared not lift herself up. Kasim moved the switch, very gently, so that it rubbed against the moist flesh-walls of her vagina.

'As your buttocks are stroked, I wish your kernel of delight to be punished too,' he said. 'It will learn discipline, as you will.'

Marietta felt completely vulnerable. The switch-tip moved inside her body with a subtle scratchy pressure. It made her long for the thrust of something thicker, something that would fill her and force her to contract and become liquid with juices. She trembled inwardly while the muscles in her over-stretched calves and thighs ached and burned.

It did not seem possible that she could maintain the position. Only the bonds at her wrists kept her from over-balancing.

Kasim withdrew the switch-tip. He ran it up her arms and flicked lightly at her armpits, rifling the golden curls. Then he stroked up and down her ribs and circled the taut muscles of her belly. He teased her nipples, flicking the undersides, snapping each one upwards until it throbbed and tingled. Marietta clenched her teeth against the pain. She tensed, knowing that this was just the beginning. Her whole body seemed to be waiting, dreading the moment when he would begin lashing her.

But Kasim handed Leyla the switch.

Understanding now what was to happen, Marietta pressed more closely against the pillar. She felt a sort of desperation. Only now did she begin to see that there truly was no escaping the punishment. She knew that she would be unable to bear the lashing with dignity. Already her buttocks were so sore. At least her belly was protected by the pillar, but her legs were wide open, so that the upper and undersides of her buttocks were vulnerable to the lash.

She prayed that Leyla would not lash her too hard. She shifted against the ache in her arms and legs, hating the position she had been forced to assume and loathing the fact that Leyla could see her like this. New colour scalded her face.

'Begin,' Kasim said. 'Do not stop until I order it.'

'Yes, my lord,' Leyla said meekly, stepping close to Marietta.

Slowly she raised her hand and lashed the switch back and forth across Marietta's already reddened flesh. Marietta cried out at the first contact. She tried to thrust forward, cringing away from each stroke. Her belly and pubis rubbed against the pillar, the contact forcing her heated sex to awaken once again. She writhed and sobbed, her buttocks bucking and jerking. Gripping the marble with her thighs, she pressed herself close to its cold surface. Each stroke of the lash forced a cry from her as the warm pain radiated through her bottom and seemed to find a throbbing echo in the erect little nub that rubbed against the marble.

Marietta longed to toss her head from side to side in her distress, but she could hardly move her head. The leather collar ensured that her chin was forced to stay high. Her cries seemed to force their way out through her stretched lips, sounding thin and high.

Oh, it was unbearable that they should watch the way she worked her hips, thrusting and rubbing against the pillar like an animal in heat. The marble began to grow warm between her legs and as her juices began to flow, she slid her pouting sex up and down. Her breath came fast as she panted and groaned, twisting this way and that, unable to escape the switch which tormented and tortured, even while it prompted her abused flesh to new and undreamt-of sensations.

Leyla flicked the switch upwards so that it stroked the undersides of Marietta's thighs and buttocks. Now and then the flexible leather made contact with her valley, slapping at the tender inner cheeks. Marietta's frantic sobs filled her ears. She could no longer tell whether she was longing for the smarting pain or trying to escape from it.

Leyla began laying the strokes up the sides of Marietta's body. She beat her armpits, where the muscles were cruelly stretched. Then she gave her attention to the sides of her breasts, until Marietta felt that the whole of her body was on fire. Perspiration beaded her forehead, tears bathed her face and dripped off her chin. She tasted salt on her lips and let out a shuddering groan of complete surrender. It was as if something in her body gave way.

She seemed surrounded by waves of pain and

pleasure, mixed. Her body thrummed as if the whole of it was a musical instrument that gave out a prolonged and perfect note.

She realised, only gradually, that Leyla had stopped lashing her. The weals covering her body burned and stung, but no more came.

'Enough.' Kasim's voice seemed to come from very far away.

Marietta gave a final sob and would have collapsed, but for the wrist bonds. Then she felt gentle hands on her.

'Hush, lovely one,' Leyla whispered.

Marietta gasped at first at the agonising touch on her reddened flesh, then she felt a soothing coolness as scented oil was applied to her buttocks and back. The soreness and pain receded somewhat, but the disturbing heat remained in her flesh. Between her sex-lips her clitoris throbbed. Her womb pulsed, thirsting for release. She was again helplessly aroused. Her flesh stirred to a point of sexual excitement, but was given no chance of a final climax. She writhed in frustration, rubbing the strongly erect bud against the warm slick marble, wanting to put an end to her torment.

Kasim drew close. He turned her face towards him and licked the tears from her flaming cheeks. His hand strayed to her sex and played lightly over it. She leaned into his hand, yearning for the thrust of his hard fingers, but he laughed and pulled away.

'Ah, not yet. There is to be no release for you until I wish it. You are not yet obedient enough. Your climax must wait.'

She felt his knuckles brushing the curls between her thighs as he touched the marble pillar, rubbing his fingertips in the patch of seepage.

'How your body weeps for love of the lash,' he said.

'This is something you cannot conceal from me. Or from yourself.'

He carried his fingers to his mouth and licked them. Then he smiled tenderly and kissed the tip of her nose. She felt her heart turn over at the unexpected kindness. When he kissed the corner of her trembling mouth, nibbling gently at her underlip, she tasted herself on his mouth.

'And now,' he said in a deceptively sweet voice, 'we make progress. You shall spank Leyla, no?'

The tears poured down her face, and, aroused past the point of no return, she nodded.

'Good.' He reached up and unfastened her wrists. Rubbing the chafed wrists, he raised her hands to his mouth and kissed the open palms.

Marietta shuddered. The slightest touch from him sent a riot of sensations through her. It seemed that her soul, as well as her body, responded to him. It made her afraid. She could not allow anyone to have such power over her, but at the same time a sort of warmth was spreading outwards from her centre. All she had to do was embrace those feelings, give in to them. As Leyla had.

She lowered her eyes, not daring to meet his. His hard face looked like a mask of shadows in the candle-light. A small satisfied smile curved his mouth. It prompted her back to reality. She felt a surge of disgust at herself. Was it so easy to win her? At the first real testing she had been ready to give in, to welcome him as her master.

Now she raised her eyes and let him see the defiance that blazed there still. He laughed, the sound low and husky.

'Ah, Marietta. How valiant you are! You warm a man's blood.'

He turned to Leyla. 'Ready yourself.'

Marietta stepped away from the pillar. Her legs felt shaky. Each step brought a little shiver of sensation from her bruised flesh. She advanced on Leyla, knowing that she would do as Kasim ordered. There was no alternative. Besides, Leyla had beaten her without restraint.

She watched appreciatively as Leyla, breathing hard from her exertion, tossed back her ringlets of black hair. A few tendrils clung to her damp forehead. Her shapely body was covered in a sheen of sweat and the skin looked a soft peach colour in the candlelight. Leyla's full red-tipped breasts rose and fell as she tried to catch her breath. She smiled tremulously at Marietta and held out the switch. Marietta raised her hand slowly and reached for it, but Kasim stepped forward.

'No. Use your hands only. You will spank her. Wait...'

He opened his velvet tunic and began to unbuckle his belt. 'You will spank Leyla's buttocks while I allow her to pleasure me.'

Leyla threw herself at Kasim's feet and gripped his booted ankles. She rested her forehead on his feet. 'Thank you, my lord,' she whispered.

Kasim stroked Leyla's bent head and looked into Marietta's eyes. His expression was eloquent. One day you will thank me for allowing you to pleasure my body, it said. Marietta allowed her lip to curl with disdain. A long, slow smile spread over Kasim's handsome face. He walked to the platform and laid down on the divan.

'Come,' he said, crooking his finger. and Leyla hurried forward.

Kasim arranged himself so that he lay facing one end of the divan, his back supported by cushions. His legs were stretched out, his boots braced against the padded and rolled arm, and his knees were lightly flexed. He pointed to the padded arm.

'Bend over, Leyla. Leave your buttocks for Marietta and give your breasts to me.'

'Yes, my lord,' Leyla said meekly, arranging herself as he ordered.

Her heavy breasts hung forward like ripe fruits; they rested between Kasim's booted feet. The long curve of her back was arched and her full rounded buttocks were thrust up and out into a perfect heart shape.

Marietta moved forward and stood behind Leyla.

'Kneel, Marietta,' Kasim said. 'But do not sit on your heels. I want you to see everything.'

Marietta did so, feeling the tension in her thighs and stomach as her upper body remained upright. Kasim made a hand movement and Leyla freed the velvet tunic, letting it fall open at his chest. Then she opened the folds of his full leather trousers and pulled them down over his hips. Kasim's powerful upper body was laid bare.

For the first time Marietta saw his chest, the slabs of hard muscle there were crested by dark brown nipples. There were ridges of muscles on his flat stomach. A line of silky black hair trailed downwards from his navel, flaring out into a thick curly bush at his groin.

Leyla did not draw the trousers down fully, but left them to lie in folds around the tops of Kasim's muscular thighs. She drew out Kasim's penis, making a sound deep in her throat at the sight of it, sturdily erect and topped by the swollen bulb. The sight of Kasim, naked to the hips, with his cock jutting upright was powerfully erotic. The black trousers and high leather boots, clothing his lower body, added a poignancy that complete nakedness would not have.

'Pleasure me with your hands, my Leyla. I wish Marietta to watch everything you do. Now. Begin to spank her, Marietta. At once.'

Marietta landed an open-handed slap on Leyla's lush backside. Leyla winced, as the flesh trembled. She gripped Kasim's shaft in one hand and began to work it up and down. As Marietta spanked her, Leyla jerked forward, making little cries of pain. Despite the discomfort she caressed Kasim's stomach with a featherlight touch, then dipped her hand down to stroke the heavy sac.

She groaned as the spanking continued, tossing her head so that her fall of hair spilled on to the divan, covering Kasim's boots. Marietta spanked Leyla again and again, feeling the firm flesh tremble under her palm. Soon the buttocks grew warm and began to glow. Marietta could not deny that she felt pleasure in spanking Leyla. Her palm stung as it connected with the now-burning flesh. The sound of the slaps echoed around the room.

Marietta's lips parted as her breath quickened. She was aware of Kasim's dark eyes watching her, slitted with pleasure, holding her gaze with hypnotic force.

Leyla's hips rose a little to meet Marietta's hand as she pumped his cock up and down. The swollen end was reddish-purple, shiny, and weeping a clear fluid. Leyla drew her thumb over the moist end and smeared the fluid over the bulb, squeezing the little mouth shut and anointing the tip of the cock.

Kasim groaned and shifted his hips while Marietta felt a throbbing deep inside her belly. She wondered how it would feel to straddle Kasim and press her soaking sex onto the head of his cock. She imagined it slipping into her, filling her until the tip nudged her womb. Kasim smiled, his tongue moistening his lips. It was as if he knew what she was thinking. She did not care. The liquid heat inside her was demanding that it be slaked.

As she watched Kasim's pleasure, she felt keenly what it was to desire a man; to want him to thrust his hard cock into her, again and again, while she bore down on to it, grinding her bud against the slick cock-stem.

She imagined Kasim holding her buttocks, dragging them apart, his fingers digging into her as he worked her up and down. The pressure built inside her.

She was not aware that she was spanking Leyla hard. Each blow followed on the previous one in rapid succession. Her eyes were held by Kasim's tension. The muscles in his belly were hard, defined into pronounced ridges, as his penis swelled and jumped in Leyla's grasp.

Leyla began to weep aloud, arching her back and trying to avoid the slaps. Her buttocks simmered under Marietta's hand. She sobbed loudly now, wincing at each slap.

'Wait,' Kasim ordered, gently chiding. 'Leyla has been punished enough. You are overzealous, Marietta. How soon you learn to enjoy such contact!'

Leyla raised her head. Her lovely face was tear-stained, the full red lips trembled, Marietta looked in horror at Leyla's flaming buttocks. They were dark red, startling against the white body. She bit her lips, feeling ashamed at her arousal, at the undeniable pleasure she had taken in spanking Leyla.

'Stretch towards me, Leyla. Leave those pretty globes to Marietta. Oil them, so that the pain diminishes.'

Marietta anointed the tortured flesh, while Leyla sighed with relief. Then she took up her position again.

'I want your mouth, Leyla,' Kasim said. 'Has she not been obedient, Marietta? Now she is to be rewarded. But not you. Not yet. You may bring Leyla to her peak of pleasure with your lips and tongue. Between her folds you will find her bud, so beautifully large and hungry to be tasted. Do not disappoint it.'

'Thank you, my lord,' Leyla said throatily as she shifted her body forward over the arm of the divan.

Her breasts were flattened against Kasim's knees and her buttocks were tipped up over the padded arm. She spread her thighs apart eagerly as she braced herself on the tips of her toes.

Marietta was stunned by Kasim's orders. Mouth Leyla's sex! She had never done such a thing. But she dared not disobey. Besides, she did feel guilty that she had spanked Leyla so thoroughly.

'Not too close now, Leyla,' Kasim said. 'I want you to stretch that pretty neck and slide your open mouth down over me. Ah, yes. Like that. Just like that.'

Kasim gave a sigh of satisfaction as Leyla's expert lips drew the swollen cock-tip in. She moved down on him, rubbing and sucking the stem. Marietta was presented with the sight of Leyla's naked and aroused sex as it hung down a little between the flushed and widely parted buttocks.

The deep red folds were wet and shiny. She could see that Leyla's clitoris was swollen and erect. It was indeed well developed, protruding from the inner sex-lips like a tiny cock, seeming to invite the touch of lips and tongue.

Marietta bent close and reached out to take a hold on Leyla's buttocks. The sex pulsed as if anticipating her touch. The smell of Leyla's arousal filled her, prompting a new and deep excitement. The musky scent was strong, clinging to the moist lips, filling the valley of her buttocks. Marietta stretched out her tongue and took a first tentative taste.

She licked one side of the open flesh-lips, feeling the warm moisture on her tongue. The sensation of the tender skin, the rain-tasting flesh and the wonderful scent were as heady as strong wine. Her reticence disappeared.

She opened her mouth around Leyla's sex and lapped at the moist folds, drawing the unusually large bud into her mouth and sucking at it gently. The smooth nakedness of the sex-lips felt strange, but exciting. They were hot and liquid, sliding against her mouth in a sort of erotic kiss. Leyla squirmed and moaned deep in her throat as Marietta thrust her tongue deep inside her. She bore down and pressed backwards, so that Marietta felt the parted globes of Leyla's buttocks against her cheeks. The moist scented valley was pressed closely to her mouth and chin.

Marietta moved her mouth up and licked at the little hole between the buttocks. She thrust in a little way with her tongue tip and felt Leyla shudder. Kasim, too, moaned and thrashed. It seemed that the three of them were locked in some primaeval dance. Marietta craved a release. She had been aroused to the brink of orgasm since the dream of last night and her body cried out to reach a peak of pleasure. She thought she would die if she did not climax soon.

While she continued to mouth and lick Leyla's sex, and listen to Kasim's groans, which had become frenzied, she stretched one hand down to her own clit. It pulsed under her fingers. Quickly, she stroked herself to a fever pitch of tension. Oh, she was near. Let it happen. Let it happen now.

Leyla tensed suddenly and gave a series of little yelping cries. Her whole body shuddered as her climax wracked her body. Marietta felt her spasms as Leyla's flesh convulsed around her buried tongue.

She rubbed harder at herself. The wetness had dripped onto her hand. She felt her pleasure drawing to that one burning point, then the first waves began to sweep over her. She pressed frantic kisses to Leyla's sex, her heated bottom-cheeks. Then she sagged against Leyla's inner thigh as her climax encompassed her totally.

She choked back a scream. The pulsing was deep and hard. It went on and on and the final waves took a long time to ebb. For a moment she thought she had fainted. When she could think again, she found that she had slumped to the floor. The carpet was soft under her cheek.

Suddenly she felt a strong hand on her wrist.

'And who told you that you could pleasure yourself?' Kasim hissed. 'I told you it was forbidden. Ah, how disobedient you are still. I hope it was good. Because for that illicit pleasure, you will be chastised further. Here you must earn the right to pleasure yourself. Only I can give that permission. Now, what shall I do with you?'

He looked from Marietta to Leyla. Marietta hung her head but she was unrepentant. It had been worth it. Kasim cupped his chin. He smiled slowly, the smile she was coming to anticipate and dread at the same time.

'I shall bring the date of the banquet forward. In two weeks from now, my friend Selim – the jewel merchant – shall visit. He will bring with him Gabriel, his favourite slave, whom you may remember. If you have not become obedient by that time, I shall ask Selim for his advice. As you saw, Marietta, he knows what to do with troublesome slaves. But for now ...'

He reached into a carved cabinet and drew out a gold casket. Inside was a small object made of gold mesh and chains. He beckoned Marietta to come close and fastened the chain around her waist.

'Part your legs,' he said, drawing the specially shaped piece of gold mesh between her thighs and securing it to the chain at the small of her back. 'That will stop you pleasuring yourself. Leyla, you will ensure that Marietta wears this at all times, especially at night. Remove it only when she is bathed or needs to expel body wastes. Until the banquet she is to be stimulated in every way possible, but her pleasure is to be withheld. I want her hot and eager on the night. Selim – Gabriel too – will take great delight in the entertainment I have planned.'

Marietta was too shocked to protest at this new indignity. She stood where Kasim left her, looking down at her caged sex. The device was beautifully made, as decorative as a piece of jewellery. Wearing the device was worse than being fully naked as everyone would see it and know of her torment. Her eyes filled with tears. How could he be so cruel? Surely he cared nothing for her feelings.

Kasim rang a bell for refreshments to be brought, then sank onto his divan. Ignoring the two women, he began to smoke a water pipe.

Marietta crossed the room and sank on to a divan next to Leyla, as Leyla bade her. The metal felt cold against her skin. She hardly tasted the food and drink they were served. Her mind was reeling. She must wear the device of mesh and chains until the banquet. What then?

And Gabriel. Gabriel was coming here with his master? She had thought of him often since seeing him in the marketplace. He was magnificent, there was no other word for him. There had been that one moment of undisguised absorption between them, when she had impressed upon him her admiration and highest regard — had it been love? And he had responded, his tear-bright, grey eyes holding hers just for the space of a moment.

She was eager to see Gabriel again. But she felt very afraid. Now that she knew a little of Kasim, she knew that he had some dark motive for arranging the banquet.

Leyla reached out and closed her fingers over Marietta's hand. Marietta returned the friendly squeeze. Leyla's long dark eyes were liquid and full of warmth.

'You gave me great pleasure,' Leyla whispered. 'I wish to help you. Will you trust me now?'

Marietta smiled shyly. The last vestiges of resentment toward the Turkish woman faded. Whatever Kasim had planned, at least Marietta had Leyla for comfort. She knew at last that she had found a true friend.

Kasim flashed them a searching look. His black brows drew together. Leyla and Marietta quickly lowered their eyes, but their fingers remained entwined.

Kasim's scowl lifted. He did not look displeased at the open display of affection between the women. 'You may return to the harem,' he said at length. 'Remember, Leyla. Continue to train Marietta in all the ways to please the flesh. I will visit every day to supervise your progress. Now go.'

Marietta followed Leyla. The gold mesh against her sex had grown warm from her body heat. She resented it intensely, but had to admit that its caress was intriguing. Now that she was forbidden to pleasure herself, she found herself longing to do so. Already the little bud within her folds was growing warm and beginning to pulse.

8

In the house of Selim the screened windows let in the late afternoon sunlight. The light in the small side room was smoky and diffuse, yet not dark enough for lamps to be lit.

Gabriel approached the figure on the divan. He held a brass tray. On it was a bowl of jasmine-scented water and a pile of hot damp towels.

Selim yawned and stretched. As he sat up his silk robe fell open and the great bowl of his belly was revealed. He was sweating; runnels trickled down his forehead and had collected in drops on his top lip. He passed a meaty hand over his face. The still-handsome face, slack at the jawline and with a look of dissipation, was blurred with sleep.

Gabriel smiled and greeted his master. Once Selim had been strong and vital, the imprint of his intelligence giving his face a singular distinction. The young Gabriel, purchased in the slave market, had been drawn to his new master by the power of his mind. But that bright intellect seemed to have dulled lately. Selim was overly fond of bodily comforts and, as he grew richer, he had allowed his senses to rule his life completely. The only exercise he took now was on his back, with the most handsome slaves for company; male and female – Selim liked to vary his pleasures. The only task he set himself was to think up new ways to punish and humiliate the slaves for real or imagined slights.

Since that day in the marketplace Selim had ordered

Gabriel to come to the chamber, where he took an afternoon rest at the same time every day. Gabriel knew what was expected of him. With the memory of the public whipping fresh in his mind, the humiliation of having his agonised sexual release witnessed by the common crowd, he took pains to appear good-natured and willing, whatever Selim's taste should be. But though he was willing, eagerness was beyond him at any price. Selim's bloated body held no attraction for him.

'Ah, Gabriel.' Selim swung his thick legs over the side of the divan and planted his feet on the tiled floor. 'You gladden my eyes indeed.'

Gabriel inclined his head in a respectful gesture. He had come fresh from the small bath house. His thick fair hair was secured at his nape. His powerful body was oiled and perfumed with sandalwood. As Selim requested, he was naked. He put the tray on a side table and stood ready, waiting for Selim to order his actions.

Selim stretched his hand out indolently and reached into a covered dish. While Gabriel waited for his command, Selim chewed on a pastry flavoured with honey and rosewater. Finishing the sweet, Selim licked his fingers then pushed himself to his feet and stood with his arms out to the sides. He nodded to Gabriel.

Gabriel eased the silk robe off Selim's fleshy shoulders and folded it neatly. He half-turned, reaching for a damp towel and the bowl of scented water, and felt Selim's hand at his neck.

'That can wait until ... after,' Selim said, sinking down to sit on the edge of the divan. His head was on a level with Gabriel's navel.

'As you wish, master,' Gabriel said, as Selim's hand moved down to his chest and toyed with his nipples.

Selim pulled Gabriel close and wound both arms around his waist. His thick lips pressed moist kisses down Gabriel's stomach, nuzzling the oiled and perfumed curls at his groin. Grinning up at him Selim whispered, his voice thick with desire.

'You be good now, Gabriel. No more thoughts of escape, eh? Lest you favour a few more strokes of the lash. All you have to do is please me. Not so difficult. And if you perform well, I shall reward you. Kasim is giving a banquet. Would you like to come with me?'

Gabriel felt a frisson of interest. 'If you wish it, master,' he said, careful to keep his voice neutral.

'I do wish it. I want Kasim to see you,' Selim said, closing his fingers around Gabriel's cock-shaft and squeezing hard. 'He is envious of me. I have seen how he looks at you. He covets you. Well, let him. You are mine alone. I shall enjoy watching him squirm.'

Gabriel winced at the pinching, rolling pressure of Selim's hands, but he hardly heard him. His mind was full of a perfect oval face and the most incredible blue eyes. She would be there, at Kasim's house.

Selim's fingers moved down to Gabriel's buttocks. He probed between the small firm cheeks, squeezing and kneading the flesh, stroking the root behind the heavy testicles. He grunted with satisfaction as Gabriel's cock swelled and jerked into life. Selim licked his lips, then bent forward. His questing mouth nibbled at the end of the crested cock. His tongue snaked out and the pointed tip poked under the loose foreskin, describing a circle around the plum and the tiny central slit. Then Selim pursed his lips and used them to push the cock-skin right back, exposing the whole of the moist swollen tip.

For a while he collared the plum with his lips, flicking at the underside where the skin formed a ruff around the stem. Despite himself, Gabriel sighed with pleasure as Selim drew the shaft into his mouth, sucking and licking down the full length of it. His buttocks clenched as he leaned into Selim. The sensations gathered in his belly.

Selim gripped the base of his shaft in one hand and worked it up and down while he collared the tip with his mouth. The other hand searched between Gabriel's legs, found his anus and stroked across the tight little mouth.

Gabriel closed his eyes, shutting out the sight of Selim's bulging cheeks, his bent head, the bare patch on his scalp. He held the sides of Selim's head, his fingers were curled around the ears. He tugged at the fleshy lobes, as his master liked. Gabriel imagined that he was thrusting himself into the woman – into Kasim's blue-eyed slave. How smooth and tight her sex would be. Would her fleece be light or dark, or would her body hair have been removed?

His penis seemed to swell at the thought. The heavy balls tightened, becoming as firm as a plum. Selim moaned, deep in his throat, and drew Gabriel's shaft in more deeply, relaxing his throat so that the blonde pubic curls brushed against his lips. The sweet, pulling sensations were almost unbearable. Gabriel moaned, thrusting at Selim's warm mouth.

Selim's fingers dug into Gabriel's buttocks, dragging them apart, searching for the tight opening between them. As Selim's fingers worked their way inside his body Gabriel spasmed helplessly. He grasped Selim's head tightly as he pumped his buttocks, rimming Selim's throat. Selim sucked hard, making small sounds of delight as he swallowed the salty emission.

Gabriel sagged, his thigh muscles trembling. Selim

released Gabriel's cock, after licking the drippings from the tip. He smacked his lips and nuzzled the pubic curls.

'You were good, Gabriel. Very good. Delicious in fact.' He laughed as he threw himself back on the bed. Under the loose skin of his belly his stubby penis was erect. 'My turn now,' he crooned. 'You were hot for me this day. Perhaps that whipping did you good. You appreciate me more now, eh? Come. Show me how good you are with your hands.'

Gabriel poured oil into his palms and bent over Selim. He closed his fingers around the short thick cock and began working oil into the stem. Selim pulled him close and pressed his mouth to Gabriel's. The thick lips prised Gabriel's mouth open, and his tongue slipped inside. He gave a sigh of rapture, murmuring against Gabriel's mouth:

'Ah, you will enjoy the banquet, my treasure. Let Kasim imagine how good you are. But only I know it. Oh, yes. Just like that. Now bend over. Spread yourself for me. Ahhh. You are so tight inside. Just a little resistance at first ... Like hot silk. My Gabriel ...'

Marietta bowed her head and slipped on the short transparent waistcoat. The sides barely covered her nipples and were linked with a gold chain. The garment was designed to draw attention to her breasts rather than conceal them. From the waist down, she was to remain naked. The small gold device that cinched her sex was clearly visible.

Everyone else in the harem was dressed in loose trousers and tunics or gowns. She felt horribly self-conscious and set apart from them all, which, of course, was Kasim's intention. Leyla gave her no immediate orders so she decided to make her way to her sleeping cubicle. There she could close the curtains around her bed and hide herself away for a while.

In the corridor she passed a slave girl holding a pile of linen. Lowering her eyes she made to walk past, but the slave girl dropped her burden and rounded on Marietta.

'You. French woman. Stand still,' she said in peremptory tone.

Too surprised to refuse, Marietta paused. Whereupon the slave moved close to her, grinning in a way that lacked any respect.

'Stand for me!' she said again and, reaching out, stroked Marietta's bare buttocks.

Another slave, passing by carrying a jug of sherbet, reached out and took hold of Marietta's gold waist chain. She snapped the chain between her fingers, pulling it up high so that the mesh was pulled even tighter between Marietta's legs. Marietta gave a sound of protest. Both slaves laughed. The first stuck her tongue out, picked up her pile of linen, and walked away with insolent slowness. Marietta pulled free and ran away, her heart beating fast.

Just before she reached the bedchamber two more slaves stopped her. Again she was ordered to stand still. One of the slaves pushed her against a wall and held her wrists above her head. The other opened her waistcoat and began roughly to fondle her breasts. When Marietta cried out in alarm a hand was clamped tightly to her mouth. A voice close to her ear mouthed an obscenity, laughing huskily.

Her nipples were pinched until they were sore and then her breasts were slapped until she sobbed with the warm ache in them.

'Stop. Please. Stop ... Why are you doing this?' she

moaned against the fingers that forced her mouth open and tugged at her underlip.

Ignoring her, one of them stroked the mesh that covered her sex. Marietta was ashamed at the rush of sensation that rose in her. The grip on her wrists, her hands pressed flat to the cold wall, reminded her of how Kasim had secured her to the marble pillar. The hand at her sex pressed harder, slapping with a gentle but eager pleasure. A slim finger traced the outline of the cage, lifting the edge so that it could tease out the golden curls within.

Marietta writhed. Her breasts burned and her sex throbbed maddeningly. She could not help thrusting her hips towards the teasing fingers. They were withdrawn abruptly.

'Naughty naughty,' the slave smirked, and slapped her buttocks hard. Marietta almost wept with humiliation. She hated the way she responded to their rough treatment. She bit her lip and began to struggle against the grip on her wrists. But the slaves only laughed harder as she tried to jerk free.

'Not so high and mighty now are you, French woman?' they teased, making free with her in whatever way they wished.

Marietta closed her eyes, enduring the pinches and slaps, holding back the tears of pain. Until, tiring of tormenting her at last, the two slaves sauntered away. When they had gone Marietta sagged against the wall, shaking and afraid.

'This is how it will be until you are willing to do as you are told,' Leyla told her later. 'While you wear the caging device anyone may handle you as they wish. Your status now is that of a slave. You must obey all commands. To refuse will earn you a spanking or worse.'

Marietta hung her head, blushing furiously. How would she bear it? There was a wicked delight to be had in being the object of so much attention, as she had found already. But the cage ensured that she was denied any pleasure. It was cruel. Oh, Kasim, she thought, you know how beguiling all this is. You are testing me still, willing me to become your creature. But you will not break me.

'It is hard for me to resist you,' Leyla whispered. 'Your flushed face moves me greatly. I am tempted to free your pretty sex ... I dare not. Yet I must touch you ...'

Leyla clasped Marietta in her arms and kissed her. Marietta responded ardently as Leyla ran her hands gently over her sore breasts and buttocks. With a shuddering breath Leyla put Marietta from her.

'You will make me forget my duty. Come, I must teach you the many ways to please a man. Kasim will test you and punish you further if you do not find favour with him.'

Over the next days Leyla showed Marietta the ways to draw out pleasure from a man's body with dance, hands, lips, and tongue. Despite her initial resistance she enjoyed her lessons. For everything she learned seemed designed to tantalise and delight her own senses also.

It was also impossible to remain unmoved by all the luxury around her. The colours of tiles, stained-glass and rich furnishings delighted her eyes. The harem was filled with the smells of incense, exotic musky perfumes and fruit blossom. She was served soft eggs with cream and sliced fresh figs for breakfast. Later there were fragrant lamb stews, fish stuffed with almonds, soups flavoured with cumin, artichokes in oil. All this was followed by squares of sweet rice jelly sprinkled with rosewater, water lily sherbet with violets and honey and the many sticky sweetmeats with voluptuous names. There was the thick sweet coffee and Russian tea to drink.

After the plain fare of the convent, Marietta ate and drank with relish. Soft music soothed her to sleep. The cries of peacocks floated into the open windows on hot damp nights. There seemed no escape from luxury, no way to avoid the pleasures of all the senses.

Marietta was kept busy with her lessons and with avoiding the slaves who took every opportunity to fondle her. She did not see Claudine for some days. At first, she was not unduly worried. The harem was a warren of corridors, ornate rooms, and secret gardens. It was not difficult to lose oneself. She assumed that Claudine was being trained also. But when Claudine's bed space remained empty one morning, Marietta began to get worried.

Then she heard the women whispering and glancing sidelong at her. One of the slaves, a thin severe-looking girl, who singled her out regularly for special intimate attentions, told her that Claudine was keeping Kasim's bed warm. The slave relished passing on the information, while she smacked Marietta's breasts and buttocks, only smiling when Marietta paled and called her a liar.

'But surely you are not jealous? Perhaps you think your friend finds more favour with Kasim than you?'

Marietta dismissed the slave's words. Of course she was not jealous. She was just worried about Claudine. What would happen when Kasim tired of her? Would he then turn his attentions back to herself?

Kasim came often to the harem unannounced. Late one evening he appeared, looking striking in a loose white linen shirt and full trousers tucked into high boots. Leyla and Marietta were alone. The lessons for the day had just been completed. Leyla greeted him deferentially. Kasim beckoned Marietta to stand close. He checked first that the cage was secure. After toying with her waist chain, his long fingers trailing down the curve of her hip, he ignored her and spoke to Leyla.

'She has not been pleasured by anyone or herself? You are certain of this? Was she watched during sleep?'

'Yes, my lord. Though she burns she has not been sated.'

'Good. Very good. The banquet is tomorrow night. I want her hot and ready. She has completed her training as I ordered?'

'Yes, my lord,' Leyla answered. 'As you have seen these past weeks, she has been diligent.'

'Diligent? Hmmm. But is she obedient enough I wonder. I would test her. On your knees, Marietta,' he ordered suddenly. 'Show me how you would pleasure a man with your mouth.'

Kasim made himself comfortable on a divan and sipped at a glass of cherry sherbet.

Marietta arranged herself into the required position: shoulders back, hands linked behind her, and her knees spread widely apart. Leyla stood to one side, holding a carved ivory phallus. Kasim watched closely as Marietta opened her mouth and took the head of the phallus between her lips. Trying not to think of his dark eyes on her, Marietta worked her mouth up and down the object. She closed her eyes briefly, concentrating on performing as she had been taught. I must make my lips loose, peel them back over the rim of the plum, then suck gently as I slide my mouth down the shaft.

'Sit up straight,' Kasim ordered. 'Thrust out those breasts.'

The gold chain tightened around her waist and bit

into her flesh-valley as Marietta obeyed. Her buttocks too were thrust out by her position. She felt intensely vulnerable, knowing that Kasim was gazing on all the secret parts of her body. The fine open-work mesh fitted closely to her mound, outlining rather than concealing the shape of her sex.

Kasim admired the look of it. 'Your pretty curls protrude through the mesh and I can see the shadow of your parted flesh-lips. It really is tantalising. Perhaps I shall imprison your breasts in this way too. Ah, how lovely they would look with their fullness contained and yet revealed, with your nipples pushing against the gold mesh. The metal would chafe and excite them...'

Marietta lowered her chin, concentrating on sucking the phallus. She closed her eyes against the sudden intensity of his face. An image of Kasim pleasuring Claudine flashed into her head. Claudine knew how his full mouth tasted, his skin, his cock ... Claudine had seen those hard dark eyes brighten with desire for her. Marietta felt consumed by a mixture of emotions.

Kasim watched her silently as she drew the thick pale shaft in and out of her mouth. His face was unreadable. She gave a little shiver. Perhaps he would wish her to practise on him? Her cheeks warmed with anticipation. How would he taste? She longed for the scent of his skin in her nostrils; for the feel of him under her hands, her lips.

She was damp already between her thighs. For days she had been aroused, shadowed by the presence of the horrid little cage clasped so firmly around her. The pressure of it was both a deterrent and a potent reminder of her leashed sexuality.

The ivory phallus had warmed in her mouth. It felt smooth and so hard. She circled it with her tongue and flashed Kasim a look from the tail of her eye. The gold chain, pulled tight between her buttocks, began rubbing at her as she moved slightly. Never had her body seemed so beyond her control. Never had she hungered so for anyone's touch . . .

Kasim laughed suddenly. 'She is ready. Almost. You have done well, Leyla. Make her beautiful. I will return for the final preparation.'

Marietta spent hours in the hammam being steamed, scrubbed with pumice and massaged. Every part of her, except her sex, was stroked and kneaded. Exotic perfumes were rubbed into her skin with long and languorous strokes.

The intimate attentions were a form of torture to her. The weeks of training, the teasing and spankings had stirred her to a fever pitch of arousal. Leyla watched her carefully, gauging her reactions. Marietta felt an echo of her own leashed torment in the Turkish woman's demeanour. Only Kasim's express orders had stopped them exploring each other's bodies in the dark scented night.

Marietta held her breath when the mesh cage was removed so that her sex might be cleansed.

'Draw up your legs and hold your knees apart,' Leyla said.

Marietta did so, feeling Leyla's dark eyes on her. Warm scented water was poured over her open flesh-lips. Marietta almost moaned aloud, filled with unbearable tension. Her hips began to work as she strained towards the warm, caressing, flow. Leyla ordered the slave to stop pouring.

'Direct the water away from the bud of pleasure,' Leyla said.

The stream was redirected when Marietta had

gained control. She almost wept with frustration. Leyla only smiled and kissed her lightly on the mouth. 'I understand. I feel it too. But the waiting is almost over. Now we must decorate your body.'

Marietta felt a sweet heavy ache as her pubic curls were brushed, teased, and oiled until they stood out in a glistening curly halo.

'I regret having to do this,' Leyla said softly as she replaced the gold mesh between Marietta's thighs and secured it to the waist chain. She fluffed out the golden curls so that they protruded around the sides and top of the mesh.

'Only Kasim can order the cage's removal. Take care that you please him when he next orders it, and he will free you.'

Marietta felt a fierce joy at the thought. When would he order her to pleasure him? What would he make her do? Her thoughts seemed crowded with him. After so much time, when she had seen him only as a fleeting visitor, she longed to be alone with him. For him to take her to his apartments. Perhaps to secure her wrists to that slim marble pillar . . .

She sat still while her nipples were rouged; her hands and feet decorated with henna. Then her hair was brushed out so that it hung free in a cascade of silver curls. The tresses were perfumed with musk-rose oil, then threaded with gold chains and looped with ropes of pearls.

When Marietta was ready, Kasim came into the harem. At a sign from him Marietta assumed the posture of submission. Without a word he reached for the chain at her waist and removed the cage.

Then he ordered her to lie on her back on a nearby divan. There was a small knot of excitement in her stomach. She did as he asked, lying back and parting her legs. He made a small sound of appreciation. Still without speaking he took a small jar and dipped his fingers into it. Then he reached between her legs and began to anoint her with a spicy scented oil. Already aroused, she trembled like a leaf in the wind.

Kasim's dark eyes gleamed and a satisfied smile played over his hard mouth. The touch of his fingers maddened her. The pressure was firm, almost impersonal, but so welcome that she felt her sex-lips become liquid. Her sex felt heavily engorged. She knew that her labia were full and pouting, resembling a firm plum. She closed her eyes, feeling her pleasure mounting. A moment more and she would climax. The tips of Kasim's fingers probed inside her, then brushed lightly over her clitoris, anointing it with the spicy oil.

It was too much. She broke all at once. The waves rolled over her in great wrenching spasms, consuming her, blinding her to everything but the moment.

'Oh, oh,' she gasped as her womb convulsed. Her thighs closed on Kasim's hand as she rubbed shamelessly on his fingers. His hand closed over her, pinching the lips together hard as if he could stop the pleasure which was only now beginning to ebb. She pressed towards him with a little sob, hearing him curse under his breath, but not caring that she had lost control. It was some moments before she recovered. The afterglow was sweet but brief. Her thighs fell open as lassitude spread over her limbs.

Kasim frowned and withdrew his hand. His mouth was a hard line. Then he smiled and, leaning over, brushed her lips with his. 'You should be spanked for that loss of control, but I feel generous this night. Besides, I should not have handled you so gently. I will allow you that one moment of delight. Wait ... Give me your mouth.'

Marietta lifted her chin and pursed her lips. Kasim swept his finger over her mouth. She tasted sweet spices and her own musk, before her lips grew warm and swollen.

'Now, get up,' Kasim said.

Only then did she become aware that the whole of her sex and flesh-valley felt warm and tingling, the same as her mouth. Her erect bud throbbed with almost painful intensity. It did not seem possible, but Kasim's touch had brought her to an even more extreme state of heightened arousal. Her release of a moment before had done nothing to assuage her desire.

'There,' Kasim replaced the lid on the jar. 'That mixture of spices I rubbed into your sex and mouth will ensure that you remain so hungry for pleasure that you care not who gives it. But your task this night is to *give* pleasure only. All you have to do is obey me. You will hunger, but you will not be eased. See that you hold yourself back. For I warn you, I shall not forgive another lapse. Your pleasure must wait until I order you to take it. Do you understand?'

She managed to nod, her thoughts in a turmoil.

'Good. The guests are about to arrive. Follow me.'

Kasim's private apartments had been transformed for the banquet.

Candles in stained glass containers cast pools of green, blue and red light on to the rich carpet, while the corners of the large room were in complete darkness. The divans around the central cleared area were filled with guests. Others stood around the room chatting, helping themselves to food from small tables. All the guests were richly dressed in silks and brocades. Jewels flashed from turbans and sashes. Slaves moved to and fro serving glasses of sherbet from gold and silver trays.

Marietta was displayed prominently, chained to the marble pillar as before, this time in the submissive posture. Guests walked around her, lifting up her long hair, feeling the weight of her breasts, murmuring idle compliments. Now and then she felt the stroke of a thin cane between her legs. Her nipples were stroked until they became erect. The many touches, the small attentions, were light, careless, almost throwaway, as if she were of little account. She suffered them in silence, betraying her reactions by shuddering very slightly. The sense of being worthless was deeply humiliating but exciting too. How did Kasim always know how to reach inside the deepest recesses of her mind and draw her out, expose her darkest desires, and make her ever more naked to him?

She began to long for the casual attentions of the guests, but wished that she could dip her chin so that she need not see their faces. They all looked so smug, so soft with good living. Perhaps she could hide her face with the heavy fall of her hair, but a stiff gold collar set with pearls and moonstones prevented it. The number of people, the noise, terrified her. She had somehow imagined that Kasim would take her to his apartments and use her for his pleasure alone. But she and Claudine were to remain on show, displayed like the prized ornaments they were.

Claudine was chained in similar fashion to the marble pillar opposite. Her friend looked magnificent. She did not look afraid and seemed to be enjoying all the attention. Like Marietta she was naked and arranged in the posture of submission. Above a high collar of gold, set with cornelians and rubies, her chin was thrust out haughtily. The wide golden-brown eyes flicked over the guests with interest. The thick red-gold hair, threaded with strings of rubies, tumbled over her naked shoulders.

Claudine smiled at Marietta. Her eyes looked dreamy and unfocused. She stretched luxuriously and arched her back. Marietta saw the newly naked sex, the outer lips agape, and the inner flesh hanging down slightly. She saw how red and wet the sex was and realised that Claudine too had been anointed with spicy oil. As Claudine thrust her full breasts forward, Marietta noticed for the first time that Claudine's pale-brown nipples were encircled by gold rings. Somehow the erect nipples had been teased through the tiny rings so that they remained hard. The tender nipple-skin was shiny, elongated into a tiny jutting teat, collared by the unresisting metal.

Though she resisted the thought, Marietta found herself imagining wearing such rings. Could she bear that pressure, the exquisite feeling of constriction? Claudine seemed proud to wear them. Had Kasim forced them on her? His cruelty was unrelenting. Marietta shivered as she remembered his hard fingers working the spicy oil into her secret flesh.

Just then a rather handsome merchant with gold teeth smiled at Marietta, distracting her from studying her friend. Moving aside his full-skirted robe, he stroked the bulge at his groin, at the same time cupping her chin and squeezing her cheeks so that her mouth opened. Marietta blushed violently. The merchant crowed with delight and freed his erect penis, pressing forward so that the tip pressed against her lips.

His cock was long and rather thin. The tip was naked with a pronounced collar of flesh around the plum. As her mouth closed over the warm swollen tip and she began sucking, she lowered her eyelids, glad to shut out the sight of his shiny red face and lustful eyes. But it seemed that even that luxury was not allowed her. Kasim appeared at her side.

'Your pardon, my friend,' he said to the merchant, who drew away regretfully, his own hand continuing to pump his cock.

'Ah, you must chastise this disobedient slave?' The merchant grinned. 'No matter. I will use the other's mouth.'

Claudine accommodated the merchant's hardness with relish. While he plundered Claudine's throat, the merchant turned his head so that he might watch Kasim's actions.

'This night you are to look the guests in the eye as you pleasure them,' Kasim said to Marietta.

Marietta was confused. Normally, in the posture of submission, she was made to keep her eyes lowered. She tried to stammer a reply, but her hesitancy was taken for resistance.

'Do you not answer your master? Then take this for your disobedience,' Kasim rapped, beginning to slap the underswell of her breasts.

He slapped each breast in turn, snapping their weight upwards until they glowed with warmth. Marietta twisted and sobbed as his hand connected again and again. Each time he allowed the breast to drop before he slapped it again, so that the bruising ache added to her torment. She had never been slapped in that way before. It seemed that she was consumed by a mixture of pleasure-pain. Her whole body shook. She squeezed her thighs together and felt her sex pulse as her oiled labia closed together. Her nipples contracted to hard little nubs like pink stones. She began to moan between the sobs, the sound supplicating even to her own ears. Something within her reached out to Kasim.

In his beautiful hard face, the set of his mouth, she sensed that he was highly aroused and she felt glad that she could stir him to such a pitch.

The merchant nearby groaned with pleasure as Marietta's flushed face became streaked with tears. He plunged himself into Claudine's mouth until he climaxed with a hoarse groan. A small group had gathered to watch Kasim chastise Marietta. She heard the sighs of pleasure, the comments on her beauty. The watchers drew away a little as Kasim stood back and lowered his hand.

Marietta sagged. She bent over at the waist as if she could shield her tormented breasts from the sea of eyes. She sobbed without restraint as the warm pain flooded her breasts. Her belly jerked with the force of her distress ... but inside her there was a hard peak of excitement. She was frightened by the delicious drowning feeling of submission. It had come stronger this time. Stronger even than when Kasim had lashed her in front of Leyla.

Kasim ran his hands over the vibrantly blushing breasts, squeezing hard and holding them up. He admired their colour. The pink nipples, cresting the dark-rose flesh, were startling in contrast. There were murmurs of approval and admiration from the watching guests. Kasim tugged on the chain attached to Marietta's beautiful gold collar so that she straightened up further and was forced to lift her chin even higher.

'Keep your head high, Marietta,' he hissed. 'Thrust out those breasts so that everyone can admire them, and keep those legs well spread. I want all my guests to enjoy your beauty.'

Marietta bit her trembling lips. A final sob was forced from her as she opened her knees wide, pushing backwards until the joints at her groin ached.

'Good. Good,' Kasim said gently. 'Now you are obedient.'

He tweaked her pubic curls, rubbing the oiled strands between his fingers, fluffing them up and stroking them back from the exposed and parted sex. Marietta felt herself bear down. Her sex seemed to push out. She managed to stop herself swaying towards his hand only with a great effort. Her sex burned and throbbed, yearning for any contact. It seemed that all her thoughts of rebellion, her wish for freedom, had sunk somewhere below her immediate consciousness. There was only the heat in her breasts, the hungry ache in her belly, the craving for sexual release.

Kasim patted her head then left her and walked over to Claudine. Claudine smiled, anticipating his approval. She licked her lips as if still tasting the merchant's thin milt. She brought her hands forward and placed them on her thighs. The fingers, spread and pointing inwards, drew attention to her hot little sex. As Kasim stopped in front of her, Claudine drew in her belly and looked up at him through lowered lashes. She thrust her hips forward so that the little purse of her naked sex was lifted invitingly.

Kasim's mouth thinned. 'You are too eager! Hands behind your back,' he said, and pinched her nipples until she gasped with pain.

Hurriedly she clasped her hands behind her back. Kasim slapped her large breasts hard. Once, twice, three times on the outswell of each breast. Claudine's mouth opened with shock. It was plain that she had not been chastised in this way before. Marietta felt sorry for Claudine but her whole body pulsed with pleasure as she watched Kasim slap the rich outer curves. The upperswell and deep cleavage of Claudine's breasts remained their normal shade of light gold, speckled with freckles, while the outer slopes – pulled taut by the held-back shoulders – were flushed deep rose. The effect was most enticing. Claudine's lovely mouth trembled violently and her eyes watered.

'You should know better by now. What are you? Tell me.' Kasim's voice was deceptively gentle as he waited for the reply that did not come fast enough. He reached between Claudine's thighs and tapped the parted flesh-lips with two fingers, spanking the tender exposed flesh smartly.

'Your ... your obedient servant,' Claudine whispered, finding her voice. She winced and writhed as he grasped the whole of her sex and pinched the naked lips together. Tremors passed across her belly.

'See that you remember that at all times,' Kasim rapped, removing his hand. He strode across the room and began speaking to one of his guests.

Claudine stared after Kasim, her face flushed and tear stained. She still looked shocked. Glancing at Marietta, she whispered in a shaky voice:

'I thought I was special ... that after the past few days... But he treats me like a common slave...'

Marietta understood. It seemed that sharing Kasim's bed did not raise one's status. She was inexplicably glad of the fact, but she trembled with fear. Kasim appeared so cold, so detached. What else would he expect of them? Was it not enough that they must display their naked bodies to all those lewd gazes; make their mouths available to whoever wished to use them and be forced to look into the eyes of each lustful guest? Even now she felt the merchants' eyes on her rounded arms and shoulders, on her breasts, and especially between her thighs.

She had heard the many comments and the laughter. Some of the merchants were fascinated by her difference, others were appalled.

'Have you seen the pale slave? The new girl?'

'Beautiful, is she not? Such pretty breasts.'

'Yes. But she has hair on her sex! Disgraceful!'

'I agree. But it's rather compelling. So pale and fine. One feels driven to feel it. To taste it. What must it feel like to plunge into a sex with hair on?'

'Ah, yes. Or to bury one's fingers inside that pretty fleshpot while plundering her tight little anus.'

'You only have to ask Kasim. He'll let you sample the goods. Is he not famous for his generosity?'

Marietta blanched at the last comment. Surely Kasim would not give her over to be used in that way. The thought of being penetrated, of her shrinking flesh sleeving those hard male organs while others watched, horrified and tantalised her. She knew that she would not be able to help showing her pleasure if anyone used her so intimately. How terrible to have to hold herself back as Kasim had ordered. But how much more awful to be viewed with her back arched, her buttocks working shamelessly, and her avid bud grinding against whatever surface presented itself. She shivered with the horror of it.

For though much time had passed since Kasim anointed her with spicy oil, she was still at a peak of intense arousal. The breast spanking had only added to the feeling. How wet and swollen she was. The normally pink flesh must be shockingly red and plump. It seemed dreadful that her open flesh-lips, the mouth of her central orifice, and the tormented swollen bud, were spread so wide to the hungry gaze of Kasim's guests.

Once she had hated the gold cage that masked her

intimacy, now she wished for it back. She did not think she could bear this new humiliation. If only she could crawl into a dark corner and hide. Her rosy breasts throbbed and tingled, but she must still bear the strokes and pinches of the guests. Now and then she must suck an erect cock, or suffer a mouth to cover hers and a thrusting tongue to circle the inside of her lips, questing for the last faint taste of some other's salty emission. And all of this was viewed by so many. Her expertise, her willingness, her physical perfection, everything was commented on. Oh, there could be nothing in the world worse than this.

Then she heard Kasim speak, and knew that she was mistaken.

'Ah, Selim, my friend, and your entourage. You are late. No matter. You were ever one to make an entrance. Welcome. Welcome. Come sit by me. And I see that Gabriel is with you. Excellent.'

9

Marietta watched, wide-eyed, as Gabriel followed the jewel merchant across the room.

The tall blond slave was even more handsome than she remembered. His mane of light hair was loose, framing the hard planes of his face and his sleeveless leather jerkin was tight over his bulging biceps. It was laced down the front, revealing his upper chest with its frosting of blond hair. A broad studded belt cinched Gabriel's narrow waist. His full white cotton trousers were tucked into leather boots and he wore broad leather wristbands.

Marietta could not believe he was really here. It seemed so long ago since that day in the marketplace, but every detail of the scene she had witnessed was imprinted still on her brain and senses. Just looking at Gabriel made her long to touch him; to stroke her hands down those strong arms; to kiss his mouth – surely it was too beautiful to have been placed on a man's face. Wicked thoughts rioted through her. She imagined the taste of his skin. It would be salty-sweet, perhaps per-fumed with some woody scented oil. Oh, to cup those tight buttocks; to lift herself on to his erect penis . . .

She tried not to stare; to veil her thoughts. In the marketplace, Gabriel had looked like a bruised angel. Now he looked like a field worker – strong and vibrant, attractive in a different, more earthy way.

Suddenly she was newly aware of her position. What was she thinking of? She was Kasim's slave, displayed like the object of pleasure she had become. By an ironic quirk of fate, her role and Gabriel's previous role had become reversed. She shrank within herself.

It was unthinkable that Gabriel would now look on her humiliation. Would he pity or desire her? She remembered the sight of his anguish, the appalling sexual tension, and that final jet of seed when he could hold back his pleasure no longer. The sight had stirred her to a shattering climax. Now she was displayed in a similar state of helpless arousal.

But she was not set apart, as he had been – she was accessible to all who wished to use her. Would Gabriel too be allowed to play with her as the others guests were – or were slaves denied such privileges? She did not think she could bear it if Gabriel handled her as the merchants had. What if he should wish her to pleasure him with her mouth? She knew that she would accept his casual lust – her desire for him was so strong that she would deny him nothing – but she wished for so much more. Ah, to have his mouth cover hers. To have his fingers search out her tender places, draw the moisture from her willing flesh. She doubted that Kasim would ever allow it.

Marietta stared ahead as Selim, his women and Gabriel approached Kasim. Perhaps Gabriel would not know her; they had exchanged only the briefest of glances in the marketplace. Her face had been framed by the black hood of the robes of concealment. Would he recognise her as the owner of the stark oval face in which a pair of blue eyes had kindled with desire?

Gabriel glanced across at her and she saw his face quicken with interest. Perhaps he saw only two singularly lovely pale-skinned slaves, chained and arranged in postures of submission. All at once she had to know if he knew her. On an impulse she raised her eyes to meet his. Deliberately, she smiled. Recognition blazed in his face immediately. A fierce joy raced through her. She and Gabriel held eye contact for what seemed a long time. For just that space, she forgot her humiliating position, the fact that she was little more than an ornament to Kasim. She was once again a free French woman: a woman who could choose the man she was drawn to. She put all the warmth – the naked desire – she felt for Gabriel into that one scorching contact.

Gabriel responded. Deep within his grey eyes a spark burned, just for her. He felt the same. She was certain of it. Her heart seemed to lift as Gabriel's mouth curved in acknowledgement before he looked away and took his seat.

Only then did Marietta look at Kasim. The unfathomable dark eyes glistened as they looked slowly from her to Gabriel and back again. Her blood seemed to grow cold. At once she regretted her actions. She realised now that Kasim had been watching her closely. His face was unreadable, his eyes hard as stones. The well-shaped mouth was little more than a line. Giving no sign of anything amiss, Kasim acted the cordial host, pressing food and drink on Selim.

Marietta watched the banquet progress with trepidation in her heart. She sensed that Kasim was displeased and she knew what he was capable of. Though time passed and nothing amiss happened, still she remained tense. Selim's slaves provided entertainment while everyone ate. The jewel merchant had brought many pretty women with him. Some of them were skilled jugglers, others were gymnasts.

Kasim seemed to be enjoying the entertainment, but Marietta – who was beginning to know him very well – perceived a contained excitement in those lean limbs of his. So casually did Kasim cup his chin and stroke one long finger down the pale flesh of his cheek. The knuckles of his other hand, curved around the stem of a glass of ruby-coloured sherbet, were white. From time to time Gabriel glanced at Marietta, but she took pains now not to appear too interested. She felt afraid for herself, for Gabriel too, and did not wish to anger Kasim further.

The most beautiful of Kasim's harem women now appeared and handed out sweetmeats, pipes and tobacco. Kasim clapped his hands and musicians appeared. A figure swathed in veils stepped on to the floor.

It was Leyla. Her dancing costume was of aubergine silk, sewn with brass sequins. Under a transparent waistcoat her large breasts were bare, the nipples rouged, berry bright. She began whirling and stamping, marking time with snaps of her slender fingers. Her long ringlets and jewelled skirts flew out into an arc with the momentum of the dance. She batted kohl-rimmed eyes at the guests, flirting with them, making suggestive movements with her hips. Stopping in front of Selim, she kneeled back, moving rhythmically until her head touched the floor. As she rose her mouth shaped itself into a kiss. Then she wagged her pointed tongue in an unmistakable gesture. '

The guests watching clapped and called out in admiration. As Leyla dipped and swayed amongst them they pulled at her silken skirts, peeling off and discarding the layers. Selim, his florid face shiny with sweat, joined in enthusiastically. Soon Leyla wore only the waistcoat and a wisp of silk worn like a halter, slung low between her legs and tucked into a thin gold chain which encircled her waist.

She leaned forward so that her heavy breasts hung down. Her cleavage was deep and shadowed; the full globes brushed her thighs as she dipped right over and rotated her shoulders. The shiny black coils of her hair spilled around her on to the carpet. Selim gave a low growl and grabbed for her.

'This prize is mine!'

Leyla smiled and dropped to her knees in front of the jewel merchant. She assumed the submissive posture but raised herself up so that her pelvis was thrust towards Selim. The thin silk clung to her pouting sex, outlining its shape and fitting closely to the indentation made by the slitted lips. Selim was breathing fast. Leyla wriggled her hips invitingly. The heavy breasts jiggled.

'Impatient for me, eh? You beauty,' he said thickly.

'Not so fast. Selim knows how to pleasure a woman.'

His meaty hand stroked her soft flat belly, toying with the gold chain at her waist. Then his big fingers strayed down to the halter of silk that cupped Leyla's sex. Two fingers reached between her legs and gathered up the silk halter into a thin ribbon shape. Selim pulled on the halter to loosen it a fraction from the waist chain, so that Leyla's sex was freed. He made a slight adjustment, bringing the ribbon down the centre and tightening it again. Grasping her flesh-lips where they joined her groin he exerted pressure so that they opened and then settled back. Now the naked lips were parted around the narrow strip of fabric, pouting out one to either side.

Selim began moving the ribbon slowly up and down, exerting a subtle pressure on Leyla's clitoris. With one finger he caressed the strip of thin silk, stroking softly in an upward motion. Soon there was a slight, but definite, bulge against the thin fabric. A little longer, and the silk grew dark with Leyla's moisture. Selim sighed with pleasure.

'Ah, see how the kernel of delight swells against the silk. Why, it is extraordinary! So firm and swollen. Never have I seen such a one. I must taste it. My tongue demands this woman's sweetness. I cannot wait.' Selim flashed a glance at Kasim, awaiting his approval and getting it as he expected.

'Of course,' Kasim said smoothly. 'You may have the use of this slave. Any others you wish also. And I may have the use of one of yours?'

Selim's glistening eyes were fastened between Leyla's thighs. He did not seem to have heard Kasim. Now he drew the silk halter slowly, so slowly, through Leyla's legs. At last the pouch of her sex was free. The rim of red flesh, visible between the swollen outer lips, was moist and shiny.

'Spread for me,' he ordered hoarsely.

Leyla complied, using her fingers to open the flesh-lips. She pulled them up slightly, so that her remarkably developed pleasure bud stood out hard, glistening redly. Selim was transfixed. His eyes narrowed with pleasure. His full cheeks trembled as he moistened his lips with his tongue. He pressed the musk-scented silk fabric to his face and inhaled deeply.

'Perfume of the Gods!' he groaned. 'Forgive me Kasim. I was quite overcome for a moment. This woman is a treasure. Take whichever of mine you wish. All my women are well trained and submissive. Their delight is to serve.'

Kasim stood up. An enigmatic smile was printed on his hard face. Across the room Marietta gave a shiver of apprehension. Claudine was watching Selim, who had gripped Leyla's waist and was lapping at her sex like a dog. Everyone in the room seemed to be watching the little scene. Leyla's head was thrown back. Her buttocks trembled. She began to moan as her fingers stroked Selim's thinning hair. Some of the other merchants were also being pleasured. While they thrust into willing slaves, or lay back accepting the attentions of lips and tongues, their eyes were fastened on Selim and Leyla. Sounds of skin on skin, rustles and sighs, filled the opulent, shadow-painted chamber.

Only Marietta, alert to Kasim's mood, noticed the determination in his gait as he walked some distance from the erotic tableaux. She followed him with wide eyes, knowing his destination even before he stopped. The moment before he reached Gabriel, he looked full at her.

He makes this decision to punish me, she thought. He knows that I desire Gabriel and he will use this occasion to humiliate him. Kasim reached Gabriel. He pinned him with a glance.

'You heard your master,' he said. 'Take off your clothes and spread yourself for me.'

Realisation flooded Marietta. Kasim was not going to lash Gabriel, as she had expected. He was loosening his belt, freeing his strongly erect penis.

'I'll have your mouth first. Then I want your arse,' Kasim said crudely. 'And if you do not please me it will be the worse for you.'

She could not stand it. Kasim was doing this because of her. He meant to humiliate Gabriel utterly. Already the other guests were showing interest. They were all going to watch. Gabriel got to his feet slowly. A deep flush stained his cheeks but he began to disrobe as Kasim ordered.

'No! Kasim ... please ... don't ...' The cry left Marietta's throat before she could swallow it.

She froze at once. There was no help for Gabriel. She knew Kasim never responded to pleas for mercy. She cursed herself for being a fool. But the damage could not be undone. With a face like thunder Kasim re-fastened his belt. Suddenly he was at her side.

He slapped her face, almost playfully. Then took hold of the chain and jerked her upright. For her ears alone, he whispered:

'Still so rebellious? I judged you well. You have not disappointed me. Come then, my treasure, you shall watch. It will add to my pleasure.'

Marietta realised too late that she had been manipulated. Kasim had wanted her to protest. He had sensed that there was a deep attraction between herself and Gabriel. Now he would use that fact to his advantage. Never would he waste such an opportunity to humiliate them both. Her throat burned. How heartless Kasim was.

The blackness inside him was deep and fathomless. Ah, but his sensuality burned so brightly. She could not help but be drawn in by it, to find the reflection of herself in him. Even as part of her recoiled, another part responded, reaching out, aching for what was to come. One day she would punish him for this, for his piercing insight. She hated him for having such power over her, even while she longed for him. If ever she penetrated that reserve, the coldness that he wore like a cloak, she would take her revenge.

As she was pulled to her feet, her sore breasts swayed. The movement of her thighs chafed her oiled flesh-lips. The hungry sex awoke, demanding release. Despite her churning thoughts, her fears, the spicy oil still worked its sensual spell over her. She caught her breath at the sight of Gabriel's body. He was naked now except for a leather pouch that fitted tightly over his already swelling cock.

Gabriel was perfect in his male beauty. He was strong, defiant as she was, and proud. Even as she had seen him last, slimed with sweat, marked by the lash, and shuddering in the aftermath of sexual release, she had been impressed by that stubborn pride of his. It had taken a lot to break Gabriel. Perhaps she did not need to fear for him; he must have endured much in all his years of slavery.

But deep inside her heart she knew that Kasim's personality, incandescent for her like a darkly glowing jewel, eclipsed Gabriel's beauty, his strength, like the sun burnt out the moon. Kasim, dark and slim and dangerous, was a past master in the subtleties of chastisement. Inside him was a rod of iron. Cold, unbending.

Gabriel, and she too, would be spared nothing.

Marietta felt a stirring within her that was not entirely sexual. It seemed that she was at the apex of this forced triangle, and in that there was a sort of power. With a defiant set to her mouth she allowed herself to be led into the centre of the room.

Gabriel's hands reached for the leather thong that encircled his waist and kept the leather pouch in place.

'Leave it,' Kasim rapped from across the room. He was bending close to the chained slave, whispering to Marietta as he freed her from the pillar.

Gabriel allowed his arms to fall to his sides. He stood with his shoulders back, his strong legs slightly apart. Kasim made a movement of his hand and Gabriel sank into the submissive posture, taught him by Selim.

He was not afraid of what Kasim would do to him. Selim had trained him well. There could be no act, however debased, that would shock him. He thought of those early times, when Selim had broken him to service the way a horse is broken to the saddle.

He had been required to stay naked at all times. To

wait on his master, sleep curled up on the floor beside his bed, and to clean Selim's then hard-muscled body from head to foot, daily, with his tongue. While he learned to use his hands and mouth to coax pleasure from Selim, he must suffer his stem and balls to be bound with thongs. Sometimes he thought he would explode with the sweet pressure. All pleasure, even self-inflicted, was denied him until he had proved that he deserved to be rewarded. It had been a time of torture. The harness around his waist, which held the ivory phallus in his anus, had chafed and maddened him.

But oh, the joy, the feeling of hot and willing surrender, when Selim allowed him his first climax. Then Selim had allowed him women to pleasure. And he must hold himself back as before. At the time he had hated his master. But now that he had acquired the taste for sensual pleasures he looked back on those times with affection.

Kasim advanced towards him, leading the blue-eyed woman behind him. The old memories faded. All Gabriel could think of was his joy in the moment. He had eyes only for her. Her face was as he remembered it: perfectly oval, with a small straight nose and a sensual mouth. The eyes were as blue as flax flowers, bluer than any eyes he had ever seen. As for the rest of her – nothing could have prepared him for the wonders hidden under the black robes she wore that day.

What a marvel her hair was! So pale, almost silver. It tumbled over her shoulders in a riot of curls. The gold collar, set with moonstones, was a perfect foil for her colouring. He had to admire Kasim's taste. The woman's body seemed perfect to him. Her limbs were long and gently rounded. She was not opulently curved like the dancing girl who had so captivated his master;

rather, she was almost slender. The deepest curves were where her waist flared into generous hips. Her breasts were not over-large, but very high and round. There seemed to him to be a wonderful symmetry to her form. And between her thighs was another wonder still. He had glimpsed, but briefly, the pink shell-like sex, surrounded by more curls of silky blonde hair. Kasim had dared to break with tradition and leave hair around the pubic lips of this choice slave.

Gabriel found the sight almost overwhelmingly erotic.

Kasim clapped his hands and slaves ran to remove Gabriel's pile of clothes and bring a small low table.

'Bring more lamps too. I want to see everything clearly,' Kasim rapped. He had unclipped the chain from the woman's collar and was feeding it idly through his fingers.

'So, Marietta, we have Gabriel to ourselves this day. There is no crowd to interfere with our enjoyment of this rebellious slave.' He grinned. 'But perhaps he is obedient after his public lashing. Shall we test his obedience?'

Marietta. Gabriel absorbed the name. Marietta. She looked uneasy. Her hands hung at her sides. She glanced through lowered lashes at Kasim, obviously unsure whether to assume the usual submissive posture. Gabriel sensed the tension between them. Why does Kasim not order me to pleasure him at once? he thought. Then he understood.

Kasim was punishing him and Marietta. He had seen the looks that passed between them.

Gabriel began to feel uncomfortable. It was unwise to provoke this man. He knew Kasim's reputation. It was said that this man could stir you to pleasure until you felt that your soul was peeled bare. And after, you would be gasping for more. It was also said that Kasim's passions ran deep, and he was reputed to have shown an extraordinary amount of restraint where Marietta was concerned. The gossip amongst the slaves was that Kasim had not yet taken her to his bed. Gabriel did not believe that. Such a thing was unknown.

But the stories he heard about Kasim must contain a grain of truth. He was an enigma and he would be an implacable enemy. A muscle ticked in Gabriel's jaw. He waited, aware that the spice of danger had fanned his excitement. At his groin the leather pouch grew tighter as the fabric strained to contain his erection. He found the thought of being spread for this man, of having to take his cock into his mouth, more disquieting, more arousing, by the moment. His earlier bravado seemed foolish now. This was not a man who would be ensnared, weakened, by the power of his senses.

Selim was one thing. Kasim was quite another.

'Move closer to Gabriel,' Kasim said to Marietta. 'Does his strength not make you afraid? But you need not fear. For this is a well-trained slave, docile and willing to offer himself for his master's pleasure. Is that not so, Gabriel?'

Gabriel answered. 'Yes, lord.' His voice was deep. Marietta thought she detected the slightest trace of a tremor in it. She felt an answering response. He is wary of Kasim, she thought, as well he might be.

Marietta stood looking down at the kneeling slave. Close to, he looked enormous. His powerful shoulders were pulled back, showing the planes of his chest and belly off to advantage. The thighs, wide apart, were taut and corded with muscle. He was as tall as Kasim but more strongly built. It was odd to see a man in the submissive posture. In the harem all the slaves were female. The only males in Kasim's household were guards and they were refused access to the private apartments.

Gabriel's calm grey eyes stared back at her. There was no sign of that earlier intimacy in his direct gaze. She felt an almost unbearable urge to touch him, to stroke back the unruly hair which tumbled over his brow. There was an innocence in Gabriel's remarkable face. The high cheekbones, the straight brows, and the deep-set eyes were those of a man who had suffered and triumphed. But in the set of the jaw, the curiously soft mouth, she detected traces of the pure young boy he had once been.

The poignant insight promoted a curious tenderness in her – something she had never felt, nor expected to feel, for Kasim. Perhaps the feeling was prompted partly by the sight of this powerful young man holding himself in check. Gabriel looked as if he could crush Kasim between his two hands, but he did nothing. He just waited. He was a prisoner of his flesh, she realised, as were all the women of the harem. For surely Gabriel had been trained by his master to do exactly as he was bid and to savour the pleasures of submission. Surely he felt that delicious retraction of will which gave a peculiar freedom to the senses and imparted power to a slave.

Oh, yes. Gabriel had been trained well, as Kasim was training her still. She was learning much and discovering more about herself with each day that passed.

Kasim said nothing. Content, it seemed, to let her look at Gabriel. Not a muscle of his face moved. It might have been carved from marble. Not a breeze stirred his outer robe of emerald velvet. It did not dare, Marietta thought, with a shiver. But she detected

Kasim's wry amusement. Very slowly and deliberately, Kasim folded back his deep cuffs, then positioned himself on the low table which had been placed next to Gabriel. Comfortably seated, his booted feet apart, hands on his hips, he ordered Marietta to stroke Gabriel's shoulders.

She began to do so, trying to subdue her churning thoughts by concentrating on the marvellous configuration of bone, muscle and sinew that made up Gabriel's upper body.

'I wish you to test this slave for me,' Kasim said with grim humour. 'I have not used him before. I confess, the thought of doing so is singularly enticing. But is he worthy to receive my attentions, do you suppose? Tell me, Marietta, how does his skin feel? Is the skin of his neck the same texture as that on his chest?'

Marietta slid her palms across Gabriel's shoulders and then up the thick column of his neck. Kasim watched her every movement, searching her face for signs of emotion. She hated the game that he was making them play, but she dared not refuse. Besides, she clutched at the chance of any contact between herself and Gabriel.

Gabriel's skin was warm, stretched like living silk over the firm muscles. It felt wonderful. She could smell his scent of clean hair and sandalwood and, under the other smells, a spicy musk that was his alone. She slid her fingers under the warmth of his hair, feeling the weight of it tickle the backs of her hand, then pinched his earlobes gently. Finding the hollow at the base of his skull she circled it with both thumbs. There was the slightest pressure against her hand as Gabriel moved towards her touch. She knew that if he had been allowed, he would have rubbed against her like a cat.

'Well?' Kasim said impatiently.

'It ... it feels ... good, my lord,' she stammered.

'Hmmm. No more than good? I think you must explore further. I need to be convinced that this slave is excellent, outstanding in fact. Move your hands down. Feel his chest. Is it firm? Well-muscled? And the nipples – suck them. How do they taste?'

Gabriel's face remained impassive as she trailed her fingertips over the bulge of his pectoral muscles where the nipples, small and copper-coloured, pointed slightly downwards. At the indentation near his breastbone she paused. Under her fingers she felt the rapid beat of Gabriel's heart. So he was not as calm as he outwardly appeared. She marvelled at his control.

The beautiful tender mouth was relaxed, the lips parted slightly. She felt a rush of heat as she imagined that mouth fully open and pushed out, forming a receptacle for Kasim's penis. Bending her head, so that she might mouth his nipples, she felt again the slightest movement of Gabriel's neck. Then came the merest brush of his lips on her hair. Her heart turned over at his daring.

'First his arms. Work down to the nipples. Are those arms strong enough to bear his weight as he takes mine on his back? Tell me quickly, for I long to bury myself inside him. Can you imagine how he would feel, Marietta?' He laughed harshly. 'Of course not. How could you. And yet ... perhaps ...'

She hardly heard him. She had tensed, afraid that Kasim had seen the moment of tenderness. But he gave no sign. His face was self-absorbed, bright with some new thought. Turning his head, he rapped out an order. At once a slave ran to do his bidding. Marietta's hands trembled as she reached out to caress Gabriel's biceps. This change of mood unnerved her. What new refinement was Kasim planning? She knew that gleam in his eye.

Despite her trepidation she felt the oddly familiar stirring of excitement, the fear, that concentrated her pleasure. The slave returned and gave something to Kasim. Marietta caught only a quick glimpse of the object. It seemed to be a contraption made of leather, something attached to a pad with straps.

'The arms?' Kasim said, distracting her.

'His arms are indeed strong, my lord,' she managed to say.

'Good. Good. The nipples?'

Slowly now she sank to her knees in front of Gabriel. She reached out to lap at his nipples, careful to restrict the contact to her mouth only. There was but a short space between them. Gabriel's leather-pouched penis was jutting out strongly. If he moved it would graze her soft belly, nuzzle the halo of the pubic curls. Her breasts were so close to him. Her nipples were no more than a finger's width away from his skin. It would be easy to sway forward, to press herself to his chest. She felt a surge of desire for him. Her nipples grew hard. They were still sore from the spanking and they tingled and burned. She longed to draw the tips of them across his silky skin, to feel the heavy heartbeat pulsing against her rigid teats. But she knew that Kasim would never forgive such blatant behaviour.

She must be content with a smaller, less visible, rebellion. She closed her mouth over one of Gabriel's nipples, then circled it defiantly with her tongue and bit down gently before releasing it. Oh, it was worth risking another spanking. The little rush of Gabriel's indrawn breath was sweet music to her.

'The nipples are sweet, my lord,' she said, hiding a smile.

'And that full leather pouch he wears is jerking as I watch!' Kasim said. 'Have a care, Marietta. Lest you take too much upon yourself. I alone order your actions.'

She drew back a little. 'Yes, my lord. Forgive me,' she said, instantly contrite.

Kasim had missed nothing after all. She held her breath, expecting him to order her to stand up, move away. Perhaps he would punish her while Gabriel watched. Or he might order Gabriel to spank her buttocks. At the thought her cheeks grew hot and there came a liquid pulsing between her thighs.

But Kasim said only: 'Remove the leather pouch. I want to see the phallus. To judge this slave's readiness.'

Marietta untied the thong around Gabriel's waist and drew the pouch free of his straining member. Released from restraint the rigid cock jutted upright between Gabriel's spread thighs. It was so strongly erect that the swollen plum had slipped free of its skin and was glistening with clear liquid. The plum was large and dark in colour and the ridge around it was prominent and collared by ruched skin. Dark blond curls clustered around the thick base of the cock-stem. The heavy sac could be seen, hanging in the space between his legs.

At the sight of Gabriel's genitals Marietta felt a subtle pressure inside her. Something seemed to open and then flow outwards. Warmth spread into her belly and between her thighs. Since her first sight of him in the marketplace she had wanted to feel that thick stem slide inside her ...

'A magnificent organ indeed,' Kasim pronounced. 'Stand away now, Marietta. That treasure is not for you. When you are completely submissive, when you hold nothing back from me, then you shall be given your full reward. For now, you may watch. And if you please me, you shall take a turn at this fine rump. Come attend me. Disrobe me. Free my manhood.'

· Kasim dropped the object the slave had handed him. The leather phallus, attached to a triangular-shaped pad, fell to the carpet. Gabriel saw the movement and understanding showed in his face. His mouth set in a stubborn line.

Marietta knew that Kasim planned something for her, but she did not know what. She backed away from Gabriel regretfully, managing to throw him the briefest of smiles before she went to stand between Kasim's spread knees. While he shrugged off his outer robe she drew off his knee-high boots, then unbuckled his belt. Next she removed the emerald leather trousers. She unlaced the front of the velvet tunic, but Kasim stoped her slipping it over his arms.

'Enough. Stand behind me, Marietta. Let your body form a backrest.'

She did as he asked and Kasim moved to the edge of the table, so that his buttocks were resting on the polished wood surface. Then he leaned back against Marietta. Lifting his heels, he placed his feet on the low table, then parted his knees. His sex was now displayed prominently. His erection swayed slightly, standing up from his belly and jutting out towards Gabriel as if eager for his touch.

Marietta saw the look of desire cross Gabriel's features. Her heart constricted. She did not know who she envied more, Kasim or Gabriel. She braced herself to take Kasim's weight. The velvet of his tunic prickled against her breasts, sending little shocks through her sore nipples as she adjusted her position. Looking down over Kasim's shoulder she could see his broad chest, bisected by the loosened laces of the tunic. The emerald fabric fell away from his pale body and lay in deep folds on the wooden table. She looked lower to the slope of his muscular belly and the line of dark silky hairs that trailed downwards from his navel. The powerful thighs, raised up and allowed to fall open, were corded with flexed muscles. At his groin the hairs grew in a thick bush, masking the place where his cock-stem joined his belly.

Kasim's position was almost one of submission. The role of master and slave might have been reversed. But though Kasim might be displayed as enticingly as any slave, he was still very much the master. His beautiful pale hands were pressed flat to the table. Only the slight movement of the sinews on the back of one hand betrayed his tension.

Marietta had forgotten everyone else in the room. The pool of lamplight was bright around the three of them, but the rest of the room was in partial shadow. Now and then a sigh or a groan could be heard. Sometimes a whispered endearment. Even so, it was easy to imagine themselves alone.

When Kasim ordered it, she looped her arms under his armpits and took his weight as he relaxed. Her hands fitted into the slight hollows at the joining of his shoulders with his chest and his head fell back on her shoulder. The realisation of their peculiar intimacy came over her gradually. She felt consumed by Kasim's proximity; never had she been so close to him. All contact had been restricted, until this moment. She knew the feel of his fingers on her flesh; or probing inside her; his hands as they spanked her, rubbed oil into her, chained her to the pillar. There had been the occasional brush of his lips against hers, but the luxury of his whole self he had held back, always.

Now she held him in her arms for the first time and was astonished at the emotion that welled up inside her. Moments ago she had been sure that she would never feel tenderness towards Kasim. Now that very emotion stabbed her through, fragmented her, swept her up and dashed her down on some bleak shore. She shuddered. It was altogether terrifying.

The dark waves of Kasim's hair, silky-textured, perfumed with ambergris, spilled against her skin. Her cheek lay next to his. She felt the rasp of his newly emerging beard, the clean line of his jaw. Moved to impulse, she pressed her lips to his forehead and could not suppress a smile of triumph when he jerked against her with shock.

Kasim lifted his head abruptly. 'Gabriel. Crawl over here, and pleasure me,' he ordered. There was an unfamiliar quality to his voice but Marietta thought that only she noticed it.

Gabriel dropped onto all fours, buttocks high in the air, chin down. His flaxen hair brushed the carpet as he crawled towards the low table and settled himself on his knees facing Kasim. His strong hands slid up Kasim's calves, massaging them and pressing them inwards, moving the bare feet even nearer to the undersides of the raised thighs. Kasim gave a sigh at the increased tension in his legs as his cock was thrust out even more prominently. It jerked as if it had a life of its own.

Gabriel brushed his fingers down the dark pubic curls and cupped the tight sac, stroking the firm pad behind it. Then, with the other hand, he grasped Kasim's stem and squeezed it, continuing to milk it, until a drop of clear fluid appeared at the tip.

Raising his body up, but staying in a half-kneeling position, Gabriel leaned over so that his long hair swayed forward to brush Kasim's belly. He began licking the sex-head, then sucking it with soft and relaxed lips. He slid up and down the plum, lipping over the swollen rim, anointing it with saliva until it was shiny and a deep purple-red in colour. For a while he restricted his attention to the plum, using his mouth to draw on it, pulling sweetly on the tender flesh. Deliberately he restrained from sliding his mouth down the shaft. He licked around the rim, flicking his tongue to the underside of the cock-head, exerting pressure on the site of the healed scar-tissue where the skin had been removed in infancy.

Gabriel's fingers strayed over the whole exposed area between Kasim's thighs. Sometimes his touch was gentle as he stroked the swollen sac or circled the puckered bottom-mouth. By turns he was rougher, digging his fingers into the insides of the thighs, holding on to the base of the shaft and pumping it hard.

Kasim's hips moved as Gabriel pleasured him expertly. His eyes closed and his hard mouth parted on a series of breathy moans.

Each of those sounds seemed to go straight to Marietta's womb. She felt how Kasim strained against her. Saw how his long white fingers clenched and unclenched. He was beautiful in his passion. She wished that she, and not Gabriel, was the instrument of it.

Gabriel shifted position suddenly, grunting with pleasure as he jammed his head down hard on the cock-stem. Kasim's back arched as he rose up to meet the downward shafting. Gabriel's hands cupped Kasim's buttocks and dragged them apart, digging his fingers into the firm globes. Kasim moaned loudly and tried to draw away, but Gabriel held him firm. The downward motion became more rapid. Gabriel drew the cock deeply into his throat and ground his lips down hard against Kasim's pubis.

'Stop ...' Kasim groaned as his hands curled into fists.

But it was too late. He threw his head back. The cords stood out in his neck. His stomach jerked as he spasmed.

Unable to contain herself any longer, Marietta leaned forward as Kasim's head lolled against her. His face was contorted by the strength of his climax. She pressed her mouth to his, drawing his moans into her, circling his warm tongue with her own. For a moment Kasim responded, kissing her deeply, grinding his hard mouth on to hers. She felt such exaltation that it seemed her soul would fly free. Kasim lifted one hand and cupped the back of her head.

Quickly, Gabriel spat into his hand and rubbed the ejaculate around the end of his cock. He was already in position. Easing Kasim's tight buttocks apart he nudged his lubricated tip towards the secret mouth he so desired. Before Kasim had recovered from the afterglow of his climax, Gabriel was inside him. The hot flesh-ring closed around him, scraping deliciously against the rim of his plum. Gabriel sank forward with a moan of triumphant delight.

'And ... now the ... slave becomes the master,' Gabriel ground out through clenched teeth.

Kasim jerked back against Marietta, seeming to rise up with a great straining of his back muscles. She regained her balance with difficulty, while Kasim wrenched his head away and gave a growl of pain. Confused and still drowsy with passion Marietta looked down and saw with horror that Gabriel was pressed up hard against Kasim's buttocks.

Gabriel's face was taut as he thrust deeply into Kasim's body.

'How do you dare ...?' Kasim cried, his face consumed with rage.

Selim, watching, gave a cry of dismay and rushed forward, ready to pull his rebellious slave off Kasim. Kasim clenched his teeth.

'No! Leave him!'

Gabriel laughed triumphantly. He spoke softly so that only Kasim and Marietta heard. 'Like it, do you? How long is it since anyone used you like this? Or this?'

Swiftly he grabbed Kasim's legs and slung them over his shoulders. One huge arm, pressed on Kasim's stomach, holding him down, and stopping him from twisting away. Kasim began to pant as Gabriel rotated his hips and worked away at him ever more strongly. Marietta braced herself to take the extra weight. Kasim was forced back against her breasts, again and again, as his whole body jerked with the force of Gabriel's onslaught.

Kasim's cock, which had begun to subside, stood up more strongly than before. It was forced down against his body as Gabriel leaned into him. Gabriel's stomach rubbed against Kasim's erect cock as he tensed and drew back, then thrust forward again. Kasim's penis beat against his own stomach.

Kasim set himself to suffer the ordeal. He was strong, but not strong enough in the position he lay in to throw Gabriel off. Though his face was deeply flushed with shame, his eyes soon became hooded with a sort of grim pleasure. All at once Kasim shuddered as his pleasure crested and broke for a second time. He gasped and moaned as a thin trickle of seed seeped from his penis and was soon absorbed between his and Gabriel's bellies.

At last, with a great cry, Gabriel emptied himself. He hunched over Kasim, bracing his weight on his arms. Sweat pearled his brow and his mouth hung open as he drew in great lungfuls of air. For a moment, as if in submission, he laid his cheek against Kasim's heaving chest. When he looked up again the marks of the tunic-lacings were imprinted on his cheek. The clear grey eyes burned into Kasim's.

'Is not submission a sweet drug, my lord?' he whispered.

Kasim seized Gabriel's long hair in one lightning swift movement. He dragged Gabriel close, his fingers curled like claws around his head, and kissed him hard on the mouth. When Gabriel pulled away his bottom lip was marked by one bright bead of blood.

'For that stolen delight you shall pay, many times over,' Kasim said icily, 'and it shall be my pleasure to watch as you are punished.'

Consternation broke out amongst the guests as Selim dragged Gabriel away from Kasim. Marietta helped Kasim to his feet and draped his robe around his shoulders. Then she stood back a little. In all the drama of Gabriel's unexpected attack, Kasim had forgotten her completely. Their brief contact had been eclipsed totally by Gabriel's actions. Her disappointment was bitter. Her lips seemed to have retained the impression of that one burning kiss and she was furious with Gabriel for stealing Kasim from her.

But her own feelings paled as she saw how furious Gabriel's master was. Selim was white to his lips. His full cheeks wobbled, his hands were clasped together, and he seemed to be having difficulty in controlling himself. He spat curses at Gabriel who knelt before him in the posture of submission.

'After all I have done for you, this is how you repay

me! You ingrate, you ... you snake! You'll not eat for a week.'

Gabriel's chin was lowered, his face hidden. He spoke no word in his own defence. Marietta felt suddenly very afraid for Gabriel, though she admired his spirit. If only she had the courage to be so rebellious.

'I ... I am mortified, my friend,' Selim stammered, turning to face Kasim, 'that this slave should so insult you! And in your own house. Oh, I could weep for the shame of it. I feel this as a blow to myself, to my honour. I must make reparation at once. We have been friends, business partners, for so long. What can I do to atone for this ... this ... wretch's actions?'

Kasim walked slowly over to Gabriel and looked down at him. There was silence in the room. Kasim smiled, long and lazily.

'You can sell this slave to me,' he said.

10

The deal was swiftly made and Selim took his leave of Gabriel.

'I shall miss you, Gabriel. But by my honour, you leave me no choice. I am forced to sell you. Be sure that you atone for your behaviour. And be as loyal to Kasim as you have been to me.'

Selim glanced at Kasim and said quietly, 'It is well that we shall continue to do business together. I value your custom. One thing only ... Perhaps you will bring Gabriel to see me when you visit?'

'I will do, certainly,' Kasim said shortly. 'Fare you well, old friend.'

Selim departed almost at once, taking with him his entourage of slaves and many of the other guests.

Gabriel watched his old master leave. His face was expressionless, but his hands were clenched into fists. In his own way Selim had been a good master. What was he to expect now? Well, it was too late for regrets. He remained kneeling in the submissive posture, waiting for his new master to order his actions.

Kasim played the host to his remaining guests. Leyla, Marietta and Claudine mingled amongst them, handing round water pipes and tobacco. Kasim gave Gabriel over to the guards.

'Tell the body slaves that he is to be washed and groomed and fitted with a gold collar – the one set with grey quartz and citrines. Also, fit him with a waist chain. His hands are to be fastened behind his back until his obedience is assured. When he is ready take him to the small bedchamber. Restrain him there. I will follow shortly.'

While Marietta moved amongst the last few guests she thought of Gabriel. She was worried that the guards might torment him, even force him to pleasure them. It was known that guards delighted in using the choicest slaves whenever they could get them alone. No doubt Kasim knew this and allowed it. But she comforted herself with the thought that Gabriel was too valuable for them to actually harm him.

Some time later, as Kasim began seeing each guest out, he called her over.

'Go through that archway and down the corridor to my bedchamber. Wait for me there.'

Her heart beat fast. Gabriel would be there by now. What was Kasim planning? She entered the small richly decorated room. It smelt of lilies and incense. Red and gold tiles covered the walls. A platform bed, upholstered and curtained in red velvet, dominated the room. There were a few wooden chests, some brass tables and an exquisite carpet, also red with gold fringing. Apart from this the room was bare. It had an air of intimacy. She sensed Kasim's preference in the colour scheme. Was this where he had brought Claudine? She imagined their bodies entwined on the red velvet covering and was surprised by the sudden hot flare of jealousy.

Gabriel sat against one wall on a bench. He was naked. His neck was encircled by a gold collar. A chain, clipped to the collar, secured him to a ring set in the tiled wall. Around his waist was a thick gold chain. His skin looked pink from the bath and gleaming from a fresh application of scented oil. The long blond hair hung to his shoulders in damp waves.

He did not speak as she walked over to him, but she sensed his surprise at finding her there. They held each other with their eyes.

'Kasim sent you?' he said.

She nodded. 'I am to wait here for him.' After a moment she asked, 'You knew that it was dangerous to cross him. Why did you do it?'

Gabriel smiled. 'I don't know. Perhaps the devil was in me. Perhaps to be with you.'

Marietta coloured. 'But you took such a risk. Kasim will not tolerate disobedience in any form. He could have ordered you to be beaten publicly. How did you know that he would buy you?'

'Because he is not done with tormenting me. Or you. He desired us both. Did you not know that? He wishes to watch us together. He will force you to use me, as he planned to do earlier.'

'How so?'

'Did you not see the phallus-harness? Surely you know what use he would put it to.'

Marietta shook her head.

Gabriel smiled. 'You have never worn such a thing? I did not expect to find one so innocent in the house of Kasim. You are charming, Marietta, and worth the risk I took. If I could reach you,' he indicated his chained wrists, 'I would kiss your sweet mouth and explore that innocence until you begged me to stop—'

'Then it is well that you are secured!' Kasim said, striding into the room. In his hand he held the object Gabriel had referred to. 'And you read me well. No doubt you thought you could avoid the public humiliation of having Marietta use you. But no one escapes my will. Ever. I have simply decided to view the deed in private.'

Gabriel's eyes grew hard. 'Why humiliate the

woman? Beat me if you must. Use me however you wish. But leave her alone.'

'How gallant,' Kasim sneered. 'Oh, I shall beat you. But that alone would not be punishment enough. Besides, I would not deny myself the sight of Marietta's lovely body as she toils over you.'

While he spoke he had been loosening the chain that secured Gabriel to the wall. He allowed just enough slack so that Gabriel could be made to kneel and bend forward over a wooden chest. Gabriel's chained hands rested in the small of his back. With his heel Kasim nudged Gabriel's legs apart. He placed a stinging slap on the tight, rounded bottom.

'Spread those knees and buttocks. Wider. Split that crease for me. You are mine now. Display yourself as you have been trained to do.'

Gabriel grunted and struggled, while Kasim laughed. 'You are not eager for this chastisement? You amaze me. For surely you know that Marietta will be punished too if she does not obey me – or if you do not comply. Do you wish that? From what I have seen of you I thought you cared about her.'

At once Gabriel stopped resisting. He pressed his stomach to the wooden chest, opened his legs as wide as possible, and arched his back.

'Beat me then – master,' he said with derision.

'Shall I use the belt or the switch?' Kasim said equably. 'No. My hand I think. I shall relish the feel of your flesh as it warms and trembles under my hand.'

Kasim spanked Gabriel across the buttocks and the backs of his thighs until the taut flesh was a deep pink. Now and then he paused to admire the colour, then began again. Each slap landed squarely, sounding crisp and hard. Gabriel's flesh quivered. After some time he began crying out. The sounds seemed forced from him, each one muffled behind closed teeth. He flinched as each slap connected, but he did not try to pull away, nor to close his thighs.

Marietta felt a movement deep inside as she gazed on Gabriel. Those bulging thighs were turning a deep shade of red. His shadowed flesh-valley gaped obscenely. She found it impossible to look away. There was the puckered bottom-mouth, pink and clean, surrounded by damp blond curls. It looked so vulnerable, a velvet aperture in the midst of the hard flesh of his rosy buttocks. The sounds of the slaps, the spectacle of Gabriel as he strained for control, trying to bite back his cries and failing, aroused her strongly.

Kasim took a long time over the spanking. He was breathing hard and rubbing his sore palms together when he stopped.

'You are lucky the beating was so restrained, Gabriel. Another master would have used the strap on you. Remain as you are, but take a moment to savour the sweet pain. I must ready Marietta. What a pretty boy she will make.'

Marietta dragged her eyes away from Gabriel. She waited, chin lowered, for Kasim's instructions. So Gabriel had been right. She was to be part of his punishment.

'Come here,' Kasim said. 'Open your thighs so that I can put this on you.'

He held out the phallus-harness and she saw it in detail for the first time. The harness was made of black leather. Set in the centre of a curved, triangular pad was an enormous erect phallus of black, leather-covered wood.

'This is a fitting punishment, is it not? He will remember what happens if he disobeys me after you use this on him!'

Marietta shrank inwardly at the sight of the harness and at the thought of what Kasim wanted her to do. The phallus looked impossibly huge. Surely Gabriel could not admit the whole of it into his body. The thought of wearing the thing horrified her. She hung back, but knew that there was no point in refusing. If she did, Kasim would chastise her and then force her to the act anyway, willing or not.

'So?' Kasim said.

Marietta squatted slightly and parted her knees so that Kasim could position the harness. His hands brushed almost affectionately across her pubic curls.

'Your obedience pleases me. You will enjoy this, Marietta. You do not wish to, I know. But I wish it. I want to see you pleasuring yourself – unable to control the sensations that flood your loins. See? There is a cunning little protuberance on the inside of this pad.'

She shivered, thinking that she could never find enjoyment in shaming Gabriel in such a way. But Kasim was right again. Her pleasure was assured. Looking down, she saw the slim, elongated oval shape that stood proud of the leather pad. As Kasim pressed the harness close to her pubis, her flesh-lips were opened and forced to settle around the protuberance. The cool contact of the leather, pressing directly against her oiled inner-flesh, sent a shock of pleasure deep into her.

Kasim pulled one shaped strap through Marietta's legs, fitting it closely to the crease of her bottom, and fastened it to the thick strap that encircled her waist.

'You see, Marietta, everything comes to pass as I plan it. When I wish to withhold pleasure, you are denied it. When I wish you to feel pleasure, as now, you will do so. Despite your resistance, your repugnance for this act, you will feel the most exquisite delight as the leather slides against your oiled sex.

Gabriel too will enjoy what you do to him, precisely because it is you who does it. And I shall enjoy watching, knowing how much Gabriel hates me for forcing this humiliating delight on him! Are we not all performers in the same dance?'

Marietta's cheeks were flushed poppy red. It was true. She could not help the feeling, the warmth throbbing richly between her thighs. The phallus-harness fitted so closely, rubbed so maddeningly against her pleasure bud, that she knew she would not be able to contain herself for long. The shaped strap pressed tightly along the length of her crease, holding her bottom-mouth firmly against the cool leather. The thick buckled strap constricted her waist, so that below it her hips seemed to flare out more prominently than ever. All that tightness, that hard leather containing her flesh, made her feel vulnerable.

The sweet feeling of submission began to rise in her belly. Her desire, which had been held in check for so long, kindled anew. She felt ready to explode right now.

Kasim ran his long fingers down the curve of her hip and over the tight leather straps. He tugged playfully on the huge faux penis that jutted up lewdly in front of her, smiling when a spasm passed over her face.

'Now you must get to work. Go gently at first.' He pressed a small pot into her hand. 'Use this oil to ease the way for Gabriel. I do not want him damaged. My new slave will provide me with many hours of pleasure.'

Kasim folded his arms and stood back to watch as Marietta unstoppered the jar. She dipped her fingers into the oil and smeared the leather object until it gleamed.

'Good. Now anoint Gabriel. Work the oil well into him. Push your fingers inside him. That's the way.'

Marietta knelt down behind Gabriel. He made no sound as she rubbed the oil around and inside his anus. The blond curls, lining his flesh-valley, glistened with excess oil. Runnels of it ran down the insides of his thighs.

'That's enough. Enter him,' Kasim said hoarsely. He had positioned himself to one side of Gabriel so that he could see clearly.

Marietta edged forward. Holding on to the shaft of the phallus, she nosed the enormous bulb towards the tight pink mouth. Carefully she pressed inwards. Gabriel gasped and thrust back and out, causing his anus to open around the tip of the leather staff. Making tiny thrusting movements with her hips, Marietta eased the head inside Gabriel.

Gabriel grunted and tossed his head back. His shoulders rose and fell as he drew in deep breaths.

'Lean into him, Marietta. Bury the shaft fully,' Kasim ordered.

'Wait!' Gabriel said. 'For pity's sake. Take it slowly!'

Kasim laughed dryly. 'Better do as he says, Marietta. Besides, I wouldn't want this to be over too quickly.'

Marietta continued to work the huge phallus inside Gabriel. It was difficult to control the thrusting of her hips. The pleasure of the now warm and slick leather, sliding up and down her wet channel, was intense. She felt the urge to work her hips back and forth, to thrust deeply into Gabriel, until the pleasure built to breaking point.

Half of the thick shaft was now buried in him. He held himself very still and seemed to be holding his breath. The oiled bottom-mouth was stretched widely around the black leather. She circled his orifice with her oiled fingers, scratching gently between his legs at the firm pad above his balls. The pad was hard, pushed out by the pressure of the leather shaft. The balls were tight, the skin around them shrunk to velvet tautness. Marietta grasped Gabriel's cock-stem. She squeezed it hard as she pushed the leather a little further into him.

Gabriel's back was rigid. Every muscle stood out across his shoulders. He turned his face to the side, with difficulty, and she saw how his mouth was stretched over his teeth.

The sight of his troubled beauty spurred her on. Suddenly she wanted to plumb the depths of his shame. To make him tremble with passion as she was doing. She pumped his erect cock, using firm strokes until his breath came fast and his hips began to work.

Then she could hold back no longer. She let go of Gabriel's shaft. Her own passion demanded her full attention. She placed her hands firmly on Gabriel's buttocks. The heat of them seared her palms as she squeezed the flesh. So hot, so delicious. She could not help making a convulsive jerk forward. The phallus slipped in further.

Gabriel's buttocks trembled, and he gave a groan. She slid the leather object the whole way into him. The triangular pad dripped with oil. Hot bottom-flesh was pressed to her belly. Powerful reddened thighs were pressed to her cool legs.

All control deserted her now. She had been kept on heat for so long. The need to climax was all consuming. She ignored Gabriel's moans as she thrust into him, again and again. The tight strap around her waist dug into her, compressing her, forcing all feeling downwards. The shaped protuberance rubbed back and forth across her erect bud. She bent over Gabriel's body, her hips working obscenely, not caring that Kasim saw.

There was only the feeling of building pleasure. As she made rapid, shallow thrusts, the strap between her buttocks pressed on her bottom-mouth. Her moisture had soaked the leather, making it hot and slippery. Soon. Oh, soon. She could hardly bear it.

Then she felt Kasim's arms encircle her. His mouth was at her neck, biting gently into the skin.

'You are beautiful, my Marietta. How does it feel to use a man this way? Is power a more potent drug than submission? Tell me truly. For I would know your secret thoughts. Perhaps I shall indulge them. Are you ready to be a master instead of a slave?'

'No ... no, my lord,' she gasped, on the very brink of dissolving, suddenly not at all clear about what she wanted.

The thin strong body bending over hers, the contained hardness of his cock rubbing against her thighs, drew a fresh wave of sweet surrender from her. Kasim's scent enveloped her, his lips burned her skin. This was what she wanted. How long could she continue to fight the knowledge?

Kasim's long fingers pinched her nipples, milking them gently outwards into hard pink teats. She groaned as he turned her head towards him and claimed her mouth. And this time his kiss was all for her. The taste of him filled her. He sucked her tongue into his mouth, and nipped gently at her under-lip. Her whole body tensed. Now. The shattering waves of pleasure broke over her and she cried out at the intensity of it. The feeling seemed to go on and on. The pleasure of being plundered by Kasim's lips and tongue added an almost unbearable note to her climax. Dimly she was aware that Gabriel too cried out. The three of them were locked in fleshly combat. For a moment everything went dark, then she heard Kasim calling her name. She had slumped across Gabriel's broad back. His chained hands dug into her stomach.

'Come away now, Marietta,' Kasim said, freeing the phallus. 'It has been an exhausting day for you. I am pleased with you, my treasure. Now it is time for you to return to the harem. You can bathe, rest. I will visit you soon.'

Kasim clapped his hands and a slave appeared at once. She helped Marietta to unbuckle the harness. Marietta looked back at Gabriel who still lay bent over the wooden chest.

'Do not concern yourself about Gabriel,' Kasim said. 'You have punished him enough for now. Quite beautifully in fact. He is now my body slave. You are not likely to see him again. Ever.'

Gabriel got painfully to his feet. His muscles were cramped, his reddened thighs and buttocks burned, and his anus felt scaldingly tight and sore. A trail of semen marked his thigh, where his pleasure had spilled past the pain barrier and he had lost control. The huge phallus had stretched him wide, filling him with a wonderful sensation of helplessness, devastating in its purity.

The leather straps had scraped his buttocks and balls as Marietta thrust into him as strongly as any man. She was cruel in her passion. He wondered how long Kasim had starved her. Near to climaxing, she had bent over him and, for the briefest moment, he had felt her breasts graze his back. Her hard nipples had brushed against his skin, causing him to draw in his breath sharply.

That was the moment when his passion matched hers, but he was sure that Marietta had hardly noticed him by then. She was too absorbed in her own release and in Kasim's attentions. Gabriel felt cheated. He wanted so much more of Marietta. He wanted to stroke her mane of silver-blonde hair; tell her that she was the most beautiful woman he had ever seen; he wanted to see those clear blue eyes turn drowsy with passion; then there was her body . . .

Their few moments chatting together, before Kasim arrived, had been so brief. The erotic tableau that Kasim had forced upon them had been brief also, but intensely pleasurable. He had hoped that Kasim might order him to pleasure Marietta while he watched. Now he realised that Kasim would gain no pleasure from watching Marietta sigh in his, Gabriel's, arms. It was plain that Kasim had decided to keep the two of them apart from now on.

Gabriel smiled grimly, finding little pleasure in the clear indication that Kasim must therefore count him as a rival. He did not think that Kasim felt threatened by any man. He was too sure of himself for that. Perhaps it was part of Kasim's plan to punish him. Who knew what went on in the convolutions of his new master's mind?

'You are nicely broken in,' Kasim said to Gabriel, unbuckling his belt. 'And I do not feel ready to seek my bed. Show me how you can work those fine buttocks against my belly, Gabriel, and I might – only might – consider letting you watch Marietta while she is being bathed. On the bed now. Press your face to the cover and open yourself for me.'

It was not much to hang on to, Marietta at her bath. But it was enough for now. Gabriel's eyes filled as he pressed his belly to the velvet and presented his sore buttocks to his new master. If there was a way, he would have Marietta. Whatever he had to do to get her, he'd do it.

He did not wince as Kasim applied more oil to his

flesh. The velvet prickled his chest and belly. He leaned down and held his bottom-cheeks apart with his hands.

'So you are now an obedient slave?'

'As you wish, my lord.'

'We have permission to go on a picnic!' Leyla informed Marietta and Claudine.

Marietta was wearing a short tunic of silver brocade over sheer trousers of blue silk. The trousers had separate legs, attached to a waistband and leaving the crotch free, so that her unique fleece might be displayed by merely parting her thighs. Leyla made sure that Marietta was always dressed this way. If Kasim were to visit unannounced he would see that his orders had been observed.

'A picnic? How wonderful. It seems so long since we saw anything but the walls of the harem,' Claudine said.

Marietta looked up and smiled at her friend. Her arms were full of lilies which she had been picking to decorate the low chest in her curtained bed space.

'You have only to put on outer veils and gloves. Everything is ready. Come,' said Leyla.

Marietta lay back in the grass of the riverbank and closed her eyes.

The sunlight brought out patterns on the insides of her eyelids. It was warm and the breeze smelt of the river. On the far bank was a domed pavilion. Boats passed to and fro on the calm water.

Marietta supported herself on one arm and sipped at a glass of boza, a fermented barley drink, served cool and sprinkled with cinnamon. The other women, screened by the trees, had slipped off their shoes and were paddling in the shallows. Female guards stood some way off, smiling indulgently and chatting amongst themselves.

Marietta looked around at everyone enjoying themselves and wondered why she did not feel like joining them. Perhaps it was because the river, the sight of the boats and the people waving, reminded her of the freedom she once possessed. She realised how long she had been in the harem and thought of all the luxury she was surrounded by: the beautiful women who were her friends; all the new pleasures she had been taught; the wonderful clothes and jewels she wore. But all of that was unimportant. It was her relationship with Kasim that was central to her.

Kasim had not been to the harem since the night of the banquet, a week ago. She had sensed that things were changing between them. There had been an imperceptible shift in the role of master and slave; the distinction seemed to grow ever more blurred. When Kasim kissed her, she thought she glimpsed a new possibility – and then there was Gabriel.

Now she was confused. Yes, she desired Gabriel, as did Kasim. But Gabriel was not Kasim. Gabriel did not prompt her to such depths of sweet anguish. In all his golden beauty there was no hint of the shadow-beast that lurked in Kasim's character. The shadow-beast that was mirrored in her own psyche. If only Gabriel were allowed to pleasure her; the fire would soon be slaked, she felt sure.

But Kasim in his jealousy was cruel. He kept Gabriel from her deliberately. And it seemed that now Kasim had withdrawn his presence from her also. Perhaps he had simply lost interest in her. If so, then the focus of her life in the harem was gone. How ironic. She was his prisoner. Without him, she was still a prisoner of her emotions. Her life seemed filled with confusion.

She turned on to her stomach and nibbled on a grass stem. Around her the laughter of the women sounded like broken glass on the breeze.

Dusk was falling as the women started back. Marietta pulled the long gloves on and settled the veil around her face as the carts trundled towards the town. The carts swayed and bumped as they rumbled over the uneven cobbles. Marietta hung on grimly as they passed narrow dark alleys and shuttered houses. There were few people about, mostly just tradesmen shutting up shops and children carrying home water or firewood. Suddenly, with a sharp crack, a wheel of the cart gave out. With screams and yells the women were tipped out on to the street as the cart lurched to one side.

'Hold!' shouted a guard, dismounting quickly and running to calm the carthorse.

Marietta picked herself up. She had rolled part of the way into a darkened doorway. Women seemed to be thronging the street. Another cart, bringing up the rear, slewed to a halt, narrowly avoiding crashing into the broken one. The guards wheeled around trying to quieten mounts which were panicked by the noise. For a moment all was confusion.

There was a narrow alley next to where she crouched. At the end of it was daylight. Freedom beckoned. Marietta was filled with a crazy impulse. She ducked out of the doorway and, without a second thought, bolted for the alley.

No one pursued her. There came no shout of discovery. She ran on, threading through the quiet streets, ducking in and out of alleys until she stopped at last to catch her breath. Leaning against a wall she looked around. This street looked just like the one where the cart had crashed. She had no idea where she was, or where she was going. Suddenly she realised how foolish she had been. She had no money and she wore only the impractical harem clothes. It had been madness to think of escape.

The dark street was unfriendly. The shuttered houses seemed to mock her. Were those shapes in the shadows robbers?

Perhaps if she hurried back she could rejoin the others. The cart would take some time to repair and in all the confusion there was a chance that she had not yet been missed. She began to retrace her steps but soon she realised that she was completely lost. As she hurried along, feeling more panicky by the moment, rain began to fall. Drops spattered her face and silvered the thick black veils that covered her.

Emerging from a warren of streets into a courtyard she stopped suddenly, then backed into a side alley. There was a carriage parked in front of a large house which had a screened balcony overhanging the street. She recognised the insignia emblazoned on the door. Surely it was Kasim's carriage! And, as if she needed further proof, there was Gabriel at the carriage window.

There was no sign of Kasim or of a coachman. She started forward and wrenched the carriage door open with trembling hands. In her haste she practically fell inside.

'What the . . .' Gabriel sputtered.

She dragged the wet veil from her face. 'You must help me. Please, Gabriel. I've been so foolish. The . . . the cart that was bringing us back to the harem. The wheel came off. I ran away. But I got lost. I must get back before I'm missed . . .'

'Marietta! You cannot imagine how I've longed to see you again. But this is terrible! If Kasim discovers that you tried to escape ... I'll help you of course. But how?'

He put his hand up to the thick gold collar at his neck. Though his hands were free, a gold chain led from the collar to a ring set high up in the side of the carriage. He could move freely inside the carriage, but he was a prisoner.

Marietta could have wept with frustration. She looked around. The interior of the carriage was spacious. It smelt of polished leather. The walls and seats were of black leather, deeply padded and buttoned. The windows were small, glazed with stained glass. They let in only filtered light.

'There!' She pointed to a pile of folded rugs that had been pushed under the seat opposite. 'If I crawl under the seat you could pull the rugs to cover me. Kasim wouldn't notice anything amiss in this gloom. At least I'd get back into Kasim's house.'

She turned to Gabriel; her face was flushed from running and her cheeks were damp with rain. 'Do you think it will it work?' she said anxiously.

Gabriel reached out and drew her close. He kissed the corner of her mouth and curled a strand of her hair around his finger.

'It might do. It's worth a try. I'll help you. But Kasim will not be back for some time. You don't want to be all squashed up under there for hours, do you? Let us grasp this time we have. Oh, I so want to talk with you, to hold you. But most of all – I want to possess you. There might never be another chance.'

As he enfolded her in his arms, Marietta leaned into him. She felt weak with the desire that was sweeping through her at his touch. It was true. They might never be alone together again. She kissed Gabriel passionately, shrugging free of the clinging black veils. He pressed kisses to her neck and nibbled along her jawline. Then he bent his neck and kissed the swell of her breasts where they emerged from the scooped neckline of her silver tunic.

'Wait,' she said breathlessly, as she unfastened the tunic and let it sway open.

With a groan Gabriel gathered up her breasts, pressing them together and burying his face in her scented cleavage. Marietta let her head fall back as he began flicking her nipples with his tongue. He sucked gently on each nipple until they rose into hard pink cones. She felt his teeth graze the tender nipple skin and drew in her breath sharply. She was ready for him at once. The moisture gathered between her thighs.

Marietta ran her hands under his silk shirt, easing it off his shoulders. He wore loose silk trousers tucked into boots, both of which he removed in a fluid motion. Underneath he was naked.

He was so beautiful. She had almost forgotten how perfect his body was.

'I'm sorry if I hurt you that day. The phallus . . .'

'Shhh,' he said, pressing his fingers to her mouth, 'it doesn't matter. Nothing matters but this moment.'

He smelt of spearmint and lemon. She gazed down at his erect penis, imagining it inside her. Suddenly she clutched at him with desperate passion.

'Do it now. I want to feel you inside me. I cannot wait.'

'You are greedy,' he whispered teasingly. 'Don't you know that you must savour a fine dish?'

Gently he pressed her back against the wide padded seat as he kissed her stomach and bit gently at her navel. Then his hand went to the waistband of her trousers.

Marietta covered his hand with hers. 'There's no

need to remove them. See?' She parted her legs and drew up her knees a little.

The separate legs of the trousers fell apart, leaving her lower belly open to Gabriel's view. Gabriel smiled ruefully.

'You wear this garment for Kasim's pleasure?'

'Yes. He desires that I display my "golden fleece" at all times.'

'At this moment, I am glad of it,' Gabriel said, sliding down her body so that his cheek grazed the slight pout of her belly.

The collar at his neck was cold against her skin. The chain tickled. She felt his lips nuzzling her pubic curls, his hands pressing on her inner thighs, easing them gently apart. His breath was hot on her flesh.

'Since I first saw you in the market I wanted you. And I didn't even know who you were. It seemed that you were the only one there. The crowd was nothing to me. And then, at the banquet, I longed to kneel before you and do this . . .'

She moaned softly as his mouth brushed over her sex. He breathed in her scent, rubbing his face all over her pubis. She felt his smooth cheeks against her thighs as he kissed the soft skin. Then his questing tongue probed between her flesh-lips. He licked her slowly, savouring the taste and texture. Marietta twisted her hands in his long blond hair, caressing his ears, uttering little sighs of pleasure.

The sensations were exquisite. Her flesh-lips grew swollen and the moisture seeped out of her as Gabriel lapped at her entrance. He then gave his attention to her erect little bud. As she held herself apart with two fingers, Gabriel licked gently in an upward movement, drawing the bud free of its hood of flesh. Now and then his hot tongue stabbed into her. When that happened he continued stroking the pleasure bud, ever so gently, with the ball of his thumb.

Marietta arched her back and thrust up to meet his hot mouth, his expert stroking. She gave a little gasp when she felt him slip two fingers inside her and begin to work them slickly in and out.

'You are ready for me now, but I would bring you to the brink before I enter you fully,' Gabriel said huskily.

'I ... I am almost ... there,' Marietta whispered as the fingers slid in deeply and his knuckles pressed against her liquid flesh-lips.

'Then let it come,' Gabriel said. 'Let me feel you shudder against my mouth,' and he pressed his lips to the hot jutting bud and sucked gently.

Marietta cried out as the pleasure was drawn out of her. She felt a bearing down, a giving sensation, as her inner flesh convulsed around Gabriel's deeply buried fingers. He pressed on her bud with his tongue, holding the sensations back, prolonging the moment of sweetness.

Before the pulsing died away completely, Gabriel slid up her body to kiss her mouth. She tasted the smoky musk of her juices on his mouth as she sucked at his tongue. She gloried in the feel of him as his weight covered her and his hard chest brushed her breasts. Then came the pressure of his cock against her parted flesh-lips. He moved in a circle, rubbing the head in her moisture, pushing at her entrance.

It felt so big. She could not help drawing back slightly. Gabriel kissed her deeply. Slipping one hand under her, he lifted her bottom and pulled her gently on to him. She felt the swollen cock-tip open her and tensed at the slight pain. Gabriel withdrew at once as she winced. He looked down at her.

'So the stories are true. You have not yet lain with

any man? Yet you have been in the harem of Kasim Dey for many weeks. It seems impossible that he would deny himself this particular pleasure. For what purpose, I wonder.'

'What do you mean? What stories?' Marietta said, confused. 'I know nothing of any stories. It is true that no man has ... penetrated me with his flesh. Does it matter? I want this. I want to feel you inside me.'

Gabriel grinned and kissed her cheek. 'Your wish is my command. I'll try not to hurt you.'

And he did not. After the initial tightness of her entrance was bridged, he slipped inside slowly. For a while they lay still. His cock was sheathed inside her. She felt it pulsing and was touched by the way he held himself back. Marietta closed her eyes as he began to move, gently at first, then with mounting passion. The pressure inside her was wonderful. He filled her, drawing sweet sensations from the whole of her sex.

Seeming to know what she would like, he held her bottom tipped up to him slightly so that her sex was upturned and he must plunge down into it. In that position his cock-stem rubbed against her pleasure bud. It was still sensitive from her earlier climax, yet it seemed to crave a new and deeper release.

As Gabriel drew almost all the way out, then plunged inside her again, her entrance pulsed. The blunt head of his penis nudged against the neck of her womb on each in-stroke. She felt his fingers digging into her buttocks. The tips moved inwards and caressed her bottom crease. His heavy balls stroked softly against her.

Their bodies were slick with sweat. Gabriel held her as if she were made of china, but he slammed into her, grinding his pubis against hers. The contrast in pressures was wildly erotic. She tossed her head from side to side, moaning as she clutched at his thrusting buttocks. The pleasure poured over her like wine and the second climax was more intense. Having Gabriel move strongly inside her lifted her to new heights of sensation.

Her inner tremors brought Gabriel to the brink. Giving a hoarse groan, he stopped suddenly and pulled out of her. He pressed her close and she felt the hot jet of his seed spatter her stomach. As Gabriel convulsed, he buried his face in her neck and cried out her name. She felt his teeth clamp on to her skin and smiled. There'd be a mark there next day – a badge of their shared passion.

For some time they lay entwined. The light grew thicker inside the coach. Gabriel brushed his lips against her hair.

'You must hide yourself now. Kasim will have soon completed his business and will wish to return to his house. He values you highly, you know. More than you realise. What would he say if he saw us like this?'

Marietta smiled, about to reply, when the door was flung open and a blast of cool air blew into the carriage.

'I would say,' Kasim said, tight-lipped and beside himself with fury, 'that I do indeed value this slave highly. Which is why she will be spared the full force of my anger!'

Marietta looked at Kasim with horror. She scrambled upright and began rearranging her clothes. Kasim's face was like marble. His eyes were as hard as jet. Yet she sensed something behind his anger. Sorrow? Surely not.

'You shall be displayed naked on the public punishment block tomorrow!' Kasim snapped at her. 'And you, my friend, will be given to the guards as a plaything.'

11

Marietta tossed the rain-wet hair back from her face. Though the air was warm and balmy, she shivered.

It was growing light. Soon the townsfolk would be pouring into the marketplace, setting up their stalls, driving herds of animals into waiting pens.

And then they would discover her.

Her earlier courage had deserted her completely. She waited with a sort of fatalistic dread. She would not be harmed unduly, she knew. The crowd would delight in ogling her nakedness, howling for her to be beaten. But the placard, erected above the punishment platform, bore Kasim's insignia and male guards stood ready to repel anyone who was too vigorous in tormenting her.

Still, she shrank inside herself.

The wooden boards felt reassuringly solid against her bare legs. Around her shoulders was the Captain's cloak. She did not need its warmth, but the cover was welcome. Soon enough she would feel all the prying eyes, the hostile glances, and be unable to hide any detail of her body from them; the body that the guards had just finished using for their pleasure.

'We've had our fun, lads. Best leave her to the common folk now. They know how to treat a rebellious slave,' the Captain of the Guard had chuckled as he planted a last kiss on her trembling mouth.

He winked at her before he walked away and she felt a brief flare of warmth at the kindness. The Captain joined the other guards who were drinking from a wineskin. Marietta felt sure that Kasim had not sanctioned that, but perhaps he did not care if they drank. Like he did not care whether the guards thrust their hard cocks into her, grasped her hips with greedy hands, and worked her back and forth for their pleasure alone.

But they had not all done that. Only one had claimed her in that way.

She shifted on the hard floor, aching slightly in her leg and stomach muscles. Despite her fears of what was to come she felt an inner languor. It was a good feeling. All the pent-up feelings of sexual arousal, those that lingered even after Gabriel had pleasured her so soundly, had left her now.

It was no surprise that the guards had taken advantage of her; she expected it. But she felt ashamed at the eager way she had responded to them.

'This is what the farmers would like to do to you,' they had grinned as they felt her breasts and bottom.

She twisted away at first, getting tangled in the trailing chains. Her wrists were attached to the two wooden posts, the chains left long deliberately. Seeing this, the guards took full advantage. They made her kneel, then lie on her back, admiring her from all angles. Then she was ordered to stand with her hips thrust forward and her knees spread so that they could admire her fleece. Marietta's cheeks flamed as she turned round and round, pushing out breasts and buttocks, sucking in her stomach, arching her back, and spreading her legs wide for their hungry gaze.

They continued to stroke her and kiss her, standing around her in an admiring half circle. One of them, glancing at the Captain for permission, ordered her to kneel in front of him. Then he took out his cock and began stroking himself. His face was lit by anticipation. Grinning at the others he said:

'Now this pampered beauty will show us all what she can do with her pretty mouth. Aye, and her hands. Are not the harem women taught the many ways to draw out pleasure?'

Marietta had been expecting this. She bent her head and nodded, beginning to suck obediently on the guard's cock-tip, flicking her tongue around the ridge and over the tiny mouth. Then she drew the shaft right into her mouth. Holding the base with one hand she slid her mouth expertly up and down. The guard was so excited by her beauty and willingness that he climaxed after only a few moments. The next guard she pleasured with her hands. He trembled, not meeting her eyes as she brought him to a shuddering peak. The others pressed close, awaiting their turn.

All but one of the guards were young and, despite their show of bravado, unsure of themselves. She pleasured them all. Their freshness and the almost deferential way they treated her excited her in a strange way. So did the fact that they did not care about her pleasure. They cared only about themselves. Ah, the selfishness of the young. Their hard aroused maleness, their eagerness, the different shapes and thickness of their cocks, their voices, their smells – all of these things drew an unbidden response from her.

The Captain, a strongly built man of middle years, watched the proceedings with narrowed eyes. He did not join in. He was handsome, with his square chiselled features and thick brown hair cut closely to his skull. When the others were finished he drew near and loosened his belt. She expected to pleasure him in the same way, but he had other plans. A wooden pot appeared from the folds of his cloak. When he opened the pot she smelt the faint scent of harness polish.

Scooping up a generous pat of grease, the Captain reached between Marietta's legs. He smeared the grease all over her flesh-lips and up her bottom crease. The fat was thick and sticky at first but it felt cool as he rubbed it into her folds, the thickness of it dragging slightly against her flesh. As it grew warm it liquefied, turning the whole of her sex slickly wet, dripping down both thighs. His soldier's hands moved over her flesh-lips, opening, stroking and pinching gently. Her pubic curls were clotted with the grease. The Captain tickled and pulled at them, twisting them into shiny coils.

It was a crude imitation of the perfumed oiling that was given in the harem. The grease smelt faintly of leather and horse sweat and there was no finesse to the Captain's touch. But the feel of the warm grease dripping down her thighs, the thick fingers that slid up and down her flesh-valley, made her long for the stroking to go on, to become even more intimate. When he inserted one finger into her body she bent her legs and rubbed against his hand.

'Don't want to hurt the pretty slave, do I, lads?' the Captain grinned. 'Now, you lot. If you've any juice left over, you'll spill it for sure as you watch this!'

His hands moved over Marietta's body, cupping her breasts, leaving greasy smears on the skin. Her nipples gleamed between his oily fingertips like shiny pink beads. He kissed her, hard. His mouth was hot and tasted of cheap wine. But the kiss was pleasant; his thick lips nibbled at her, his tongue probed her mouth deeply. To Marietta's horror she found herself responding to the man with enthusiasm.

He pressed her backwards, so that she lay flat. She felt the wooden boards against her spine. The long chains rattled into a heap, one on either side of her body. The Captain knelt between her legs while the others watched enviously, the bulges swelling again at their groins.

'That's it, girl,' the Captain groaned. 'Part those knees and let me in.'

Belly pressed to hers, he buried himself to the hilt inside her. Marietta could not help crying out as the rigid shaft slid deliciously into her.

'Slide forward. That's it. Ah, you're slick as a seal inside there. Feel me all the way up you, eh? I've a fine big staff to pleasure you with. Am I not as good as your master? Shall I make you pulse, my pretty? How'd you like that, eh?'

Though the eyes of the other guards watched her closely, she writhed and moaned against the Captain. He reached between her legs and rubbed at her clitoris with the pad of his big thumb. The caress was scarcely gentle but it aroused her strongly. He stroked her in time with his thrusting. As he pushed in he pressed down on to her bud, smoothing the flesh-hood towards her greased opening. When he drew out he exerted an upward pressure, so that her bud slipped free of the greased hood and rubbed against his calloused thumb.

She felt hot and slippery from the grease and her own moisture. The thick cock felt good. Almost as good, she realised, as Gabriel's had. It felt good when the Captain drew his cock right out of her and rubbed it up the length of her greased valley, playing the swollen tip over and over her slick bud. It was more than good when he slid back inside her, pumping his hips in a fast and shallow motion, so that the big head nudged at the neck of her womb.

She had not known, until Gabriel, how wonderful it was to be filled by hard flesh. To feel how strong men trembled with their desire. The Captain groaned, burying his face between her breasts, and his greasy hands clutched and slipped at her waist. His hardness slipped smoothly in and out. She rose to meet it, straining to draw him in ever more deeply. His thumb rubbed at her in that same roughly knowing way. And it did not matter that he had forced his will on her. She forgave him. She was filled by the hot sensation of bearing down, of giving herself to this man. She felt glad of the weakness he now drew out from her – a reflection of his own. It seemed a fair exchange for the pleasure. The Captain sighed and paused, holding himself in waiting.

And then – within the workings of her flesh, the feeling of becoming liquid, the gathering and concentrating of pure pleasure – her mind, for a moment, became razor sharp. Marietta came upon a sudden truth: there was a weakness in men when they thrust into a woman. Some could not admit to this, it seemed. Rather they hid the fact behind a show of power, exerting control over the woman. This was why Kasim had denied himself the pleasure of entering her. This was why he had not let her share his bed. He had not allowed her to sleeve herself around his shaft – as she now realised she had been longing to do.

Kasim was afraid. Afraid that he would lose part of himself if he gave in to that weakness.

And she had thought that Kasim cared nothing for her as a person. That he desired only to torment her as his newest slave. She had been wrong. For did he not desire her strongly? Leyla had told her so. Gabriel had even commented on it. Others had seen the truth before she. Here was the source of the shift in power which she had perceived and been confused by. It was so simple really. The more enamoured of a woman

Kasim was, the more he held himself back. He had worked so hard to keep a part of himself detached, whilst teaching her to relish the act of submission. In that way he could always act the master, remain in control.

She saw through him now. Just wait until I return to the harem, she thought. A new fear possessed her. What if Kasim left her here?

The Captain's beard prickled her skin as he mouthed her neck and breasts. The novelty of the sensation dragged her back to the present. He began thrusting into her again. And now she could not think. All thought, all action, was condensed into the moment. She gave a throaty moan. Lifting her legs, she wrapped them around the Captain's broad back and surged forward, rubbing her pubis against his. The Captain crowed with delight at this evidence of her enjoyment. He plunged into her more deeply than before. His hairy sac scraped lightly against her upraised bottom. She whispered in his ear, urging him on.

'Fill me with your big cock, my Captain. Oh, I am near to breaking now. Feel how hot and wet I am for you. Make me ache with pleasure.'

Her words tipped him over. He began grunting as his thrusts became faster. She gripped his hairy buttocks. The chains trailed across his thighs. Pulling the cheeks apart, she scraped her long nails across his bottom-mouth. The Captain cried out. Marietta shuddered under him, her breath coming in hoarse gasps as her pleasure matched his. She threw back her head, her eyes tight shut, as the wrenching waves flooded her body.

Her inner pulsing seemed to go on and on, stroking the Captain's cock, drawing out the last drops of semen. He jerked with reaction, then lay on her belly, resting his stubbled cheek on her breasts. The moment was oddly tender.

Marietta closed her eyes and imagined that she lay with Kasim.

Afterwards the Captain cleaned her himself, wiping her sex free of grease and semen with a piece of soft kid leather. He stroked her loose hair with his big rough hands and kissed the corner of her mouth.

'You've made me very happy, girl. It's been a long time since I felt like that. Don't you worry now. Me and the lads here will make sure these farmers don't hurt you too much. They'll maybe ask the public punisher to spank you a little and make you dance for them. But you can bear that, eh? Here now, you can lay on my cloak until it's full light.'

So now she lay looking up at the lightening sky, waiting for the farmers, the tradesmen, and the torment. Perhaps it would not be so bad, except that she wished they would hurry. There was too much time to think just now.

What of Gabriel? Was he receiving such gentle treatment?

Gabriel was cleaning out the stables.

If he concentrated on his tasks he could sometimes stop thinking about Marietta for whole minutes at a time. His head seemed full of her. He was torn between elation at the memory of their joining and fear at what she must be suffering. His own situation would not be so bad if he knew that she was safe.

He was naked except for the leather pouch at his groin. The straw prickled his legs and feet as he moved between the stalls, sweeping out and replacing soiled straw. His powerful torso was streaked with sweat and dirt and his long blond hair was damp and dull. It stuck to his forehead and clung to his shoulders in lank strands.

The woman, dressed in the livery of the female guards of the harem, leaned on a stall at the back of the stable, watching Gabriel work. She admired the play of the powerful muscles, the slim waist, and the small tight buttocks bisected by the thin strap of the leather pouch. Even grimy as he was he looked magnificent. She had not desired any man for a long time but this slave woke almost forgotten hungers in her.

'You. Slave. Come here,' she said.

Gabriel walked towards her, his steps slowing as a group of other female guards sauntered into the stable.

'Hurry up now,' the women rapped. 'When I, Sita, give an order, you obey it. At once!'

Gabriel quickened his step. His heart sank. Sita had been the one who took immediate charge of him when Kasim had given him into the care of the guards the previous night. It was she who had ordered him stripped and restrained in the stables. After the luxuries he was accustomed to it was doubly humiliating to have to sleep naked on a pile of straw. A bowl of soup and bread had been his only food, and he had been required to pleasure two of the guards before he could eat. Sita had watched the women use him, laughing as they humiliated and teased him.

At first light Sita had awoken him, then watched hard-eyed while he threw cold water over his body and hair. There was no scented soap, or oil, no comb to pull through his hair. He was given a rough towel to rub himself down with and must cleanse himself as best he could. After he had finished Sita examined his body minutely. He suppressed a shudder as he remembered her cold eyes, her cold thin fingers that probed everywhere, pinching, pressing and opening ... and he remembered how he had writhed with shame as his body responded to her touch.

Sita was tall and thin, with the body of a soldier. It was plain that, despite her apparent lack of desire, she had taken a special liking to him. She could only have come back so soon to torment him. He was surprised. The others had made him pleasure them in many ways, but Sita had remained remote, severe and cold, giving no sign of emotion beyond the snapping of her sharp eyes.

Now Sita crooked her little finger and beckoned. Gabriel flushed, then lowered his eyes as her thin-lipped mouth curved in a smile. Curse Kasim! He had known what he was doing when he gave him to the female guards. They were far crueller, more insatiable, and more inventive than the male guards.

'Too late,' Sita said. 'You were not quick enough in responding. You four women, strip him. Press him back against that stall.'

Gabriel pressed his lips together. A hot excitement rose in him. A mixture of fear and the beginnings of the sweet helplessness he always felt when he was chastised. The fear was uppermost at this moment. He felt a strong urge to resist them. But he controlled himself, knowing that there were too many of them and that they were armed. He would not give Sita the satisfaction of seeing him struggle in his weakness.

He felt the guards' hands on him, surprisingly strong for women. Someone fetched him a slap across his bottom so that he jumped with the pain. Then he was slammed back against the hard wooden side of a stall. He grunted as the wood pressed into his sore buttocks. The previous night's weals, part of the other guards' torment, were raised and red. Someone untied the strap at his waist and dragged the leather pouch from him.

He knew he could not hide his arousal. His face grew hot with shame as they mocked him.

Sita reached out to cup his sac and tug it. Then she dragged the tips of her long scarlet nails up his cock-stem. He trembled at the feel of her hands on him.

'See. He is already hard. Ah, Gabriel, you do not disappoint me. Kasim told me that you need firm handling. See how hungry you are for punishment!'

She slapped the leather crop she held against her high brown boot, then ran the notched tip up his body. The tip quested amongst his pubic curls and stroked up his belly. She lowered the crop and stroked it playfully back and forth across the skin-covered shaft.

'Sita knows how to make you squirm,' she purred, leaning close so that he smelt her. She smelt of leather and herbal soap. Clean and fresh, almost a male scent. There was no trace of the rich perfumes of the harem about her. The uniform of deep-brown leather fitted her closely. Her black hair was pulled back from her face and tied at the nape. Her severity, her very plainness, reached out to him.

She pinched the skin that covered his cock-tip and rubbed it between finger and thumb. Then she passed the pad of her thumb over the tiny moist mouth. Closing her fingers around the tip she worked the skin gently back and forth until she eased it back fully, exposing the purple flesh.

Sita tapped him lightly on his mouth with the crop. She leaned close. 'You're ready for me now, aren't you? You long to be beaten. Ask me. Say it! Beg me for my favours.' Her eyes were narrow, catlike.

Gabriel's cheeks flamed. Rebellion flared inside him 'I . . . I will not.'

Sita laughed. 'You are wickedly disobedient! But willing. The fact is evident. Soon your groans shall speak for you. Squirm you shall. You'll buck and writhe for my pleasure, and if you do not give a good account of yourself, then . . .'

Gabriel tried not to react, but that unfinished sentence held such promise – and he sensed that Sita did not make empty threats. An ache was building in his loins. There was a tightness in his belly, an eagerness for the touch of the crop that he could not deny.

'Loop his arms over the top of the stall and hold them there. Thrust him forward.'

Gabriel found his shoulders pulled back and his chest thrust out by the new position. Someone grasped his hair and pushed his head forward. He was made to look down his body. So, he was to watch everything. The thought excited him further.

Sita kicked his legs apart. 'You and you take his legs. Hold his ankles.'

Each leg was grasped and pulled back. The knees, slightly bent, were drawn around the sides of the stall. In this way Gabriel's hips were thrust forward. His belly was pulled flat, his erect cock sticking straight out in front. The vulnerability of his position, the way his penis and testicles were exposed, almost terrified him. Sita slapped his cock from side to side, smiling coldly when the engorged flesh jerked and twitched. The other women stroked his skin, tickling his armpits, straying between his legs to nip and pinch at his scrotum. He tried to pull back, hollowing his stomach and wincing at the little darts of pain, but they laughed and teased him more roundly.

'Enough!'

Sita drew back. For a moment longer she ran her eyes over his body, admiring the perfect musculature, searching his face as if trying to read his expression. Then she brought the crop down in a stinging blow across one of his spread thighs. Gabriel drew in his breath at the pain of it. Sita began laying on the strokes steadily. First one thigh only, until it glowed a deep scarlet. Gabriel wanted desperately to pull his legs together. But they were held fast, pulled apart so widely that the tendons at his groin showed pale beneath the skin. He could do nothing but suffer the beating.

The warm pain radiated out from one thigh. Each time the sting faded the pain turned to heat. His thigh seemed to blossom, to positively glow. His cock jerked and throbbed. He was afraid that Sita might whip his balls by accident and the threat of it caused his buttocks to contract and his anus to twitch. But Sita was an expert with the crop. When his thigh was a satisfying shade of red, she turned her attention to the other one.

Gabriel sweated and heaved. The muscles in his legs bulged as he writhed. The blond curls under his arms were soaked and they gave off a musky scent. One of the guards holding his arms leaned forward and buried her face in the hollow. He felt her hot tongue lapping at his sweat, while the others laughed and spurred her on.

Sita too was sweating. Her tightly fitting leather jerkin had dark stains under the armpits. Runnels of sweat ran down her neck, disappearing inside the neckline. She paused and rested the crop against her leg. Swiftly she unlaced the tunic and stripped it off. Under it she was naked. Her torso was spare and muscular; her breasts were very small and high, the nipples large and cone-shaped, deep brown in colour and erect.

Gabriel breathed raggedly. His thighs felt as if they were on fire. His shaft was swollen to bursting point.

The sight of Sita's tiny breasts inflamed him. They would have been childlike except for the prominent nipples that were pointing at him almost arrogantly. He wanted to nuzzle those rigid brown teats, to throw her on to her back and plunge himself inside her. Oh, it was sweet torture to be denied that release.

Sita smiled slowly, looking into his troubled grey eyes. She seemed to know exactly what he was thinking. Gabriel steeled himself for the next blow, but it never came. Sita drew close. She made a gesture and his head was jerked upright. He looked into her face, and felt her hands stroking his inner thighs softly as if assessing their warmth. Even that gentle touch was torture. The heat and soreness seemed to shout at him.

Sita smiled, then clawed into his spread thighs, squeezing the tormented flesh, hard, while her tongue moistened her thin lips. Gabriel gasped as a dart of pure pleasure shot down his cock. Sita leaned over him. Her face was inches from his. She put out her tongue and licked his cheek.

He turned towards her and managed to brush her cheek with his lips. 'Please,' he whispered, not caring now if he begged.

She jerked back, a spasm of displeasure marring her face. Then she smiled. Moving down his body she rubbed her breasts across his sweat-slick torso. Gabriel felt the stiff peaks brushing his skin, nudging his own nipples, igniting and teasing them. He felt one of the other women reach for his penis. She grunted with satisfaction as she felt the clear emission from his cock-tip. She smeared the liquid around the head while he moaned and thrust into her hand.

Sita stood back for a moment. She fumbled with her belt, opening the loose trousers and pulling the legs free from her boots. She let them fall. Wearing only the high leather boots she drew close. Her arms went around his neck and he felt the hard stubs of her nipples pressing against his chest. She made no attempt now to pleasure him. Lifting herself on to him, Sita straddled his spread thighs. In one swift movement she sheathed herself on to his cock. Gabriel cried out as he was drawn deeply into her narrow orifice.

The different sensations were maddening. Her heat surrounded him, the strong inner muscles rubbing against his shaft. He felt the coldness of her leather boots as she hooked her calves tightly around his hips. Shards of pleasure and soreness filled him as Sita worked herself up and down on his straining member, her bottom bouncing on to his reddened thighs.

It was over swiftly. Sita uttered a series of hoarse little cries as she rode him hard. All at once she arched against him, throwing her head back. He dipped his chin and drew one of her nipples into his mouth. It was like sucking on an almond. He bit down gently on its firmness. Sita groaned and drew back, almost pulling the nipple from his mouth. Her inner tremors gripped his cock just at the instant that his fluid rushed out.

He had hardly time to register the pleasure. The last pulsings were still jetting from him when Sita pulled herself free. Still breathing hard, she stood up.

'Let him loose,' she ordered shortly.

The women obeyed. They slapped Gabriel's buttocks, blew him kisses and winked at him, then walked away. Gabriel stood there shakily. His cock was shining and still dripping semen. His thighs throbbed with warmth, but the pain, like the pleasure, had already become a memory. Sita dressed swiftly, her face expressionless. She pointed to the back of the stables where Gabriel had left his broom and bucket.

'Get on with your work,' she said. 'Food will be brought to you later. And you may rely on the fact that you will be punished at regular intervals. This time, you found pleasure, for you are beautiful and hard to resist. But don't expect such soft treatment every time.'

'And no soft words ever?' Gabriel said.

Sita only stared at him in incomprehension. 'Clean yourself up,' she said, turning on her heel. The others followed. One of them threw him a hunk of bread and an apple. Left alone Gabriel washed himself with cold water. He picked up his leather pouch and put it on. After he ate the food, he went back to his cleaning.

It was quiet in the stable. His head was again filled with images of Marietta. Apart from the times when the guards came to give him orders or to torment him, he thought of her. All he could think of was how beautiful, how desirable, she was. And how much he wanted to repeat their experience inside the carriage.

The fear that he would never see her again added a poignancy to the desire he felt for her. Perversely, that was why he had become imflamed by Sita; for she was the very antithesis of the lovely French woman. Sita was as cold and heartless as Marietta was warm and vibrant. Now that his brief flare of passion for Sita was over he felt disgust at his weakness.

He could never help becoming aroused by those who tormented him. Always he was spurred on by feelings of submission. Selim had perhaps trained him too well. Certainly he had been highly valued, even pampered at times, by the jewel merchant. Gabriel had respected his old master. There had been an odd sort of nobility in serving such a man.

Conversely, Sita treated him as if he was worth no more than a piece of meat. He suspected that she would have acted that way regardless of Kasim's orders. Sita, the others too, took their pleasure and turned their backs on him. The thought that he might be left in this situation forever depressed him. He leaned on his broom. Suddenly he felt drained, numbed of all emotion. All, that is, except the fear. Worse than anything – worse than the fact that he might be left at the mercy of Sita – was the thought of what Marietta might be suffering.

'Where are you?' he said aloud. 'What are they doing to you? I pray that your God will keep you safe until I see you again.'

It was daylight. Smells of dust and dung lifted on the hot air.

Marietta tried to make herself into a ball. She longed to hide from the sea of eyes.

The marketplace was thronged by a milling crowd of people. And every one of them seemed to be looking at her, pointing, shouting, making obscene gestures. The thickset man who had whipped Gabriel climbed the punishment platform.

'Stand up,' he ordered. 'You must obey the public punisher. Come now. You're no spectacle at all curled up on the floor like that. I have something here that will display your charms to advantage.'

She was made to sit on a shaped wooden block. There was a backrest and two indentations in the seat, set widely apart. The crowd shouted their approval, as the public punisher pushed her back against the rest.

'Put your feet here,' he ordered, 'and draw up your knees. Let your thighs fall apart. The crowd wants to see what is so special about a favourite slave.'

Marietta closed her eyes, feeling the hectic colour flood her cheeks. She placed her feet in the marks and felt the metal clamps fold over her wrists and ankles.

Opening her legs wide, she drew them up and let them fall apart. She was completely visible. They could all see everything – even the pink lips of her sex and the golden curls that surrounded it. She had never felt so utterly alone, so vulnerable. The feeling was devastating.

'Have you ever seen such a beauty?' the public punisher asked happily. 'Such breasts, that tiny waist, the swell of her hips. See how soft her thighs are; the skin is the colour of milk mixed with honey. And look here at the garden of delight. Did you ever see yellow hair on a female mound before?'

It was worse than she'd imagined. The crowd seemed like a beast as it surged towards her. The platform shook under their onslaught. The coarse shouts and cries ran in her ears. The thickset man seemed unconcerned by the crowd's fervour. He strode around exchanging jokes and making comments to those nearest the platform.

He came back to stand before Marietta and lifted her hair, running it through his fingers so that it caught the sun. He turned her face this way and that. Then he cupped her breasts, massaging her nipples roughly until they hardened. The eager faces craned close.

Marietta could distinguish the individual faces of the people pressing close to the platform. Their eyes were wide, their mouths slack, as they gazed on her charms. She squeezed her eyes shut, but felt her cheeks pinched hard.

'Open your eyes. Surely you want to see your admirers!'

Marietta cringed inwardly as the man's meaty hand squeezed her thigh then moved inwards. He tweaked her pubic curls, threading them through his thick fingers. She tensed, ready for the intimate touch she knew would follow. When it did, she gave a little moan of distress.

The thick fingers spread her flesh-lips, pinning them wide open. With the other hand he pinched at her bud, drawing it out and rubbing it between his fingers. His hands were dry but the residue of the grease made his touch bearable. The little bud began to swell as he tweaked and stroked it. Now he spanked it lightly with the tip of one finger. And she could not help her response. Her bud began to throb and grow warm, and, though she could hardly believe it was happening, she felt herself growing moist.

He pulled and probed at her, spreading her bottom-cheeks to display the tight orifice mouth that nestled there. He tickled the curls that encircled her anus, pulling at them cruelly so that the little mouth was forced to pout for the crowd.

Marietta blinked back her tears. Gabriel had suffered this and survived. But oh, it was hateful, hateful. Now the public punisher was pushing his fingers into her, working them in and out, and worse was the fact that her hips were beginning to move. He was gentle, deliberately so. This man was highly trained in drawing out his victims' pleasure – all the more to shame them.

The crowd loved it. In front of all the awful grinning faces, Marietta was becoming aroused – just as Gabriel had done. She could not bear it.

'Stop. Oh, please. Stop,' she begged, her voice a hoarse whisper. 'I'll do anything. I do not want this.'

'Should have thought of that before.' The public punisher grinned, hooking two fingers inside her. He drew her up a little so that she was forced to clench around his knuckles to brace herself. The fingers were buried deeply inside her. She felt him moving them slowly, circling her moistness, pressing against the soft inner walls.

'What a pretty morsel we have here then, eh? One of the pampered playthings of the harem. All she has to do is enjoy a life of pleasure and please her master. How many of your daughters crave such a life? But this one's not satisfied with her lot. Oh, no. She wanted to escape!' His voice boomed out over the marketplace.

The crowd gurgled.

'What shall I do with her?'

Someone shouted. 'I'll have her!'

A great squawk of laughter greeted this comment. The public punisher grinned, removing his fingers. He carried his hand to his nose and sniffed deeply, rolling his eyes in appreciation, while those closest whistled and stamped.

'Shame she's not for sale. And she's not to be harmed. But a tickle of the lash wouldn't go amiss. Have you had your fill of looking? Shall I make her dance for you?'

'Yes! Yes!' The sound swelled to a roar. 'Make her dance! Make her pale skin glow!'

Marietta was unfastened and allowed to stand upright. The wooden block was removed. Her wrist bonds were tightened until her arms were drawn out straight, then her legs were pulled apart and her feet fastened to the wooden posts. She stood spreadeagled between the wooden posts as Gabriel once had stood. The shame, the humiliation of it, seemed to crash down on to her. Her tears overflowed and ran down her cheeks.

How could Kasim do this to her? She had been right about him from the start. He was cruel and ruthless – and he cared nothing for her.

The first blow jerked her up straight. It had cracked

across both buttocks at once, bringing a rush of heat and pain. The blow felt more like a slap, not the expected stroke of a lash.

'How'd you like that?' the public punisher crooned, waving an oblong-shaped paddle in the air so that she could see the instrument of her torment. 'It gives a good sound wallop. And the leather makes a lovely noise as it connects. You'll soon be glowing like a cherry and dancing for the crowd.'

And Marietta did indeed begin to squirm. By the third stroke she was pulling against her bonds and twisting her hips in an effort to avoid the stinging slaps. The crowd cheered as each new blow swept across her buttocks. They clapped as she swung her hips, rotating them lewdly, thrusting forward as if to meet a lover's caress.

'Feel her. Is she wet?' Someone in the crowd called out. Hoots of encouragement greeted his question.

The public punisher plunged his hand between Marietta's legs and cupped her sex. He pressed the palm of his hand close so that the flesh-lips pouted down on to it. The touch of the man's hand brought an immediate response. Her swollen bud ticked. She gasped and pulled back, jerking her legs, trying to dislodge the probing hand. It seemed incredible that his unwanted touch could be so arousing.

When he withdrew his hand he held it up to the crowd.

'Aye. She's wet. Wet enough for pleasuring. Pity it's forbidden.' Groans of disappointment came from the crowd. They had obviously expected to see Marietta used in every way possible.

She could not hide her body's response to the punishment. Like Gabriel before her, she had been stripped naked in every sense of the word. Tears dripped from her chin as she fought the outrush of humiliating pleasure, and failed. She could not help the fact that between her widely parted legs her sex was plump and moist. As her buttocks grew ever more heated, wetness began to trickle down her flesh-lips. Her swollen breasts felt heavy and her erect nipples tingled.

She clamped her lips together on her moans as her buttocks were paddled again and again. There was nothing but the warm pain, spiking through her trembling flesh, heating her, drawing pleasure-pain from the very depths of her soul. She tossed her head and began to sob, uncaring now of the crowd, uncaring of dignity. There was a tight knot of pressure in her belly. Soon, oh, soon, it would dissolve and she would melt in that moment of release that the crowd waited for. The wrist bonds cut into her as she sagged against them. Her parted thighs trembled. She thought she could stand it no longer.

It was some moments before she realised that the paddling had stopped. The crowd was hushed. Silence was thick all around. Gradually she became aware that something had changed. A new tension was evident.

Marietta lifted her head slowly.

12

Kasim watched Marietta from the shadows at the back of the platform. He was half concealed by the wall of the narrow alley that butted up close to the platform's steps.

He had arrived a short time ago, anticipating the pleasure of watching as Marietta was punished. But he was not enjoying himself as much as he had expected to.

Instead he felt an inexplicable anger as he watched the thickset man using the paddle on her. It was similar to the feeling that had coursed through him when he discovered Marietta and Gabriel together in his carriage.

He recalled the sight of her face, soft with the afterglow of passion. With her pale hair all tangled around her shoulders and spilling on to her bare breasts she had looked so desirable. That pale skin, gleaming softly in the shadowed interior, had a quality that was heart-breaking. On her neck there was a purple mark. It had been that which had gone to Kasim's brain like a dagger. Gabriel had put his mark on her. Gabriel. The thief. He who had stolen what Kasim had denied himself.

The prize should have been his. He was not so unsophisticated as to believe that it was important for him to be Marietta's first lover or indeed to be her only lover. But he had felt disappointed – no, it went deeper than that – wounded, flayed, that Marietta had allowed Gabriel the full intimacy of her body.

Kasim had waited so long because he knew that the moment when he finally took Marietta would be deeply significant. For him there was a kind of sacredness inherent in the particular act. He allowed only his favourites the full use of his body.

Perhaps the fault was his. He had misjudged the depth of her passions. Her sensuality ran deeper than even he had imagined. He had starved her for too long, given her too many morsels, but kept the main feast from her. How ironic, when it had been difficult beyond all measure to hold himself back. Many times he had hungered to possess her. How many nights had he lain in delightfully agonised contemplation of the delights he would discover in Marietta, when the time was right?

No wonder that his rage had blinded him for a moment. Yet, what were they after all but two disobedient slaves pleasuring each other? For his crime Gabriel was to learn discipline amongst the guards. That prospect gave Kasim no trouble. But the very second he uttered the words that secured Marietta's punishment, he wanted to retract them.

He could not, of course; that would have shown weakness.

In the alleyway he pulled the enveloping dark cloak more closely about him. His dark brooding eyes travelled restlessly over the faces in the crowd. His lip curled with contempt. None of them was worthy of watching Marietta, of seeing her spread naked and exposed for them. She was too fine for that – and he had not realised the fact until this very second.

He was deeply troubled by this enlightenment. Marietta had, from the first, prompted emotions in him that he would rather not admit. Yet perversely he was enthralled by the changes in himself. He found Marietta's sensuality, her stubbornness, her refusal to accept her own nature, compelling beyond measure. And now there was anger ... As he wrenched open that carriage door, it seemed that he had been torn apart by his blinding rage – so clean and pure it was, like ice crystals on snow.

He felt a paler shadow of that same emotion as he watched the public punisher going about his business. The crowd pressed close now, baying like hounds closing on their quarry. The man stopped paddling Marietta's buttocks. He reached his hand between her legs, once more pressing his cupped palm against her plump little sex.

Kasim felt a surge of outrage. How dare he! How dare that ... creature touch the pink wounded heart of *his* Marietta! With difficulty Kasim checked his thoughts. His blood drummed in his ears; there was an unbearable pressure building inside his chest. He felt that if he did not act soon he would begin to shout, to scream, for Marietta to be released. The thought so frightened him that he took a moment to gather his thoughts, to put his emotions back where they belonged. He forced himself to view the proceedings coolly, from a distance that was mental as well as actual.

Ah, better. How stupid to have let himself be drawn so strongly into the spectacle. Disobedient slaves were a common sight on the punishment block. Yes, his inner voice said, but never such a slave. Marietta was so beguiling, so possessed of the ammunition to wound him fatally.

He'd had such hopes for her. But he had not reckoned on Gabriel. He desired Gabriel so strongly himself that he had been blind to the danger. Quite simply he had wanted everything, and now it seemed that Marietta had fallen in love with the big blond slave.

Had he lost her then? Kasim trembled. Marietta might come to despise him. Unbearable. He would be the master no longer. Kasim bowed his head. He was too proud to take someone else's leavings.

Then came a flash of insight. He knew what he must do. Of course, that would settle the matter for good or ill. But one thing at a time. The sound of the paddle hitting flesh broke into his thoughts. Kasim's head snapped up.

How crude the public punisher was. The man's big hands were pulling Marietta's buttocks apart now. Kasim's face twisted with emotion as Marietta writhed. The lovely scarlet globes of her buttocks trembled, her shaking thighs straining to close. The crowd was silent for an instant, and in the space of silence Marietta's moan was clearly audible. She turned her head, seeming to stare straight at Kasim.

Her face was prettily flushed and imprinted with anguish, the features partly obscured by the tangle of pale curls that had fallen forward over her forehead. Kasim knew she did not see him, but he lowered his eyes, his cheeks growing hot with a reflection of her shame. How beautiful she was. It was like looking into the sun. The tumescence at his groin was painful. Like every man in the crowd he ached to part her soft thighs, nudge apart her tender flesh-lips, and slide into her body.

The image moved him greatly. It was as if a white hot sword passed right through him. It was a moment before he realised that his desire was coloured by a new tenderness. He wanted to bend her to his will, to pleasure her until she cried out for mercy, to taste her smoky juices ... and, amazingly, he also wanted to smooth her hair back from her forehead, to rub soothing oil into her reddened flesh, kiss away the heat, cradle her in his arms.

Kasim clenched his hands into fists. Words rose into his throat. But his mouth felt dry. He doubted if he could utter more than a croak. Without stopping to consider his actions further, he took a step forward. His dark cloak billowed out around him, as his boots thudded on the wooden boards.

Marietta tossed back the tumble of curls from her forehead.

A tall cloaked figure was advancing on her. She knew him instantly. Her heart contracted. What new punishment was this?

No one spoke. The public punisher stood with paddle raised for another blow. Kasim wrenched it from his hand. He turned to Marietta. There was such a look of fury on his face that she shrank inwardly. He means to punish me himself, she thought, steeling herself for his blow. But he only looked at her. Two bright spots of colour burned on his cheekbones. His dark eyes glistened with emotion. And suddenly, incongruously, she thought: I have hurt him deeply.

For a moment longer Kasim held her gaze. He seemed to be coming out of a trance. Then he dropped the paddle, unfastened his cloak, and covered her with it. Turning on his heel, he rapped, 'That's enough. Free her.'

As the public punisher shrugged and began to unfasten her chains, the crowd roared in dismay and pressed forward.

'No! No! It's not finished!'

'She's only had a tickling!'

Marietta fell into Kasim's arms. He clasped her so

tightly that her sore thighs and buttocks bloomed with pain, but only a sigh of pleasure came from her lips. She was oblivious of the grumbling crowd.

The public punisher stepped forward to address the massed townsfolk. 'It's all over. Go back to your business. There'll be another slave on the morrow. There always is.'

But the roars redoubled in volume. A shower of objects rained down on to the public punisher. He was hit by a rotten apple and put his hands up to protect his face. The guards ran to take control.

'Come,' Kasim said softly, gathering the cloak into folds around Marietta. 'We are going home.'

Marietta's legs gave out. Her experiences, coupled with the lack of food over the previous day and a half, made their impression on her at last. She trembled with reaction, weak with relief. The prying eyes were no more. Kasim had come for her. Tears glistened on her cheeks.

Kasim scooped her up and carried her swiftly from the platform and down a narrow alley. His coach was waiting. Without a word he climbed inside and placed Marietta on the seat beside him.

She felt safe. The voice of the crowd was muffled. The smell of leather and polish enveloped her. It all seemed to have taken only seconds. Confused and exhausted, she could only lean against Kasim as the coach began to move. He put up his hand to stroke her hair as she laid her head on his shoulder. The charcoal-grey silk of his tunic was cool against her cheek and he smelt of some fern-scented perfume. She realised that she must smell of sweat, cheap grease and stale sex and made a move to pull away. But the gentle pressure of his hand kept her close.

The carriage wheels rolled across the cobblestones

and the outside world seemed far removed. Kasim was silent. He had not spoken since telling her that they were going home. Home? Had he chosen the word deliberately? He was so still that she thought he was absorbed in his anger. Had he come for her so that he might take her back and subject her to a more subtle, more beguiling, torment? Her head was spinning with questions. She opened her mouth to speak, but felt Kasim's cool fingers against her lips.

Then one arm snaked around her back, the other rested across her thighs. The heat from her paddled buttocks seemed to be absorbed somewhat by the fine wool of Kasim's cloak and the coldness of the leather seat under it. Kasim moved a hand inside the cloak to fondle one of her breasts. She leaned into him, finding the gesture comforting rather than arousing, and realised, with surprise, that he felt that too.

She sighed and sank more closely into the circle of his arms. There came the lighest brush of his lips against her temples. And now she dared not speak, not wanting to break the spell of tenderness. She had rarely seen Kasim like this. The new hint of vulnerability in his nature penetrated all her defences.

She had never wanted anyone so much. The desire raced through her veins, leaving her weak and mindless. She wanted Kasim to lay her along the seat and thrust himself inside her. She wanted to belong to him completely, but the ghost of Gabriel was between them. Later then. All thoughts of being comforted fled as Kasim's mere presence set her aflame. Her breath came fast and shallow as his slender fingers pinched her nipples into peaks.

The carriage raced through the narrow streets and out on to the metalled road that led to Kasim's house.

* * *

At the harem Kasim gave Marietta over to Leyla. Marietta felt bereft. She had expected him to explain his actions, to utter soft words. But that was not his way. She must do as he wished, take her lead from him. Sometimes it was hard to remain subservient. If only he would unbend – just a little. But she knew that he could not.

He was captive within his own flesh, as was she.

Infuriating. Must he always be so remote? But would she find him so devastatingly attractive if he was different?

'Have the women bath her,' Kasim said. 'The guards have been at her. She smells of the stables. Make her comfortable. Feed her, then let her rest.'

He stroked Leyla's face with one long thin finger, while she rubbed herself against him like a cat. 'Have someone bring Marietta to me this night in the small bedchamber.'

'I will see to her myself, lord,' Leyla said with meaning.

'Ah, my treasure. Your touch is ever soothing to one who is troubled. Show Marietta more of your talents. Perhaps she will not wish to leave us again.'

Marietta wanted to tell him that she regretted trying to run away already, but she was given no chance to speak. Kasim turned on his heel and strode away, as severe and cold as always. The intimacy between them in the coach had disappeared. She might have imagined it, yet the fact remained that he had come for her. She did not know what to make of him. He was still a puzzle, as enigmatic as the moment she had first set eyes on him.

She was too exhausted to think any more. In the hammam she gave herself up gladly to Leyla's attentions. After her experiences on the punishment block

the luxury of the bath seemed heavenly. The hot perfumed water washed away the last traces of sticky
grease from her pubic curls and cleansed the sweat
from her hair. It soothed her sore buttocks and calmed
her churning thoughts. The memory of her ordeal was
already fading. She had at least been spared the final
indignity of having her forced climax witnessed
publicly.

'I have been so afraid for you. I thought Kasim would
sell you, then I would never see you again. But you are
here and my heart is light.' Leyla smiled warmly at
Marietta as she dried her, then massaged her limbs.

Marietta was glad to be back. This place had become
her home. Strange that Kasim had referred to it that
way. Leyla truly cared for her. If only Kasim were
different she could even be happy here. It was the first
time she had admitted the fact to herself.

'Oh, your pretty bottom is so red,' Leyla crooned,
rubbing her with soothing oil. 'Was it terrible to be
beaten in front of all those people?'

Marietta shuddered. 'Yes. And yet ... you will think
it strange, but there is a kind of desperate attraction to
it. All those people watching as you twist and burn,
unable to escape the strokes of the pleasure you feel in
the pain.'

'Ah, yes. The pleasure. Always that. And how awful
to have everyone witness your helplessness.' Leyla's
long dark eyes glowed. 'Did you reach your peak while
they all watched?'

'No, I was spared that humiliation.'

'Then ... You burn still? I shall soothe you. For I too
burn, for you. But you know this. Kasim knows it too.
Did he not give me leave to soothe you? He wishes you
to be pleasured and made to relax. Sweet Marietta, I
feel a change in you. I cannot explain it, but Kasim too

... he is different.' She shrugged delightfully. 'Kasim tells no one what he plans, but this night you will share his bedchamber. Is that not an exciting thought? Now, we shall go to a quiet place I know. There we can rest together. Would you like that?'

Marietta looked at Leyla's sweet pale face. At her black eyebrows drawn together in a worried little frown. Her full red lips were slightly parted. She looked unsure of herself, vulnerable, and very beautiful. Marietta felt a surge of the desire that had always been present, but which neither of them had explored to the full. At this moment, when she was confused and vulnerable herself, she found it impossible to resist Leyla's sweetness. The night, Kasim's bedchamber seemed very far away. She longed to be soothed into forgetfulness, to lie in Leyla's arms and drift into blissful sleep. But first ...

She leaned forward and placed her lips on that full red mouth. Leyla sighed, opening her lips to return the kiss. It was some time before they broke apart.

'Follow me,' Leyla said, her voice breathless and filled with a savage joy.

In the little pavilion, screened by trees, Marietta lay next to Leyla on a silken couch. Both of them wore only thin silk robes, loose and low at the neck.

Marietta moaned softly as Leyla's slim hand stroked her body, gliding over every curve and hollow. The feel of the cool silk sliding over her skin was soothing and arousing at the same time. Leyla's hands were slim and decorated with henna; the nails were long and painted. Marietta watched their progress through half-closed eyes. The soft caresses made her feel drowsy with passion.

When Leyla closed a hand on her breast she arched

her back and sighed. Leyla teased the nipple until it was erect and standing up under the silk. She did the same with the other one, then slid her hands down to stroke Marietta's stomach. All the time she kissed Marietta's neck, darting out her pointed tongue to lick and nuzzle her skin. They kissed deeply, entwining their tongues, nibbling at each other's full lips.

Marietta felt herself growing liquid, melting, becoming eager for more. Her legs parted willingly as Leyla's hands moved downwards. She lifted her hips so that Leyla could gather up the almost transparent silk and bunch it on her stomach.

Between kisses Leyla used the bunched-up silk like a powder puff, blotting and stroking it all over Marietta's taut stomach and parted thighs. The silk glided over her skin in a petal-soft motion. Leyla used the pad of silk to stroke between Marietta's thighs, tickling the pubic curls, drawing the bunched folds over her pubis and down to the slightly parted sex. Marietta lay with her eyes closed, enjoying the unique sensations. They went on for a long time.

Then Leyla dipped her hand and began stroking Marietta's sex with the tips of her fingers. Marietta moaned aloud as Leyla pinched the sex-lips together and rubbed gently in a circle.

'These pretty curls are delightful,' Leyla said, stroking them outwards from the flesh-lips with two fingers. 'There. Your centre of pleasure is revealed. It's so pink and delicately folded. Moist and fragrant as the heart of a lily.'

The slowness, the subtleness, of Leyla's touch and her soft husky voice drew a strong reaction from Marietta. She reached for Leyla's body, wanting to give as well as receive pleasure. The other woman pulled away.

'No. Not this time. Let me pleasure you. I have dreamt of doing this. Will you allow me to do as I wish, this one time?'

Marietta smiled into the glistening black eyes. 'How could I refuse?'

Leyla sat up and lifted the loose silk robe over her head. Then she drew Marietta's robe from her. She settled herself down beside Marietta, cradling her head in the crook of her arm. Reaching down to Marietta's sex, she parted the flesh-lips, stroking upwards against her bud, at the same time leaning close so that Marietta could suckle her heavy breasts.

Marietta opened her mouth with a sigh of pleasure and drew a large rouged nipple into her mouth. Feeling the fullness of the breast pressing against her rounded lips she sucked with relish. Circling the nipple with her tongue she polished it with saliva, then drew it back inside her lips. The nipple was wonderfully big and hard and tasted sweet. She felt her sex becoming hotter and more liquid as Leyla caressed it. She suckled and tugged softly at the breast, loving the feel of the heavy globes as they lay against her cheek.

Leyla's busy fingers were stroking and rubbing softly, so softly, her touch featherlight. She stroked up the sides of the inner lips, leaving the clit-hood alone, until Marietta almost begged her to touch her straining bud. As if she knew when Marietta could stand that particular stroking no longer, Leyla took the clit-hood between a moist finger and thumb and slid it from side to side, then pulled it up and down, squeezing gently so that the tip of the bud received a tiny brushing motion.

Marietta shuddered. She felt the warm feeling of pushing downwards. Her sex was soaking. Leyla's fingers slid over her folds, bringing her to the very threshold, but not tipping her over. She clutched at Leyla, squeezing her breasts together with sudden violence so that she could suckle both nipples at once. She wanted something more than gentleness now. Sliding up Leyla's body she kissed her hard, grinding her mouth against those full red lips until she felt Leyla sigh deep in her throat.

Leyla reached over and pressed one shapely thigh between Marietta's legs. She lifted Marietta's thigh and settled it around her waist. Then she grasped her hips, turning her on her side, pulling her close, moving her inside her scissored legs. Cradled in that exciting embrace, with Leyla's legs curved around and under her, Marietta felt the heat of Leyla's sex as it rubbed against hers, fitting to it closely.

'The feel of your fleece against my naked sex is so exciting. It is soft, yet scratchy. Oh, I can feel the moist curls rubbing me. Oh, oh!'

Leyla moaned softly, beginning to make small thrusting movements with her hips. Marietta let out a sigh of pleasure as Leyla's well-developed clitoris slid delightfully back and forth across her own. It was like a tiny cock, hot and hard. Their inner flesh-lips cleaved together, sealed by their mingled juices. Marietta moved to meet Leyla's thrusts, grinding herself against Leyla, delighting in the leashed violence of the action.

Before long they were both shuddering in a long drawn-out release. Leyla tightened her legs around Marietta as she uttered sharp cries of pleasure. Her hands clutched Marietta's shoulders and drew her close. She pressed small kisses all over Marietta's face, gasping breathlessly,

'So beautiful you are. So beautiful . . .'

Even before the final spasm had faded Marietta felt herself relaxing into a pleasant torpor. Leyla shifted so that they were more comfortable. Marietta laid her head on the pillow of Leyla's bosom and closed her eyes. No more words passed between them. They were in complete accord. Soon they slept.

Kasim peered through the lattice screen of the window at the sleeping figures.

In the dim interior the entwined women seemed fashioned from porcelain. Their pale skins were patterned by the light pouring through the lattice and shadows formed in the hollows of their bodies. Rippled midnight tresses were spilled across a cloud of silver curls. Kasim found the sight intensely moving.

He smiled. Leyla had done exactly as he wished. It had been no hardship certainly, for he knew that she desired Marietta almost as much as he did. He knew now that a woman of Marietta's sensual temperament responded best to being soothed; by being brought to a sexual climax. If only he had realised that earlier, so much might have been avoided. Now Marietta lay sated in Leyla's arms. She would awake, renewed, refreshed, and ready to face anything. He wanted her mind to be clear by the time she was brought to his bedchamber, unshadowed by what she had suffered on the punishment block.

Though what he was about to do pained him, he was set on his course. After a final glance at the figures curved together in sleep, he slid noiselessly through the garden and made for the stables.

Gabriel got up slowly from the stable floor, where a few moments ago he had lain spreadeagled at Sita's command. He waited on all fours until she commanded him.

It had been her pleasure to have him lie down

unbound to receive his regular beating. He moved stiffly, the hot pain in his thighs and buttocks jarring right through him. The circle of female guards watching, laughed and jeered as he crawled on hands and knees to where Sita now stood waiting.

Sita had loosened the belt of her leather trousers and let them fall. Her muscular legs were parted, wreathed at the ankles by crumpled fabric. She had her hands on her hips and was watching Gabriel approach, a hard gleam in her narrow eyes.

'Not such a pretty boy now, are you?' Sita jeered. 'You look like the peasant you are with straw in your hair and your arms and legs all scratched from cleaning the stables. You can still use your tongue, though. Get over here and pleasure me.'

Gabriel knelt before Sita. He reached up and grasped her narrow hips, leaning towards the thickly furred sex. Sita pushed his hands down, then fetched him a stinging slap across the face.

'Did I tell you to touch me? Use your tongue alone. And if you do not please me, you'll feel the bite of the lash again.'

Obediently Gabriel let his hands fall. He pressed his face to Sita's sex and reached out his tongue, questing through the musky-scented hair to the flesh-lips beyond. Sita's pubic hair was very thick and curly and extended to the crease of her groin, a few strands curling around the tops of her thighs. Sita tasted of musk and salt, with a trace of herbal-scented soap. One of the other guards flicked his sore buttocks as he probed the soft inner flesh of the sex. Gabriel grunted at the sudden flare of pain and his buttocks tightened as he arched his back.

Sita laughed at his discomfort and sank towards him a little, rubbing herself crudely over his face. She grasped his hair and pulled him close so that his mouth and chin were buried in her. Gabriel gasped with pain as she twisted her hand in his hair. Sita laughed again, commenting on the hot rush of his breath. She closed her eyes, opening her thighs a little wider, as Gabriel began licking upwards towards the joining of her flesh-lips.

As she pulled his head back and forth, his tousled blond hair brushed her thighs and stomach and Sita's face softened with pleasure. Her muscular belly and thighs grew taut as she strained towards her climax. She was unaware of a sudden tension amongst the other guards. Their feet rustled in the straw as they stood back to let someone through.

'Well, well, Sita,' Kasim said, 'I see that you are carrying out my orders to the letter.'

Sita's eyes snapped open. She yanked Gabriel's head away and motioned to the other guards. While she rearranged her clothing they dragged Gabriel to his feet. Sita, her narrow face flushed scarlet, stood to attention. 'My lord!'

Kasim smiled. 'And Gabriel, have you learned obedience yet? No matter. It is time you returned to me.' He put a hand to his nose fastidiously. 'You and you throw that bucket of water over him, then secure him. I'll take him with me.'

Sita watched, almost regretfully, as Gabriel shivered under the freezing deluge. 'Shame you have to leave,' she hissed under her breath. 'I had such plans for you.'

Gabriel let her see his disdain. 'I pity you,' he whispered. 'A woman without warmth is an enemy to herself.'

Sita's narrow lips tightened. She did not answer, but she jerked the bonds tight until they cut into his wrists and ankles. Gabriel did not react. He looked at her coldly as she handed him over to Kasim. Without a backward glance, and without a word, Gabriel was led away.

Kasim was tempted to take Gabriel straight to his bedchamber. He found him most attractive in his dishevelled state. The water had washed off the muck of the stables, but straw was still flecked amidst the strands of his sweat-darkened hair. The scene he had come upon had aroused him. And, despite his obvious hatred of Sita, Gabriel too was aroused.

He was glorious in his nakedness. Water dripped down his shoulders and trailed in runnels to his groin, disappearing in the thick blond thatch. His sex stuck out straight in front of him. Kasim paused, grasped the erect shaft, and stroked it absently.

Gabriel's expression amused him. He still thinks he has a choice about whom he pleasures, he thought. Then he saw the well-shaped mouth set in resignation. The grey eyes flared with renewed desire. Gabriel was a volatile animal; it was a shame not to use him once more. Why not, Kasim thought. There was time before what he planned. He would take his pleasure with Gabriel one last time.

In the bedchamber he pressed Gabriel to the red velvet bedcover, not bothering to loosen his bonds. He reached for a pot of scented oil and began to apply it. His fingers worked into Gabriel's crevice, probing into his anus without gentleness. Gabriel gasped at Kasim's roughness.

'Spread those buttocks. I care nothing for your pleasure. See that you work your opening for me. This is my reward. Are you not grateful that I released you from the stables?'

He took Gabriel without preamble, feeling the tight opening slide with scratchy heat along his shaft.

Gabriel's groans, caged behind gritted teeth, spurred him on. He thrust deeply, digging his fingers into the sore and heated bottom-flesh, while Gabriel buried his face in the red velvet, his groans turning to sobs.

Images of Gabriel and Marietta together flashed through Kasim's mind. His jealousy and rage was a white-hot presence, seeming to spread spiky fingers down into his belly and into the pulsing shaft of his cock. His testicles shrank to a hard tight bag. The fear, the risk he was going to take – soon, so soon – added an extra note to his pleasure. It took only a few moments for his climax to swamp him.

The thrusting within Gabriel ceased. The pleasure was so intense that it blotted out all thought, all sensation, except for the sweetly tearing pulsing that went on and on. Kasim's breath left him in a harsh sobbing groan. Under him Gabriel bucked and writhed, rubbing his erect penis against the velvet cover, straining for his own release. His face was turned to one side, his eyes squeezed tight shut. Tears streaked his anguished face. His bound hands flexed, wrists straining against the tough bonds. But his pleasure eluded him.

Kasim withdrew and cleansed himself with the oil. He left Gabriel lying on the bed, breathing hard, uncaring that he rolled over on to his side, his eyes pleading for Kasim to relieve his torment. Gabriel's shaft was standing up straight. The swollen head was free of the skin. It looked moist and inviting.

Kasim flicked it with a sort of sorrowful disdain. There was no time to pleasure Gabriel. 'Get up,' he ordered. 'Stand over there. I am about to do you an honour. Your future depends on what happens in this chamber in the next few minutes. You will observe and not say a word until I call for you. Do you understand?'

Gabriel did not, but he nodded and went to stand behind the carved wooden screen that Kasim had indicated. His body was a riot of pain and sensation. The tumescence at his groin was a torture to him. He craved Kasim's touch, even while he hated to admit to it, but the last few sentences Kasim had uttered chilled him. Something momentous was about to happen. And he sensed that it concerned Marietta.

That joining, just now, had had a contained frenzy about it. There seemed a desperation in Kasim, as if he were strung as tight as a bow. But to what purpose? Gabriel was puzzled. He had been dumbfounded when Kasim came to the stables to fetch him. That Kasim was still furious with him was plain. But he sensed that there was more to it. What was Kasim planning? No one could guess what went on in the dark convolutions of his mind.

Then the door to the bedchamber opened and Marietta walked into the room. Gabriel's heart leapt at the sight of her. So Kasim had also brought her back from the punishment block. They had both been rescued. But were they forgiven? Surely it could not be that simple.

Marietta crossed the room and stood waiting for Kasim to speak. He was reclining on the wide bed, one hand propping up his chin.

'Ah, Marietta. I trust you are rested and refreshed. Leyla's attentions, while stimulating, are also soothing, are they not? You looked quite beautiful when I saw you together.'

She gave a little start of surprise, but he was smiling. She nodded uneasily. Was there anything that escaped his notice? He looked relaxed, even indolent. But she knew that his attitude was a mask. Kasim was at his most dangerous when he appeared that way. His dark eyes were watchful, shadowed by that keen intelligence of his.

'Come closer to me. I wish to look at you. In the short time you were gone I found my eyes lonely for you. Display yourself.'

There had been no word of blame, nor yet of forgiveness. She was sure he was testing her. First there was the hint of his affection for her, then the order to submit. She did not know how to react. She could only follow her instincts. As she took off the outer garment of gold tissue, she felt a sort of willing gladness flood her soul. Only now did she realise that she had been afraid that he would reject her completely. She had a strong urge to throw herself at his feet, beg him to forgive her, stammer out her thanks – but she controlled the impulse.

Kasim watched her. Did he sense her inner struggle? Though he remained stern, even cold, something had changed between them. She dared to think that it might be for the better.

Her white silk tunic, split down the front, fell at her feet. Under it she wore a breast halter made of tiny jewelled chains. A deep belt of gold leather cinched her waist. More chains were secured to the centre of the belt; they trailed over, but did not obscure her fleece – displayed prominently as always. Loose, open-fronted trousers of white silk clothed her legs and were drawn in tightly at each ankle. Leyla had dressed her with special care for this meeting. She knew she looked her sensual best.

Marietta saw Kasim's eyes widen slightly as she sank gracefully into the posture of submission. Without his prompting she arranged herself as beguilingly as possible. She straightened her shoulders, pushing her breasts up and forward, the action making the delicate chains part so that her rouged nipples protruded invitingly. Clasping her hands in the small of her back, she parted her knees widely, feeling her flesh-lips open and the heart of her sex present itself to his view. The chains hung down between her legs, swaying gently. She felt their delicious coolness tickle her open sex and thighs.

Kasim's eyes raked her face, searching. He looked as if he wanted to speak but dared not. She knew that the proper thing to do was to lower her eyes and chin, but she looked straight at Kasim and let him see her utter compliance. Then she lowered her eyelids and said one word.

'Master.'

Kasim made a sound deep in his throat. Slowly he got off the bed and came to her. He walked around her sedately, a look of wonder on his face. Still not speaking he stroked her tumble of silver curls, cupped her chin and turned her face up to him. He ran one hand over her breasts, squeezing the nipples gently, rolling them so that shards of sensation pooled in her stomach. Marietta parted her lips and smiled up at him.

Some of the tension seemed to go out of Kasim. He sat on the edge of the bed. 'The moment has come for you to make a choice. Perhaps I need not ask you this – you seem to have decided. Yet I must be sure.'

She looked at him, a puzzled frown gathering between her pale brows.

'I demand complete obedience from those I . . . regard highly. You know this. But the submission I wish for from my favourites must, ultimately, be given freely. Do you understand?'

She nodded.

'I think you do not. Not fully. I kept you here against your will because there was no other way to show you what I am. And what you are. For, make no mistake, I choose only those in whom I see my own reflection. I knew the moment I set eyes on you that we were alike.'

He spoke the truth. Marietta had felt this all along. That was why it had been so hard to resist. Deep inside her she knew that she craved Kasim's coldness, his domination. Because it was not coldness at all – it was an expression of love. Oh, yes. A departure from the conventional understanding of it, but love nonetheless – the kind that struck a note of resonance deep within her soul.

'I have made my choice,' she said, her voice husky with emotion.

A dark flame kindled in Kasim's eyes. 'I see that you have, my treasure. But there is more to this. You make your choice blindly, for you are not aware that there is an alternative to staying here with me. You and I must face this. And then there will never be any barriers between us.'

Marietta looked puzzled. 'My lord?'

For answer, Kasim walked over to a screen she had not noticed and spoke to someone. She heard the sound of a muffled conversation, then Kasim reappeared. A figure emerged after him.

'Gabriel!' Marietta breathed. 'You are safe!'

Gabriel smiled at her, his eyes kindling as they took in her posture, the charms so openly displayed. 'As you are, my heart. How I ache when I look on your beauty.'

Marietta flashed a worried look towards Kasim. Surely he would punish Gabriel for his outspokenness. But Kasim merely ignored his words.

'Gabriel has something to ask you.'

'You are certain? This is no trick?' Gabriel said to

Kasim. When Kasim remained silent he went on confidently. 'Marietta, we can leave. Together. If you wish it. Kasim gives us his blessing. Will you come with me?'

Marietta was stunned. She looked from one to the other. Kasim had a shuttered look to his face, while Gabriel was all contained excitement.

'Don't you see what this means?' Gabriel said. 'Kasim is giving us both our freedom. I heard you make your choice just now. But you did not speak from your heart, I know it. You thought you would remain a slave always. But now there is no need for compromise. No need to convince yourself that you must accept life here in the harem. You are free. Kasim is not your master unless you wish it. Tell him that you are leaving with me.'

Marietta felt torn in two. After all this time she was being offered freedom. She gave a strangled laugh. But I am no longer free, she thought. Oh, Gabriel, how could you be so wrong about me?

'Marietta?'

She turned at the sound of her name. Kasim's face, angular and strong featured, looked strained. How had she never noticed the underlying fragility? He was like a precious stone that was flawed, but the flaw only served to show off his perfection. He had never looked so beautiful to her.

He smiled gently, a little sadly, 'You have not answered Gabriel. So. Tell me that you are leaving and I shall not stop you.'

'And if I stay?' she said, trying for lightness, though her voice shook alarmingly.

He gave an elegant shrug. 'I am what I am. I make no apologies for it. You know what to expect.'

Yes. She knew. And it was what she wanted. With

all her heart and soul she wanted Kasim. Gabriel was like a comet, streaming through her life, lighting it up briefly with the brightness of its passing. But Kasim was the blood and soil of her soul. The dark tides that moved within him were mirrored in her. She had found herself in Kasim and it was quite impossible to leave him. She never wanted to leave him.

When Marietta remained silent Gabriel's brow darkened. He began to look afraid. It was painful to her to see the indecision mar his face.

'I'm sorry,' she whispered, knowing how inadequate that sounded.

How could she ever make Gabriel understand? Whatever she said he would think that Kasim had coerced her into staying. Then she must show him. It was cruel, but unavoidable.

In one fluid movement she changed position, so that she lay full length on the carpet. Clasping Kasim's booted ankles she pressed her lips to his feet.

Gabriel blanched. He took one step back. 'I seem to have misunderstood. Foolish of me ... forgive me,' he said dazedly.

Kasim raised Marietta to her feet and kissed her deeply. She put her arms around his neck and returned the kiss, pressing herself closely along his length. There was triumph in his kiss and the promise of the spiked pleasure to come. Heat unfurled slowly and spread through Marietta's body.

Neither of them noticed when the door opened and closed.

Kasim put Marietta from him. His dark eyes seemed fathomless. His voice was perfectly level and restrained when he said, 'On your knees, Marietta. Free my phallus.'

Marietta felt a strong swimming desire in her loins

as the welcome submission gathered in her belly. She sank to the carpet in front of Kasim and said softly, huskily:

'Yes. Master.'

Visit the Black Lace website at
www.blacklace.com

BLACK LACE – THE LEADING IMPRINT OF
WOMEN'S SEXY FICTION

TAKING YOUR EROTIC READING PLEASURE
TO NEW HORIZONS

LOOK OUT FOR THE ALL-NEW BLACK LACE BOOKS – AVAILABLE NOW!

All books priced £7.99 in the UK. Please note publication dates apply to the UK only. For other territories, please contact your retailer.

Also To be published in August 2009

SEXY LITTLE NUMBERS
Various
ISBN 978 0 352 34538 7

Sexy Little Numbers is a choice cut of all new and original erotic stories and the latest addition to Black Lace's immensely popular series of erotica collections. This longer collection will contain even more variety and a greater range of female sexual desire than ever before. It will be the first of an annual collection of the best erotica stories written by women. Fun, irreverent and deliciously decadent, *Sexy Little Numbers* will combine humour and attitude with wildly imaginative writing from all over the world.

UP TO NO GOOD
Karen S Smith
ISBN 978 0 352 34528 8

Emma is resigned to attending her cousin's wedding, expecting the usual excruciating round of polite conversation and bad dancing. Instead it's the scene of a horny encounter which encourages her to behave even more scandalously than usual. When she meets motorbike fanatic Kit, it's lust at first sight, and they waste no time in getting each other off behind the marquee. They don't get the chance to say goodbye, however and Emma resigns herself to the fact that she'll never see her spontaneous lover again. Then fate intervenes as Emma and Kit are reunited at another wedding – and so begins a year of outrageous sex, wild behaviour, and lots of getting up to no good.

To be published in September 2009

MISBEHAVIOUR
Various
ISBN 978 0352 34518 9

Fun, irreverent and deliciously decadent, this arousing anthology of erotica is a showcase of the diversity of modern women's erotic fantasies. Lively and entertaining, seductive and daring, *Misbehaviour* combines humour and attitude with wildly imaginative writing on the theme of women behaving badly.

NO RESERVATIONS
Megan Hart and Lauren Dane
ISBN 978 0352 34519 6

Kate and Leah are heading for Vegas with no reservations. Both on the run from their new boyfriends and the baggage these guys have brought with them from other women. And the biggest playground in the west has many sensual thrills to offer two women with an appetite for fun. Meanwhile, the boyfriends, Dix and Brandon, realise you don't know what you've got 'til it's gone, and pursue the girls to the city of sin to launch the most arduous methods of seduction to win the girls back. None-stop action with a twist of romance from two of the most exciting writers in American erotica today.

TAKING LIBERTIES
Susie Raymond
ISBN 978 0352 34530 1

When attractive, thirty-something Beth Bradley takes a job as PA to Simon Henderson, a highly successful financier, she is well aware of his philandering reputation and determined to turn the tables on his fortune. Her initial attempt backfires, and she begins to look for a more subtle and erotic form of retribution. However, Beth keeps getting sidetracked by her libido, and finds herself caught up in the dilemma of craving sex with the dominant men she wants to teach a lesson.

To be published in October 2009

THE THINGS THAT MAKE ME GIVE IN
Charlotte Stein
ISBN 978 0352 34542 4

Girls who go after what they want no matter what the cost, boys who
like to flash their dark sides, voyeurism for beginners and cheating
lovers . . . Charlotte Stein takes you on a journey through all the facets
of female desire in this contemporary collection of explicit and ever
intriguing short stories. Be seduced by obsessions that go one step too
far and dark desires that remove all inhibitions. Each story takes you on
a journey into all the things that make a girl give in.

THE GALLERY
Fredrica Alleyn
ISBN 978 0352 34533 2

Police office Cressida Farleigh is called in to investigate a mysterious art
fraud at a gallery specializing in modern erotic works. The gallery's
owner is under suspicion, but is also charming and powerfully
attractive man who throws the young woman's powers of detection
into confusion. Her long time detective boyfriend is soon getting
jealous, but Cressida is also in the process of seducing a young artist of
erotic images. As she finds herself drawn into a mesh of power games
and personal discovery, the crimes continue and her chances of
cracking the case become ever more complex.

ALL THE TRIMMINGS

Tesni Morgan

ISBN 978 0352 34532 5

Cheryl and Laura decide to pool their substantial divorce settlements and buy a hotel. When the women find out that each secretly harbours a desire to run an upmarket bordello, they seize the opportunity to turn St Jude's into a bawdy funhouse for both sexes, where fantasies – from the mild to the increasingly perverse – are indulged. But when attractive , sinister John Dempsey comes on the scene, Cheryl is smitten, but Laura less so, convinced he's out to con them, or report them to the authorities or both. Which of the women is right? And will their friendship – and their business – survive?

Black Lace Booklist

Information is correct at time of printing. To avoid disappointment, check availability before ordering. Go to www.blacklace.com.
All books are priced £7.99 unless another price is given.

- ❏ THE PRIDE Edie Bingham ISBN 978 0 352 33997 3
- ❏ THE SILVER CAGE Mathilde Madden ISBN 978 0 352 34164 8
- ❏ THE SILVER COLLAR Mathilde Madden ISBN 978 0 352 34141 9
- ❏ THE SILVER CROWN Mathilde Madden ISBN 978 0 352 34157 0
- ❏ SOUTHERN SPIRITS Edie Bingham ISBN 978 0 352 34180 8
- ❏ THE TEN VISIONS Olivia Knight ISBN 978 0 352 34119 8
- ❏ WILD KINGDOM Deana Ashford ISBN 978 0 352 34152 5
- ❏ WILDWOOD Janine Ashbless ISBN 978 0 352 34194 5

BLACK LACE ANTHOLOGIES
- ❏ BLACK LACE QUICKIES 1 Various ISBN 978 0 352 34126 6 £2.99
- ❏ BLACK LACE QUICKIES 2 Various ISBN 978 0 352 34127 3 £2.99
- ❏ BLACK LACE QUICKIES 3 Various ISBN 978 0 352 34128 0 £2.99
- ❏ BLACK LACE QUICKIES 4 Various ISBN 978 0 352 34129 7 £2.99
- ❏ BLACK LACE QUICKIES 5 Various ISBN 978 0 352 34130 3 £2.99
- ❏ BLACK LACE QUICKIES 6 Various ISBN 978 0 352 34133 4 £2.99
- ❏ BLACK LACE QUICKIES 7 Various ISBN 978 0 352 34146 4 £2.99
- ❏ BLACK LACE QUICKIES 8 Various ISBN 978 0 352 34147 1 £2.99
- ❏ BLACK LACE QUICKIES 9 Various ISBN 978 0 352 34155 6 £2.99
- ❏ BLACK LACE QUICKIES 10 Various ISBN 978 0 352 34156 3 £2.99
- ❏ SEDUCTION Various ISBN 978 0 352 34510 3
- ❏ LIAISONS Various ISBN 978 0 352 34516 5
- ❏ MORE WICKED WORDS Various ISBN 978 0 352 33487 9 £6.99
- ❏ WICKED WORDS 3 Various ISBN 978 0 352 33522 7 £6.99
- ❏ WICKED WORDS 4 Various ISBN 978 0 352 33603 3 £6.99
- ❏ WICKED WORDS 5 Various ISBN 978 0 352 33642 2 £6.99
- ❏ WICKED WORDS 6 Various ISBN 978 0 352 33690 3 £6.99
- ❏ WICKED WORDS 7 Various ISBN 978 0 352 33743 6 £6.99
- ❏ WICKED WORDS 8 Various ISBN 978 0 352 33787 0 £6.99
- ❏ WICKED WORDS 9 Various ISBN 978 0 352 33860 0
- ❏ WICKED WORDS 10 Various ISBN 978 0 352 33893 8
- ❏ THE BEST OF BLACK LACE 2 Various ISBN 978 0 352 33718 4
- ❏ WICKED WORDS: SEX IN THE OFFICE Various ISBN 978 0 352 33944 7
- ❏ WICKED WORDS: SEX AT THE SPORTS CLUB Various ISBN 978 0 352 33991 1
- ❏ WICKED WORDS: SEX ON HOLIDAY Various ISBN 978 0 352 33961 4

To find out the latest information about Black Lace titles, check out the website: www.blacklace.com or send for a booklist with complete synopses by writing to:

Black Lace Booklist, Virgin Books Ltd
Virgin Books
Random House
20 Vauxhall Bridge Road
London SW1V 2SA

Please include an SAE of decent size. Please note only British stamps are valid.

Our privacy policy
We will not disclose information you supply us to any other parties. We will not disclose any information which identifies you personally to any person without your express consent.

From time to time we may send out information about Black Lace books and special offers. Please tick here if you do not wish to receive Black Lace information.   ❏

Please send me the books I have ticked above.

Name ....

Address ....

....

....

....

Post Code ....

Send to: Virgin Books Cash Sales, Random House,
20 Vauxhall Bridge Road, London SW1V 2SA.

US customers: for prices and details of how to order
books for delivery by mail, call 888-330-8477.

Please enclose a cheque or postal order, made payable
to Virgin Books Ltd, to the value of the books you have
ordered plus postage and packing costs as follows:

UK and BFPO – £1.00 for the first book, 50p for each
subsequent book.

Overseas (including Republic of Ireland) – £2.00 for
the first book, £1.00 for each subsequent book.

If you would prefer to pay by VISA, ACCESS/MASTERCARD,
DINERS CLUB, AMEX or SWITCH, please write your card
number and expiry date here:

....

Signature ....

Please allow up to 28 days for delivery.